SIL...

STI...

OVER 100
GREAT NOVELS
OF
EROTIC DOMINATION

If you like one you will probably like the rest

NEW TITLES EVERY MONTH

All titles in print are now available from:

www.adultbookshops.com

If you want to be on our confidential mailing list for our Readers' Club
Magazine (with extracts from past and forthcoming titles) write to:

SILVER MOON READER SERVICES

Shadowline Publishing Ltd
No 2 Granary House
Ropery Road
Gainsborough
DN21 2NS
United Kingdom

telephone: 01427 611697
Fax: 01427 611776

NEW AUTHORS WELCOME

Please send submissions to
Silver Moon Books
PO Box 5663
Nottingham
NG3 6PJ

Silver Moon is an imprint of Shadowline Publishing Ltd
First published 2004 Silver Moon Books
ISBN 9781-904706-56-4
© 2007 Geoffrey Allen

AFRICANUS 3

TEMPLE OF DARKNESS

BY

GEOFFREY ALLEN

ALSO BY GEOFFREY ALLEN
AFRICANUS: ARENA OF TORMENT
AFRICANUS 2: RITUAL OF PAIN

INTRODUCTION

The girl, resplendent in her nakedness laid full length across the seat of a small boat, her head and feet resting on the gunwales. A man sitting in the stern watched idly as the great temples of Thebes drifted harmlessly by. He turned the tiller sending the craft towards a smaller river disgorging its contents into the greater waters of the Nile. Two Nubian rowers, their dark skin sweating profusely under the glaring sun had little chance to admire the girl's fine figure or her stark nakedness. The sweat pouring from their brows had all but blinded them. The girl for her part gazed absently at the cloudless sky, listening to the monotonous creaking of the oars and occasionally shifting her numbed buttocks. Another man seated at the prow plucked the strings of a harp, stealing glances at the girls' wobbling breasts. It might have been a pleasure outing, a boat making its way inoffensively up the Nile were it not for the girl's wrists locked through a wooden manacle and a chain around her pretty neck securing her to the boat's ribs. The look upon her face was not one of pleasure. She knew, as did the men in the boat what fate awaited her at the hands of Queen Hatentita.

The boat thumped dully against a stone wharf and the men moved fast, releasing the chains and lifting her over the gunwales. Leaving the exhausted rowers behind, they marched the naked girl through the portals of a now deserted temple, handing her over to heavily armed guards. The man who had been playing the harp went up a flight of steps, entered a second chamber and bowed low.

"Your imperial majesty, we have been betrayed," he informed, wondering if, as the bearer of bad tidings, he too would be executed. "The Romans have sent an army into Semna and have destroyed all our forces."

He stepped back awaiting her response.

But the enraged outburst he anticipated never came.

Instead, she continued to gaze across the desert at the distant pylons of Thebes. Not moving or speaking; lost in thought.

He had to admit she was stunningly beautiful with the sun shining through her diaphanous robe. Her full figure was silhouetted in all its glory; long shapely legs, magnificent tightly rounded buttocks forming into a darker sensuous crease, a long back tapering up from the devastating swell of her hips and terminating into square and perfectly sculpted shoulders. Bereft of her wig, her cropped scalp lost none of its beauty. If anything she looked younger, but there was nothing girlish about the look on her face when at last she turned to face him. Her high, firm breasts heaved under the robe and he clearly saw the darker discs of her pimpled areolas and puckered nipples rising like the tips of her fingers.

"Who betrayed me?" she whispered dangerously, eyeing him with smouldering eyes.

"The serving girl," he answered, taking another step backwards. "The one we sent into the governor Cellenius' harem."

Queen Hatentita screwed her face in thought. "If you send a girl to do a woman's job what else would you expect?"

The man visibly trembled for the emphasis had stealthily shifted from the plural to the singular.

"Was she tortured?" the Queen asked.

"Our intelligence is that she betrayed our secrets in exchange for sexual favours and a promise of much gold, your majesty."

"And you have her here now?"

"She is under guard and awaits your decision, your majesty."

Her face relaxed, her lips curling into a sardonic smile. "If sex is to her liking, see to it that she is well punished and then send her into the underworld."

He bowed and made a hasty retreat. There was no telling

how such volatile a woman would suddenly change and have him executed into the bargain.

"Bring the wretch along," he said to the guards, who promptly dragged her into a small, airless chamber.

How old was she? Nefru wondered looking at her small pert breasts. Not much more than eighteen summers, he guessed, and certainly not virginal. Then again, a girl with legs and a bottom like that could hardly expect to keep her virginity for very long. Leading her across the chamber, he also wondered how many men had laid between her slender thighs and penetrated that succulent peach of a slit.

Dismissing the thought, he ordered her to sit astride a stone phallus and the girl went wide-eyed. It was long and thick, not smooth like the real thing she now saw displayed from under his tunic, but with deep ridges and knobbles and ringed with a many pointed star fitted under the head. She swallowed hard and straddled the weapon, spreading her legs and slowly bending them at the knees.

"Must I suffer this?" she wept, feeling the tip nudging into her slit.

"It is the Queen's wish," he told her flatly, and placed his hands on her shoulders, exerting a strong downward pressure.

She sucked her breath as inch by inch the weapon filled her belly. Fully penetrated, she sat upright, keeping her balance, not daring to move. Inside her sex, the ridges and knobbles teased the delicate and tender petals. The pointed star rubbed against her vaginal walls. Already she was flushed with sexual arousal. The slightest movement of her hips and buttocks would have her on heat.

"Now ride," Nefru ordered. "Ride it until you're sore, and at the same time you can suck my cock."

He saw no point in wasting such an opportunity. She was defenceless with the guards now tying her hands behind her back, her slim legs thrown wide, her mouth open and there for the taking.

Nefru guided his cock into her mouth and placed his hands at the back of her head holding it rigid. A lash from the guard's belt sent the girl into a steady rocking motion, bucking her bottom and digging her toes hard onto the stone flags. Riding faster now, the muscles in her calves and thighs hardened and flexed. Her bottom cheeks clenched from the huge weapon teasing her sex. Nefru closed his eyes and sighed at the feeling of her warm wet mouth gliding up and down his shaft. One of the guards' released his own pulsating organ and rubbed the tip over her nipples. He too saw no point in wasting such an opportunity. The other guard leaned against the wall content to watch the goings on without participating. There was as much satisfaction in looking at her slender body twisting and writhing in all directions as there was ejaculating over her tits.

Soon the girl gasped for breath; half choking on the organ stuffed deep in her throat, and inside her, the phallus was already doing its deadly work. Streams of love juice poured from her trembling sex and at its base, an artfully placed ridge was driving her to distraction pushing hard on her swollen clit. A fast hot stream of male juice shot over her nipples and the guard staggered backwards laughing like a hyena. Urged on by Nefru's hands, her head bobbed faster over his cock and she felt its length suddenly harden. He thrust deeper and then suddenly erupted, filling her mouth and throat. She choked and coughed, unable to do anything but swallow the thick globules of sperm slithering into her belly.

"Please, I've had as much as I can take," she wailed, spreading her legs so widely the pelvic bones cricked.

"You're going to take a lot more," Nefru told her, wiping his cock head in her hair. "You'll ride the weapon until your arse splits."

"Do we kill her afterwards?" one of the guards whispered.

Nefru hesitated. What a waste of a magnificent little morsel of fucking meat, slitting her throat and despatching her naked and penniless into the underworld. A twinge of guilt gnawed at his conscience. There were times when he though that Hatentita was stark raving mad. The idea that she could muster an army and drive the Romans out of Egypt bordered on lunacy. Nevertheless, it was not entirely impossible. Cleopatra had almost done just that. So why not Hatentita? And there was the possibility that he might become her consort with his own harem and all the maidens he could fuck. But he had no desire to murder the sobbing serving girl now slumped exhausted over the weapon.

"If you can make it into the desert, you can keep her," he advised softly.

And he went back to report to his sovereign.

"Is it done?" she asked.

"It is your majesty," he lied, hoping that both the guard and the girl would be far away by sundown.

"I have been thinking," she said, swinging her legs from the window cill. "We have failed because we sent an imbecilic serving girl to do a job which requires both intelligence and tact. We need a grown woman to get into Cellenius' harem. She must be tall, voluptuous, willing to fuck like a goat, of keen intelligence, good with a sword if needs must. She must be quick witted and able to escape when the time is ripe. She must also be black. I've heard that Cellenius has a penchant for fucking black slaves."

Nefru stared in disbelief. "I'm sure I don't know any woman living who could fulfill those expectations," he said stunned at the suggestion.

Hatentita crossed her legs and stroked her chin.

"There must be someone, somewhere," she hissed. "It's only a matter of finding her."

CHAPTER ONE

If Quintus thought his wife, the Lady Octavia would spend the rest of her life in the House of Scorpions fucking with every ne'r do well that happened to frequent the place he was profoundly mistaken. It had taken her only a month to escape, boarding a ship and fucking all the crew and then persuading the captain to take her along as his mistress, only to jump ship at Alexandria.

Egypt was now a Roman colony and its rulers had scant respect for the Egyptians whom they regarded as troublemakers, like Cleopatra, or a race of natives useful only as slaves toiling in the southern goldmines or tilling the fields. But their women had their uses as domestics or concubines. And they were good lookers. The Roman Emperor played the part of pharaoh, but with little conviction. The once rich and powerful cities of Abydos and Thebes had declined into a collection of squalid villages, hot beds of vice and insurrection. Romans visited the great temples as tourists, and around them brothels and taverns flourished along with the accompanying slave markets and the Lady Octavia lost no time in getting in on the act. The slave women, shipped up the Nile by the boatload sold cheaply to any brothel keeper eager to replenish his stock, for under Roman rule navigation on the river was safe and reliable.

"Keep together, you worthless whores, or you'll get another taste of the whip!"

Africanus had already feasted on the leather thongs swinging menacingly in his hand. Naked, except for a strip of cloth knotted around her hips, she strained at the oars along with four and twenty other similarly attired women, most of them black Nubians, or paler skinned slaves brought from the Northern colonies. The Phoenician had wasted no time in selling her to one of Lady Octavia's agents scouting the wharves of Alexandria.

Begrudgingly, she had to give credit where it was due. The agent was a black woman like herself, but there the similarity ended. Calla was large in every respect, massive wobbling breasts, an equally large bottom and hips, and thighs that could crush a man's skull. But she was not ugly. If anything, she was quite striking in her way. One of those women that men wouldn't immediately choose as a mate, yet having met her fell strangely under her charms, what with her infectious laughter and her brilliantly dyed hair, and those enormous breasts, she was difficult to resist. She also had the same effect upon women.

"I have just the opportunity you're looking for," she told Africanus, leading her by the hand. "A strong, good looking girl like you will do well in Thebes. Rich Romans pay a lot of money for black women."

She was telling the truth.

"And Thebes is a lovely place," she added.

But did not go into details.

"Not if I'm sold into slavery?" Africanus contradicted, sipping from a goblet of mellow wine.

"We are all slaves of a sort," Calla said. "But some of us are well favoured."

The truth again.

"So what do you have in mind for me?" she asked, looking with amazement at Calla's flaming red hair, and the tightly fitting red robe stretching with difficulty over her breasts and bottom.

"A companion to complement a well respected citizen of ample means. She has her own villa, and you will have your own quarters."

The truth, if taking into account any number of companions, not all of them respectable, and her own room in which to complement them, but certainly not situated in the well-respected citizen's villa.

Nevertheless, it seemed a haven after her recent sufferings; what with being ravaged by barbarians and almost butchered by the mad priestess, and then coming perilously close to ending her days living the life of a troglodyte.

Only after finding herself chained to a group of other hapless dupes driven like animals to the dock did she realize the truth.

Plying the oar, she smiled grimly at how convincing Calla had sounded, and how easily she had been taken in.

"Will I never learn?" she muttered aloud, arching her back from the whistling tails.

There was little opportunity to view the landscape, but from a few cursory glimpses, it seemed green and verdant if sparsely populated. Huts of mud and reed clustered together in frightened huddles at the river's edge. Once or twice, she saw vast temples and palaces seemingly abandoned or in disrepair, but the river craft were abundant; boats of all kinds made their way up and down the river. Some seemed so heavily loaded with grain that the water lapped ominously at the gunwales. Pleasure craft of varying sizes drifted happily by, their occupants lolling on divans or sporting with bevies of dusky maidens drafted in for the purpose. Slave boats rowed by near naked men and women came and went, some stopping to unload their cargo, others heading in the same direction up river. Towards nightfall, a brightly painted barge passed so close, the male passengers leaned over the gunwale to get a better view of the naked female rowers gleaming and dripping with sweat.

"You there, hove to!" a voice from the barge bawled, and the order to raise oars came as a desperate relief to the exhausted women.

One look at the goggle eyed male passengers told Africanus and her suffering companions what would happen next and it was not long before they were unchained and clambering wearily onto the deck of the barge.

There were more men than women but rather than wait their turn they decided to slake their lust simultaneously.

Africanus sat astride the first and, reaching under her legs, guided his throbbing cock easily into her sweating sex. She sat upright, jerking her hips, hoping to bring him off and get the wretched business over and done with. More than anything else, she needed sleep. Both the heat and sheer exhaustion of continual rowing against the current had all but drained her. Then the flat of a hand landed neatly between her shoulder blades tumbling her forwards. She fell over the man beneath, squashing her breasts against his chest and knocking her elbows on the deck. A pair of hands seized her ankles throwing her legs wide. In the next instant, they were at her bottom, fingertips worming into her crease, pulling it open revealing her puckered bottom hole. The man behind her sighed at the beauty of her buttocks, soft, round and wobbling, so beautiful that he could not resist pinching and fondling each cheek. She grunted as his weight bore down on her back as he fumbled clumsily with his cock aiming it into her bottom hole. One vigorous shove penetrated her arse and her whole body shuddered, trapped between both men now slamming into her. Her eyes misted and she felt nothing but a dull ache spreading through her belly and buttocks. A wild shriek of laughter erupted from her assailants as they both shot their loads and then withdrew making room for the next pair who hauled her onto all fours.

It was as she expected; one man taking her from behind, the other filling her mouth. As the night wore on, she became dimly aware of the men happily changing places with each other for as long as their strength lasted. Overhead the dark, star spangled sky turned to purple, then to pink and a glorious golden sunrise illuminated the horizon.

"You did well," the last man to ravage her bottom complimented. "Where are you headed?"

Her shoulders gave a barely perceptible shrug. "Thebes, I think," she muttered, feeling his wilting organ soften inside her throbbing sex.

He made a mental note to check every brothel until he found her. A woman who could take that amount of punishment and remain coherent was well worth another pounding.

The sun was well above the palm trees when the slaves boarded the boat firmly chained to the oars. Taking the strain, they bent their backs and rowed the craft midstream oblivious to the ribald compliments coming from the barge. It was close to sunset when the first hovels of the once great city hove into view. In semi darkness, the boat master herded the women towards various brothels, pushing them through the doors and happily collecting his fee.

"What a filthy hole," thought Africanus, trudging through narrow streets of dark and airless hovels.

An overwhelming stench of dried fish frying in rancid fat wafted from the open doorways around which hordes of naked children played in the overflowing gutters. Dead dogs and cats littered the unlighted street and from brief glimpses of the hut interiors, she saw nothing much beyond a rude plank bed, a few threadbare mats and heaps of broken earthenware vessels. She even saw a man and woman openly copulating much to amusement of passers by who found nothing unseemly in what ought to have been a very private affair.

At the end of a winding street, the sad convoy halted. Along with two of her miserable companions, she went through the doorway of a three-storied dwelling towering high above the sordid huts. In the dim light, she could just make out an overhanging balcony and large windows, those on the ground floor tightly barred and shuttered those on the upper floors open to admit the cool evening air.

Flicking their haunches with his whip, the drover herded them into an antechamber and moved on, cracking his whip over the heads of the remaining convoy.

"Ah, the new girls," a woman greeted, blasting acrid breath into their faces. "We have been expecting you."

She clapped her hands and a young slim slave barely into her teens came hurrying over. "Show the new girls to the wash room and see they are fed and watered," the woman commanded.

Fed and watered? What did she think Africanus was, a beast? But she managed to hide her feelings as she and the other two slaves followed the girl into a sunken brick chamber filled with water. It might have been stagnant and of doubtful odour, but it was at least wet and warm and complemented with a cake of soap. After they bathed, the girl showed them to their rooms and Africanus thought she was really seeing things.

Far from being a dirty rat infested chamber overrun with flies and vermin, the place was spotlessly clean. A huge bed with carved feet and an abundance of fresh linen occupied the centre of the floor. A refreshing breeze wafted through the open window through which she could clearly see the sky and hundreds of twinkling stars, whilst below the flickering fires of the huts threw ghastly shadows over the hovel walls. The girl disappeared as noiselessly as she came leaving Africanus still in a state of shock, for hanging in a cabinet was a long transparent robe evidently meant for her usage, along with combs, a mirror and all the clutter that women consider so indispensable to their well being, even down to a bottle of perfume.

She was still gazing in amazement when the girl returned with a plate of fish and bread and a small jug of wine, all of which smelt delicious. But something was wrong. She searched under the bed and in the bottom of the cabinet, checked every nook and alcove. Not a whip or cane in sight, not even chains or shackles. But she did find a golden earring that the previous occupant must have lost, probably during a bout of furious lovemaking.

It was worth pocketing.

She settled down to her meal and thought that maybe Calla had not been so much of a liar that she had anticipated.

However, it seemed odd that such a refined sort of brothel should exist like a pearl in the middle of a dung heap, but that was no business of hers and, curling up on the bed, she concluded that life in Egypt might not be so bad after all.

Exhausted from the previous days' exertions, she slept soundly and awoke to the soft footsteps of the girl entering her room with breakfast, a bowl of steaming porridge and generous portions of grilled fowl. The girl left without a word and closed the door softly behind her without bolting it Africanus noticed. It just seemed too good to be true, holed up in a brothel where she might come and go as she pleased. No sign of any guards or acid faced harridans to thwart her passage. With a little imagination, she could have been back in Rome if it were not for the rising stench of the hovels below slowly stirring into life. The occupants were making their way to the fields and beyond them, she could just make out the vast temples of Luxor with their ranks of columns and massive lintels rising like the skeleton of some long extinct creature.

It was not until midday that the brothel keeper came into her room. Seen in the daylight she looked middle-aged but had lost none of her fine figure. A white robe, held tightly at the waist hugged a firm pair of buttocks and breasts and had been slit to the hip offering a glimpse of her well proportioned legs. Her hair was glossy black and tied into a long tail behind her head.

"I expect you'll want to meet your customers," she beamed, striding across the floor.

"I did wonder about that, yes," Africanus returned, rising to greet her.

"Most of the entertainment takes place in the hall downstairs, but if a customer wishes to make use of you privately you will show him to your room, after he has paid for the privilege, of course."

"I understand," said Africanus, who really did not understand at all.

Entertainment? More and more she was forming the impression that her purpose was less of a prostitute and more of a tease than anything else. But there was nothing sinister in that. It was good business having splendidly dressed women offering only the barest glimpses of their charms to prospective clients, waiting on them, bending low displaying their cleavages, but keeping just out of range, giving men enormous throbbing hard ons, then charging the earth for a fuck in the privacy of their rooms. Rome was full of places like that. It was a comfortable little niche, if one could get it.

Smiling smugly, she followed the woman downstairs to the hall of entertainment.

The room was larger than she imagined with gaily-painted walls and a profusion of couches and tables laden with copious amounts of wine. She could see at once that the clients lolling on the couches were rich Romans on holiday and indulging in a little illicit sex before returning to their wives. She was not the only finely dressed slave. The two women who had accompanied her there looked equally splendid in their transparent robes, along with half a dozen others who were busy waiting at tables.

As her eyes grew accustomed to the lamplight she saw a pair of wooden frames, two upright trestles with a long stout pole resting between them and beyond that another pole, much stouter than the last, rising from floor to ceiling and another suspended with chains directly overhead.

Africanus, following the woman's' bidding, picked up a tray from a cabinet and carried its contents to the nearest Roman who, despite her expectations, did not fondle her near naked breasts swinging deliciously beneath her robe. Neither did he make a play for her bottom cheeks, but just accepted the drinks she offered and went on conversing with his companion. Perhaps the place was more sedate than she thought, and its clientele content merely to observe beauty rather than indulge it.

The woman clapped her hands and the idle banter ceased.

"Welcome to the House of the Sphinx," she greeted, smiling a row of large gleaming teeth. "Now gentleman you must choose. Don't be shy. Every slave here is at your disposal."

"Oh," thought Africanus, dropping her tray onto the nearest table.

"The one with her hair in a knot," a voice suggested. "Her arse looks solid enough."

All eyes turned on a brown skinned Nubian, her long hair fashioned into a huge knot at the side of her head. She was not as tall as the other slaves, but her figure was good and her arse was certainly solid, as were her firm high breasts. The lower parts of her stomach disappeared under a triangular bush of thick black, pubic curls luxuriously brushed and scented.

"Remove your robe, Weral and put yourself over the pole," the woman commanded.

The girl loosened a hasp and the robe floated into a pool around her ankles. She deftly stepped out of it and advanced towards the horizontal pole. Africanus could see she was already trembling and her nipples had clearly stiffened into frightened points. She stood in front of the pole, its length passing over her deeply embedded navel. In a single sweep, she bent over emitting a slight grunt as the shaft dug into her belly. On the other side, her fingertips just managed to touch her toes. At a signal from the woman male slaves cranked handles in the trestles lifting the pole slowly upwards. Bent over the pole, her arms and legs dangled helplessly at either side, and Africanus could see her breasts swaying under their own weight, her nipples pointing to the tiles beneath. Then the male slaves seized her ankles and drew them apart until her legs stretched as wide as nature would allow. Chains hanging from the trestles were swiftly manacled to each ankle, holding them open and it was possible to see the gaping pink slit of her sex. The

18

male slaves went around the trestles and attached more chains to her wrists. In a trice, these were secured to iron rings in the tiles holding her arms fast.

"Who shall administer the punishment?" the woman offered gaily, accepting a long supple plaited whip.

"You, Akara. You shall flog her!"

The woman bowed in mock solemnity and reached for the hasp at her shoulder.

Seen naked she was more voluptuous than Africanus imagined. For a woman probably in her early forties she had kept herself in good shape. Not an ounce of fat or a crease anywhere, except from the corners of her lips when she broke into her crocodile smile. But it was her magnificent legs and buttocks that held the audience riveted. The calves undulated in a perfect curving sweep to the backs of her knees, and then broadened into the long pale expanse of her thighs. Her pubic bush had been closely shaved and her nipples were now proud and hard.

"Very well, gentleman," she bowed. "If that is your wish."

She took her place behind the suspended girl, a little to the left and at about the right distance to swing the whip directly onto the now quivering buttocks. The girl emitted a sob and clenched her manacled hands. Her bottom cheeks flexed and hollowed as Akara lifted the whip high over her head. She paused allowing the clients to feast their eyes on her flattened stomach and protruding ribs as her arm rose to full height. Her breasts lifted and formed into two perfectly symmetrical globes, and there wasn't a man in the place who wouldn't have given his right arm to have them squashed against his chest.

A hissing whistle broke the silence and in a flash, the whip smacked over the centre of the girl's buttocks. A high pierced shriek reverberated around the walls and Africanus saw the other slaves cringe from the pain burning through the girl's naked rump.

Akara stood perfectly still admiring the effect the whip

was having on the blazing buttocks. A long thin red welt gradually formed across her moons and was soon joined by another only a finger's distance beneath it. The girl jerked her hips and calves from the sudden shock. Her buttocks broke into a wobble, softened now from the searing pain burning into her skin. Akara delivered another four carefully aimed strokes, keeping them close together, leaving enough skin untouched for further assault.

She paused again and accepted a glass of wine from one of her naked male attendants, and playfully stroked his hardened cock with the tip of the whip. She played it around his ball sack and gave a harmless flick across his bare rump. The effect on the audience was immediate; some were on their feet and already discarding their tunics.

"You clever bitch," Africanus muttered, watching the throbbing organs nodding at Akara's blatantly teasing display.

Not a word had been spoken or a gesture made and she had them eating out of her hand.

She opened her legs and drew the whip slowly under her buttocks, and with a flourish of her hand glided it through her sex slit, passed it under her nose, sniffed her own juice and then ran her tongue up its entire length. Even Africanus felt her heart skip at such a devastating display of sexual invitation. One of the clients had already shot his load and the young girl slave who had previously waited on Africanus rushed forward and dropped to her knees. He was still hard enough for her mouth to suck off the remaining drops.

"Remove your robes, all of you," Akara demanded, sweeping her almond eyes over the slave women.

Quickly, they loosed the hasps and stood gloriously naked under the flaring lamps.

"This is it," thought Africanus. "This is where we get fucked until sunset."

But not a man made a move towards them. All eyes were

back on Akara, now teasing the girl's sex. Open and vulnerable, she could offer no defence against the whip sliding deep inside her quivering tunnel. The pace quickened, her wrist jerking faster and faster until a flood of sex juice dripped to the floor. The girl's moans rose above her gasping pants as she reached her climax and Akara summoned Africanus to where she was standing.

"Open your mouth and suck her come," she said, displaying her gleaming, wolfish teeth.

This was it. This was where she started earning her keep. Her jaw dropped open and she put out her tongue, licking at the juice-slicked plaits as Akara drew the whole whip through her mouth. She swallowed and gulped, tasting Weral's juice lingering on her teeth.

"Isn't she sweet?" Akara teased.

Africanus nodded and knew at once that behind that gleaming smile lay an astute and calculating mind that was dangerous to cross.

"Shall we say, another twenty lashes, gentleman?" she suggested, sending the whip viciously over Weral's back.

"Listen to how she snorts," she laughed, lashing in an upward cut, sending the whip slicing into the girl's sex.

Weral caught her breath and blasted it through her nostrils. A stream of mucus splashed onto the tiles and she snorted like a pig at the trough. Wild guffaws filled the hall at the sound of her reverberating throat.

"That sow needs seeing to," one of the men proclaimed, advancing, cock in hand.

"Wait until I've finished with her," Akara said firmly, gathering the whip into a coil.

One sharp flick of her wrist and the whip uncoiled and wrapped itself around Weral's thigh. Her legs trembled from the shock and louder snorting followed.

"This is the funniest thing I've heard in months," Akara said to no one in particular, displaying her rows of gleaming teeth.

She lashed each buttock in turn, now using her full strength, and every stroke brought forth more snorting and gasping which had her tormentor rocking on her heels. Weral's bottom was a mass of blazing welts and she felt sure it had swelled to four times its size.

"Now you can have her," Akara said, dropping the whip and summoning the young girl slave.

While she slaked her thirst, the man stood on tiptoe and rammed his cock hard into Weral's sex. The girl grunted and jerked her slender hips. Not content with just fucking her, the man slapped her flanks and thighs increasing the pain already coursing through her belly.

There was a short interlude whilst Akara searched the faces of the remaining slaves, deciding which one would be the next to entertain her clients.

"You," she said, pointing her finger.

All eyes turned on the tall and splendid black woman who suddenly felt as if the whole world had shrunk to the miserable dimensions of the Hall.

"Do you see that pole," she smiled horribly, indicating the vertical shaft. "Let me see you climb it."

Africanus swallowed and looked at the pole. It seemed much higher than when she had first noticed it, and there was no doubt in her mind what Akara had in store.

She walked slowly to the pole and reached up grabbing the shaft with both hands. Taking her weight, she lifted herself up and swung her calves around the circumference. Another tug and jerk of her hips lifted her higher. She went on climbing until her bottom was at chest height of those standing around her.

Akara, chuckled and came close, running the flat of her hand over Africanus' thrusting buttocks.

"Beautiful, isn't she?" she taunted, slapping each half in turn.

She reached under the crease and rubbed the black woman's sex, cupping the bristling mound in the palm of her hand and squeezing until Africanus' eyes watered. Then, as if the thought had suddenly occurred, she ordered one of the slaves to kneel beneath her trembling rump.

"Suck her cunt 'til she comes," she sneered, and then broke into a wild peal of laughter.

Startled at the suggestion, a pale-skinned girl knelt at the base of the pole and pressed her face deep into the join of the rippling thighs. Her head twisted and bobbed as she sucked on the black woman's sex, nibbling at the aroused sex bud and licking the pouting labia.

"These bitches would fuck with a horse if I let them," Akara proclaimed. "See how she works her tongue."

The assembled men could see right enough, but were unaware it was more from fear than lust that the girl buried her face into the black woman's bottom.

Africanus heaved a sigh and clung hard to the pole. It was bad enough taking all her weight, let alone having her sex made wet and longing. Her belly stirred and she felt her nipples tingle. Whimpering softly, she held back tears of ecstasy as the worming tongue flicked rapidly over her clit. It was only a matter of time before she climaxed. Her thighs and calves flexed hard as she crossed one knee over the other clinging to the pole like a limpet.

Meanwhile the whipped girl was hauled from the shaft and thrown over the end of a couch, her legs open, her sex still wet and dripping.

"Please help yourselves," Akara offered, turning briefly away from the black woman. "Her bottom is there for the taking if any of you fancy it."

There was no shortage of takers and the first was quickly behind her, spreading her whipped cheeks and thrusting hard into her bottom.

Africanus bit on her lip desperately fighting the rising chill in her belly. But the effect was not lost on Akara who knew a woman in orgasm when she saw it. She watched closely as Africanus' belly contracted, heaving in and out, her breasts rising and falling, her toes curling, and her eyes mere slits of agony.

Akara's foot shot out kicking the girl away from Africanus' rump. Faster than the men could blink, she snatched up the whip and sent it whistling under the black woman's buttocks. Her whole back jolted from the unexpected shock and her buttocks went into trembling spasms. But she held on to the pole, knowing that if her grip failed Akara would whip her senseless.

So much for sobriety, she thought, knowing now just what sort of place this really was.

"Hold tight and open your legs," Akara commanded. "Stretch them wide!"

Africanus' fists clenched around the shaft and, taking a whole lungful of breath, she unlocked her legs and slowly opened them.

"Wider!" Akara barked, lashing the whip into the spreading bottom crease.

The long shapely legs slowly parted until they were fully spread, each leg jutting at right angles to the shaft. The sight of her straining thighs now iron hard and breaking into splendid hollows was not lost on the men. In a frenzied shuffling of feet, they gathered around the black woman, their cocks at bursting point.

"I must fuck her," a desperate voice whispered.

"Not yet," Akara cautioned, raising her whip hand.

The plaited whip sailed under Africanus' rump, catching the under hang of her buttocks. She squirmed and lifted her hips higher. Hugging the pole, the shaft went hard between her breasts and she couldn't help squashing them against the wooden shaft, giving the impression they were even larger than they already were.

Akara whispered to one of the men who promptly creased with laughter. But Africanus wasn't laughing when the whip sailed expertly against her left flank. She clung hard but could not prevent her body from turning around the shaft.

"I'm going to whip you all the way around that pole," Akara informed her, gathering the whip for a fresh strike.

She delivered four strokes in quick succession, driving the sobbing black woman further around the shaft, and kept on whipping until her victim had turned full circle. But now her strength was failing and she locked one thigh over the other and slid round and round crashing her bruised bottom hard onto the tiles.

Akara stood over her flicking the hardened nipples with the end of her whip.

"On your knees, slave," she ordered, but did not smile.

With a painful grunt, Africanus obeyed, putting her hands behind her back as one of the male slaves tied her thumbs with twine. Akara went behind her and planted the sole of her foot between her shoulder blades. A slow, deliberate shove of her heel sent the black woman tumbling onto her chest. One of the men thoughtfully placed a cushion under her tear-streaked face.

"Have her anyway you like," Akara offered. "Her cunt is still wet and her bottom well softened."

While one of the men mounted her, driving his cock into her throbbing sex, Akara turned her attention elsewhere.

The object of her next torment was a diminutive Nubian, standing less than five foot on her bare feet, but despite her slim frame her breasts were ample enough and the areolas spread over almost half her globes. When she saw Akara's blazing eyes turned upon her, the nipples instantly rose and throbbed, a reaction that the brothel mistress evidently relished.

"Hold your tits," she said, smiling at the thought of what was going through her mind.

The Nubian placed her hands under her breasts and lifted them. The whip she thought would lash onto her raised breasts was tossed aside and it was the flat of Akara's bare hand that smacked over the risen nipples. Not content with just slapping her, Akara rolled the nipples between her forefingers and thumbs, pinching until the girl let out a cry of pain.

"You must admit, she has a fine pair," she addressed her clients. "Just the sort that men like, eh? Full and ripe and so firm."

She slapped the sides of the girl's breasts, going from right to left, striking so hard the whole breast jiggled and shook. The huge discs of the areolas had now turned almost black and the liberally sprinkled pimples stood out and throbbed, but it was her nipples that caught the clients' attention. Each teat had transformed from a soft succulent berry into a hard pointed cone.

"See how they twitch," Akara taunted, wetting the ends of her fingers and rubbing saliva slowly around the nipples.

The areolas spread wider until the palm of her hand could barely cover them, and it seemed that the girl's nipples were twitching in time with the quickening of her beating heart.

"You see how she wants it," Akara announced, now smoothing the girl's bottom cheeks.

At the touch of her mistress' fingers gliding through her arse crease, the Nubian let out a harsh gasp and held her breath. Silently she prayed that her tormentor would not touch her fleshy thighs or pouting sex lips. To her relief, Akara took away her hand and placed the tip of her finger on her lower lip, already trembling from the hundreds of tingling darts paining her breasts and sex.

"I want to hear you pant like a bitch on heat," she whispered, forcing open the girl's mouth. "Put out your tongue and start panting."

The men had crowded around the girl and the sight of her enormous breasts and cute, tight buttocks was too much. Akara was mistress of her profession and knew the effect all this was having. The girl, teetering on the edge of orgasm, longed for any one of the openly displayed erections to drive hard inside her soaking cunt, yet no one could touch her. She stood alone in the centre of the room, her enormous breasts seemingly making up half her body. Her thighs fleshy and quivering shook with desperation.

Shaking uncontrollably, she put out her tongue and started panting, her breath coming in rapid, short inhalations. The men could see her plump belly fanning in and out and her breath getting more urgent. Then Akara pulled off her masterstroke. Taking one of the men by the hand, she led him to where the girl was standing and held his throbbing erection, stroking it slowly in her palm, keeping the purple head only a hair's breadth from the girl's arse cheek. From sheer desperation, the man ground his teeth and clenched his fists. He too wanted his cock pounding inside the girl's cunt. But Akara held him back, deliberately prolonging the agony of them both. She slapped the girl's bottom and breasts, urging her to pant and gasp faster, and at the same time tease her own nipples. Tears of agonized frustration trickled down her cheeks as she placed her hands under her breasts, holding them in her tiny hands whilst she thumb flicked each black tingling bud. Akara led the man to the girl's front and rubbed the tip of his cock through the mass of pubic curls. This was too much, being so close and yet so far. Just one shove of his loins would have penetrated her, but Akara went on grazing the tip under the girl's belly and around the outer fringes of her hair.

Suddenly she tightened her grip and gave a rapid shake of her hand. The man let out a groan like a speared lion and sent his juice soaring over the girl's front. She stopped panting and jerked her head as a stream of hot sperm shot over her face. Another splashed over her breasts and belly. Akara kept her hand moving, letting the man spend all over the girl's pubic mound and thighs.

"Lick your tits clean," Akara crudely ordered.

The girl lifted her breasts, squashing them together and lapping at the streams of sperm trickling into the cleft. She sucked in each nipple, rolling the teats over her tongue and sobbing hopelessly. At last, Akara relented.

"You can have her now if you wish," she said, without a trace of emotion.

It went without saying that the men rushed forward, grabbing the girl and dragging her roughly to the nearest couch. She was on her back with a man at each calf, holding open her legs whilst the first cock rammed into her. Some had reached the point of no return and ejaculated all over her face and hair. One or two deliberately aimed their cocks at her nipples and left them piled with their combined spending. No sooner had the first man reached his climax another immediately took his place. The girl resumed her panting and gasping, but now it came from the depths of her throat, the sounds of a woman reaching climax after climax as each man filled her sex.

Africanus was back at the pole, her arms reaching upwards, her feet on tiptoe, legs widely spread as her lover took her from behind.

"These bitches are all the better for being whipped before and after having sex," Akara told him, coming over to where the black woman was standing. "If you would care to take her to her room, she will be entirely at your disposal. May I recommend a belt? Her arse is strong enough to take at least forty lashes, unless of course you would prefer my own whip."

The man withdrew and although still hard, smoothed his hand over Africanus' rump.

"I think a belt would suit her admirably," he agreed. "Am I free to whip her anywhere I choose?"

"She will do exactly what you demand. If by any chance you should meet with any disobedience, she knows what to expect."

Naked, both Africanus and her lover made their way upstairs, where the air was cooler, the furnishing softer and out of reach of Akara. Only the belt swinging in his hand made her gulp.

"Your mistress said that you are entirely at my disposal," he reminded her, kicking the door shut. "Now I'd like to hear you start panting, just like that little tart downstairs."

He gathered the belt in his hand, and then cracked it over the bed. A great cloud of dust arose from the mattress leaving in its wake a deep indentation in the fabric.

"All right," she said quickly, watching the dust motes settle on her skin. "I'll pant, if that's what you want."

She started breathing fast, taking deeper and deeper breaths. Her bare breasts shook and heaved. Her nipples were already erect and throbbing, and just like the little Nubian, her belly expanded and contracted, breaking into creases across her navel.

The belt sailed into her rump with a hollow smack.

"Faster!" he bawled. "Much faster!"

Africanus' tongue went dry and her head started to swim.

Again, he sent the leather cracking over her naked rump.

"Faster, you idle bitch!" he snapped.

A curious throbbing started in her ears and the room seemed to spin. Her heart definitely quickened and the blood was rushing through her veins. From the depths of her sex arose a strange tingling, one she had never felt before. It was not immediately noticeable but was definitely there and was spreading right through her vaginal walls. He hit her again, aiming the belt under her legs.

"Aaoof," she grunted, and jerked her hips.

"Spread your arse cheeks," he said, his eyes glinting at the tall black woman standing naked and panting like a mare.

She reached behind and put her hands on her bottom, curling the fingertips deep into her crease. Gripping tightly she forced open her buttocks.

"Keep panting," he said his voice softer now as he flicked the end of the belt at her inner thighs.

"Of all the places, he just had to hit me there," she thought, her throat now completely parched, her tongue beginning to fur.

"I'm doing my best," she croaked, taking faster gulps.

The belt struck hard over her belly and she doubled up from the shock.

"Don't answer back!"

"I'm sorry," she sobbed, pulling herself upright.

Her clit pulsed and throbbed and it seemed her labia was swelling and getting hotter. A tiny weep of sex juice dripped from her slit and she caught her breath.

"If you come, I'll thrash you senseless," he said dangerously.

Now she understood. He was going to keep her panting and gasping, making her head swim, standing naked and still, pulling open her bottom cheeks whilst he whipped her. It was all a test, a weird trial of strength to see for how long she could hold back without reaching her orgasm.

It wasn't made any easier when he started lashing the belt into her bottom crease and under her legs, hitting harder with every stroke, landing the belt where he knew it would have the most effect. Her thighs began to quiver and sweat and to her amazement, he knelt at her feet, swept his tongue up the whole length of her inner thigh, and then, after a pause, licked all the way around her sex lips.

"I can't…keep…this…up," she gasped, feeling a cold chill start through her belly.

He ignored that and angled his head into her pubic mound. Africanus rocked on her heels and threw back her head. What was he doing now? His hands were smoothing her bottom, savouring the silky texture of her skin, going all over each buttock while his mouth opened and took in her sex lips. His tongue flicked over her clit and she let out a long howl. She had stopped panting and was breathing slowly, filling her lungs, desperately trying to restore some sort of equilibrium.

But now her thighs were shaking and her legs pricked with pins and needles. To add to the torture he started running his fingertips up and down the backs of her knees and thighs. He seemed to know exactly where to touch the very spots that had her moaning and grunting.

"No one told you to stop panting," he said, coming out from under her legs.

"Please, if you intend to fuck me, just do it," she shrieked emphatically.

The belt whistled and struck the sides of her flanks, and then lashed over her buttocks. A carefully aimed stroke sailed right under her legs and whipped against her belly.

"I'll fuck you when I'm ready," he told her. "Until then I want to see your whole body shake."

He sent the leather cracking anywhere within reach, bouncing it off her bottom, curling it around her thighs, whipping it through her crease and over her breasts. The pain was not so much sharp and hot, but dull and seemingly going deep into her body, titillating every sinew and pore. Her sex juice was running freely now, running down the insides of her thighs in a steady creamy rivulet. The panting had subsided to mere gulps and she tottered and fell, crashing backwards onto the mattress.

He moved fast, dragging her to her feet and ordering her to stand upright with her hands on her head. She waited, trembling with anticipation, wondering where he was going to strike next. She heard the belt whistle and jolted when it lashed over the crown of her buttocks. He delivered ten strokes, each precisely aimed at where he knew it would cause the most sensation, whipping her until blood raced through her veins, but mostly through her sex. Perhaps more from luck than deliberation the end of the belt struck her clit and she collapsed exhausted, soaking the floor with her juice.

"You've come," he said, rolling his eyes. "You were not supposed to do that. Now I shall have to punish you. The mistress told you what to expect if you were disobedient. Now up end your arse."

Africanus struggled on to all fours and thrust out her

31

rump. He gave her ten lashes across each buttock, whipping her as hard as he could, watching with glee as her bottom wobbled and trembled under every blow. When he had finished he knelt between her throbbing buttocks and penetrated her with a single thrust. He rode her slowly, slapping her thighs and back until he came.

"Now you can suck my cock," he said softly.

Groaning from the pain burning through her sex, she got onto her knees and sucked on his shaft, swallowing the last few stray drops that lingered in his balls.

"You can sleep now," he said, "I have finished with you."

Africanus hobbled to the window, not caring whether she was naked or who could see her. The cold night air was nectar to her parched throat and she stood at the cill filling her lungs.

Below, the twinkling lights of the hovels went out one by one and the town fell into silence. It would not be difficult, clambering over the ledge and making an escape. But where was there to go? It was doubtful whether a naked slave running through the maze of streets would attract much attention. But then, having reached the land beyond she would find herself in the desert, cold, dark and inhospitable, and beyond that the mountains or an endless barren plain. She was strong enough to swim the Nile but even if she made it, there was only another squalid town on the other side where she knew no one. Then it hit her, harder and more painful than any whip or belt. She was alone with no hope of ever getting back to Rome.

She knew now that she would end her days here in this rat-infested village, used and tormented, whipped and fucked until she was sore.

She curled up on the mattress listening to the creaking bed in the adjoining room and the soft footfall of her next client coming to slake his lust.

CHAPTER TWO

Queen Hatentita was pleased with her reflection; she had the kind of body for which any man would kill, she looked devastating in a diaphanous robe, she was a good looker, she had paid great attention to her mode of dress.

She looked like a whore.

Stinking of cheap perfume, her face painted with equally cheap paint and wearing worthless costume jewelry and an enormous plaited wig, she set off through the dark, unlighted streets of Thebes. She knew her way around and never needed to stop for directions. A carefully secreted, razor sharp dagger would take of any untoward advances that proved neither profitable nor sexually advantageous.

It was not the first time she made her way to the lurid fleshpots tucked away in dark alleys. She knew most of the harlots, tipsters and clients, if not by name then by sight. She called herself Atata. She was a part time whore. A pretender to the ancient throne of Egypt. She fucked like a rabbit. She was good at it. And no one ever guessed who she really was.

But tonight was different from the others. It was not a night she would spend on her back, legs thrown open and fucking her heart out for the mere pleasure of having multiple orgasms. She was on a mission to find just the kind of woman she needed to fulfill her ambition of overthrowing the detested Romans. There were plenty of black whores in the brothels but finding the one she needed was not going to be easy, and patience was not one of Hatentita's virtues.

She picked her way through the overflowing gutters littered with animal corpses and human offal, pinching her nose and holding her hand over her mouth, dodging drunks and half-naked harlots willing to fuck anything for a penny, and found the house she wanted.

"Atata!" greeted the brothel owner. "We have sorely

33

missed you. Where've you bin, fucking your sweet arse off in Memphis, I suppose."

She shrugged and accepted the drink he offered, then, taking an earthenware tablet inscribed with a number, she hung it around her neck and seated herself on the bench with the other whores. The only other black woman there was a freed slave. A branded mark above her right breast betrayed that she had once belonged to Julius Sentonius. The name meant nothing to Hatentita, but the girl was no fool and her quick, dark eyes missed nothing. She knew all the right moves, crossed her legs when a fresh client entered the room, letting her robe fall open to the top of her thighs. She had good legs and knew how to use them. Her dress was open at the front revealing large breasts but kept the nipples half hidden even though they were erect and left little to the imagination. Her head was completely shaven except for a side lock of long braids growing at the left of her scalp. The women in the harem wore their hair like that and Hatentita wondered. It was just possible that she might be a discarded concubine, and those women often had scores to settle with their former masters.

Biding her time, she sat sipping her drink, giving the eye to the men who came and went. It was a good hour before she heard what she wanted to hear.

He stood well built and swarthy, a fine rippling torso and strong thighs, a scarred face, probably from a knife fight. He looked fit and the kind of man some women have wet dreams over.

"I'm in the mood for fucking two of your best whores," he announced to the brothel owner, casting his eyes over the assembled women.

"Then you need look no further, Anka. I have just what yor lookin' for. Let me introduce you. Atata, Philomena, on your feet."

Hatentita and the black woman arose and smiled sweetly.

"The first likes it from behind and will gladly take it up

her arse. The other will suck yor cock 'til yor balls wrinkle. Both come highly recommended and at a good price."

He strolled casually over, nodding his satisfaction.

"I'll take them both...if they're willing to fuck each other. I want them well drilled before I dip my cock in their pots."

The brothel keeper laughed at the thought of two whores fucking one another. "I'm sure they would happily oblige. Uh, I can provide the necessary tools."

"Make sure it's good and long. I want their eyes watering and their cunts split," he said, in a throaty tone.

As a rule, Hatentita was not overly attracted to her clients. Most were in need of a bath and grunted like hogs when they mounted her, but this one did bring a tingling to her thighs. She could see that the black whore was thinking the same. Her nipples had definitely enlarged at the sight of him.

"Ten silver pieces for both," the brothel owner suggested, and then accepted the five he was offered and threw in a bottle of cheap wine for good measure.

All three processed to the rooms upstairs and Philomena shoved open a door. The room, adequately furnished for their purposes boasted a large bed, a piss bucket and a row of hooks on which to hang their clothes.

The women disrobed and stood naked before him awaiting his command.

"Which one of you is going to wear this?" he asked, tossing a huge polished wooden dildo onto the bed.

"I'll fuck the Egyptian," Philomena said abruptly, her dark eyes flashing.

Without waiting for any argument, she reached out and seized the dildo. Her slim fingers moved fast, throwing the straps behind her and knotting them tightly over her buttocks. The third strap went under her legs, cutting into her sex and then up through her bottom crease. One sharp tug fitted it in place.

Hatentita looked at the dildo rising from Philomena's

pubic mound and gulped. She was thin and wiry but her buttocks were pert and compact. Her legs were slender but muscular, the sort of woman who could fuck with a vengeance.

"Don't just stand there woman," Anka grated to Hatentita. "Get your arse over that bed."

She was unused to being treated like this. Usually she took the lead on the rare occasions when a man wanted two whores and even rarer when he wanted them to have sex. However, that was his privilege and she dutifully spread her legs and bent over the edge of the bed, bracing herself for what was to follow.

The black woman stood behind her, putting her hands on Hatentita's hips and easing her bottom gently onto the dildo.

"It's too big," Hatentita protested, feeling her sex lips stretch around its circumference.

It was also long and with Philomena bent on riding her hard, the pain would be excruciating.

"Use this on her," Anka said bluntly, tossing his belt at Philomena, who, grinning widely caught it in mid air.

Already Hatentita sensed an unspoken attraction between the black whore and the client and knew that whatever would follow she was going to be on the rough end of it. But she had displayed leadership and had taken the lead with consummate skill, getting the client on her side and being the first to grab the dildo artfully letting herself off the hook.

"I can fuck without taking a beating," Hatentita hissed, looking over her shoulder at the belt swinging in Philomena's hand.

"Give it to her anyway," Anka suggested, warming to the idea of one whore beating the shit out of another.

Philomena rising to the occasion winged the belt over Hatentita's bare back.

"Aaagh, that hurt, you bitch," she snarled.

"And this is going to hurt a lot more," her assailant laughed, lashing it across the backs of her thighs.

It was then that a red mist clouded Hatentita's eyes. As future queen of Egypt, she certainly did not intend playing second fiddle to a slave. Her right foot sprang up and caught Philomena hard in the groin who recoiled and swore horribly.

The belt came flying back and cracked over the base of Hatentita's spine, and then lashed under her legs. Hatentita stood up and spun around on her heels. Before Philomena could blink, her fist shot out and smacked her under the jaw. Anka watched with a mixture of amusement and fascination unsure whether this was all part of the act, or whether it was spontaneous. Either way it was good entertainment watching the whores breaking into a stand up fist fight.

But it did not last as long as he hoped. Both women had come to the simultaneous conclusion that knocking each other senseless was a waste of energy, not to mention the damage they both knew they could readily inflict. A battered and bruised whore would not be in much demand. As a rule, men liked their whores in good shape.

"Give it me gently," Hatentita whispered, and Philomena nodded her assent.

She dropped the belt and placed her hips neatly at Hatentita's rear. She took the dildo in her hand and moved it slowly around the Egyptian's sex lips. A gentle nudge sent the polished head inside her. The tip grazed her clit and Hatentita's labia quivered in anticipation. Philomena wetted her fingers and ran them down the dildo's shaft. Her hands gripped Hatentita's hips and pulled her steadily backwards. She jerked her pelvis driving the wooden shaft deeper into the sucking tunnel. Hatentita caught her breath holding it tightly in her lungs. Then as Philomena gave a final thrust, it whooshed from her throat in one mighty gust.

"Now let me see you ride her," Anka said, settling into a chair.

Philomena now had the edge and was eager to please him. With Hatentita fully penetrated, she could do little in the way of protest or escape.

"Yes, master," she returned obsequiously, and gripped Hatentita's hips.

Roaming her hands feely over the Egyptian's back, she withdrew the dildo and played it around the labia, angling her body so Anka could see the effect it was having. Hatentita's sex opened like a flower each petal quivering a gorgeous pink. She paused and then let the dildo glide in to the hilt. Her hips broke into a dance snaking from side to side and the client's throat went dry with despair. Her gleaming ebony buttocks flexed and tensed and then each half wobbled against the next seemingly acting of its own accord.

"Phew!" he breathed, his eyes fixed on her bottom crease.

"The Egyptian has a good body, master," Philomena complimented, stroking Hatentita's thighs.

But she knew the master was watching her twisting hips and buttocks. There wasn't another whore in Thebes who could shake her arse like that. He could see the flushed face of Hatentita and her fingernails tearing at the fabric.

"Slap her thighs," he commanded. "You're being too gentle with her."

Given that the instruction came from a paying client, she had no choice but to obey regardless of her earlier promise. She looked slyly at Anka who grinned in return. The unspoken understanding had again been reached and both knew what the other wanted.

A slap from Philomena was no light thing and the sound of her hand striking against the broader expanse of Hatentita's thigh echoed around the room. A livid imprint of her hand formed on the paler skin and she hit her again, slapping each thigh in turn until the skin blazed.

"You fucking bitch," Hatentita muttered, gritting her teeth.

She swore that when she became Queen, her assailant would be the first buried up to her neck in sand and left to rot. But at that moment, there was nothing she could do but clench her fists and suffer the flat of the hand now slapping her flanks and back. Then Philomena pulled her masterstroke. Keeping the dildo engulfed to its fullest depth, she reached down and grabbed Hatentita's ankles. A sharp tug bent her legs at the knees and she toppled forward. But Philomena kept the dildo rammed tight in her sex and now started riding her. Slowly, as her arse broke into another orgiastic dance, she spread her arms away from her sides, forcing open the Egyptian's thighs.

"That's good," Anka breathed, watching Hatentita's arse splitting.

He also heard her groaning with pain and delighted in seeing her face screwed in agony as the black woman jerked her hips so fast the buttocks turned to jelly.

Hatentita's sex was hot and burning, every thrust ripped at her sex petals and it felt as if her labia had been torn in half. She was no stranger to cock and had some big ones in her time, but nothing compared with what she was taking now.

"Please," she begged, "I can't take any more."

"Just another few minutes, master," Philomena suggested spitefully, gathering her strength for another fearful insertion.

"Ride her for as long as you like," Anka encouraged, in no hurry to see the spectacle end.

Flexing her biceps, Philomena brought Hatentita's ankles hard over her buttocks and the Egyptian howled in pain.

"See how her cunt opens," Philomena taunted, twisting her hips left and right, deliberately driving the plum of the dildo into the vaginal walls.

She released her grip on Hatentita's ankles and fell

forward, leaning over the length of her back, reaching under her chest, groping for her breasts. Her thin, pointed fingers squeezed each nipple bringing tears to the Egyptian's eyes. Sweating from the exertion of fucking the woman beneath her, Philomena slithered like an eel, slapping her belly against the spine and squashing her breasts over the shoulder blades. From where Anka was seated, it looked as if both women had become joined at the hip and as the dildo teased the throbbing clit, both women broke into a confused array of thrashing arms and legs. It was almost comical watching Hatentita struggling in agony beneath the jerking black whore, nudging with her elbows, striking viciously at anything within reach, and the black woman in turn struggling to remain inside her.

Again, he wasn't sure if this was all contrived, or whether the Egyptian really was sobbing in agony, her legs wide spread as the black woman rode her hard. The dildo creamed with juice and the polished wood shone in the dim light, but despite Hatentita's love juice pouring from her sex, the pain was still unbearable.

But Philomena loved it. Ever since having been sold into slavery she had dreamed of getting her own back on the Egyptians. The chance rarely came but now it had she was determined to make the most of it and Hatentita's howls were music to her ears as she gathered her strength for one last savage thrust of her hips.

Her lips contorted into a snarl and she slammed her pelvis against Hatentita's rump. Anka could smell the musky scent wafting from Hatentita's sex and could see her juice dripping. Then as a final act of vengeance, Philomena raked her talons down the whole length of the Egyptian's back.

Anka rose from his seat and ambled to where the women were lying exhausted and panting.

"You both did well," he complimented, patting Philomena's rump. "I never expected such a display. Now I'm going to have you both. Take off that thing and lie over her."

"You're going to take us both from behind?" Philomena asked, releasing the straps.

He nodded and pushed her forward, sending her tumbling over Hatentita. Both woman lay face down, their legs spread and cunts wide open. Hatentita was still hot and dripping and he plunged straight into her.

A feeling of masculine strength came over him as he fucked Hatentita, taking possession of her body whilst the other whore lay over her, her sex open and waiting. He could also fondle both of them at the same time, playing his fingers around the Egyptian's sex and then smoothing his palms over Philomena's arse. He rode Hatentita with surprising gentility, taking his time and savouring the warmth of her sex tunnel, then withdrawing and plunging into the black woman's expectant sex, riding her with greater gusto and relishing the wobbling of her soft buttocks. Beneath her Hatentita moaned in ecstasy, her body tingling with longing and the satisfaction of reaching orgasm. But Anka kept her in suspense until she begged again for his cock. He slipped out of the writhing Philomena and saw his cock slicked with juice. Another feeling of masculine power came over him, mixing the juices of both women, and he marveled at how differently they smelled, the musky aroma of the Egyptian contrasting with the stronger and earthier aroma of the Nubian. When Philomena's sex started to flow, he watched her rich creamy juice dripping onto the crown of Hatentita's arse and running through her crease, gathering at the portals of her sex, and then greasing his cock as he plunged into her. But now as his ball sack tightened and his cock suddenly throbbed he was faced with a painful decision, which one would receive his spunk. He thought he could pleasure them both if he was quick enough and with masterful self control he let the first jets of juice empty into Hatentita and, as she squirmed like a serpent, he pulled back and dived straight into Philomena. He let his cock spend of its own accord, keeping his loins as still as he could while his spunk ejaculated into the depths of her sex. He clenched his buttocks and came fast out of her intending to give Hatentita the remainder, but his rampant cock thought otherwise and he shot his load over her thighs and he cursed himself for not holding back. He stood upright and Philomena rolled off Hatentita, lying on her back and gazing at him with enraptured eyes. It was a real man who could fuck two women at once and then come into both of them. Hatentita rolled over and lay on her side, her hands clutching her soaking mound. She looked at the gaze in Philomena's eyes and knew at once that this was not the woman she had come to seek. The bitch was practically begging for it, reaching out and stroking his cock. If he told her to stuff her cunt with nutmeg, she would be weak enough to do it.

She closed her eyes inwardly cursing at so much effort for so little gain.

Philomena was off the bed and on her knees, jerking his cock and aiming the plum over her breasts. The look in her eyes was pure joy as his load spilled over her nipples. She also sensed victory and was soon rewarded.

"I'll take you for the rest of the night," he said looking down as she took his cock in her mouth. "I hope you can take a good thrashing on that pretty bottom."

"Beat me as hard as you like," she offered, licking his balls. "As long as you fuck me afterwards."

He cast a censorious eye at Hatentita. "You did well," he complimented. "But this whore is more to my liking."

There was nothing personal in his choice, and he preferred the company of one whore and besides, beating them both would be an unnecessary waste of strength.

Hatentita put on her robe and went downstairs to the washroom. She did not like what she saw. She looked a total mess. Her face ruined with mascara running all over the place, her wig fallen askew and her bottom well bruised.

Inwardly she wondered how much more of a battering she would have to endure before her mission was brought to completion. There were hundreds of black slave whores in this city and she despaired.

"Atata, you leavin' so early. I've got just the man for you," the fat brothel keeper announced.

She ignored that and made her way along the street determined to make one more play before returning home.

Africanus couldn't concentrate. Her next client had all but worn her out insisting he fucked her four times in succession, and then ordering her downstairs to fetch him more wine and bread. After he had gone, she had a few minutes peace, doing nothing more arduous than sluicing her sex and dousing away the last drops of juice that clung stubbornly to her pubic fleece, before returning downstairs and offering herself to the next man who wanted her. There was something about male spunk clinging to her hair that she found distasteful, huge globules that looked like cold porridge and, grimacing, she brushed her fleece until the curls shone. She felt better seating herself on the cill and watching the late revellers staggering home. This place was a gold mine for any brothel owner. This part of the world that had once been the centre of the mightiest and most glittering empire on earth had now degenerated into a seedy backwater where there was nothing better to do than till the fields and fuck oneself stupid.

With the light behind her, she made a splendid profile, her long legs bent at the knees, her naked breasts forming a perfect silhouette of feminine beauty. In the darkness below, footsteps she heard coming along the street had suddenly halted and she peered into the gloom, but saw and heard nothing except the dim light of a hovel and the terrified shrieks of a woman receiving a sound thrashing. She thought she discerned a figure standing stealthily opposite, keeping out of sight but watching her every move.

"I'm losing my mind," she muttered, and sloshed a mouthful of bitter wine round and around her teeth.

She threw back her head and sent the liquid cascading over the sill. She heard it hit the stones with a resounding smack and laughed.

The shadow below moved abruptly and, illuminated for an instant by the light of the hovel, Africanus saw the vague form of a woman. She looked up at the window, hesitated, and then came out into the light. The door of the brothel opened and closed emitting in that brief interlude the raucous din of the revellers.

Africanus entered the waiting room paying little heed to the heavily painted Egyptian whore got up to look like some long extinct princess.

She was well known it seemed and several whores greeted her by name and inquired as to where she had been keeping herself.

"Oh, Atata, long time since you favoured us with your presence," Akara said sarcastically.

The Egyptian pulled a face and slowly crossed her legs, giving the impression that the brothel mistress meant nothing to her.

Africanus liked that. Most of the other whores seemed afraid of her. For a couple of minutes their eyes met, both women coolly appraising each other, as women do. Then a sudden distraction diverted their attention.

"Marius Aquinus," Akara beamed, flashing her teeth. "Welcome to my humble house. Your pleasure is our pleasure."

"You never change," thought Hatentita, watching Akara embrace the Roman with her usual false frozen smile.

"I'm in need of cheering up," he announced. "Something to distract me from the constant nagging of my horrible wife."

"Then you need look no further. Everything you need is here. I'd like to recommend Zaida, a fresh young country girl, an unspoiled creature whose family have regrettably fallen on hard times." She gave him a playful nudge. "And she likes it up her bottom," she whispered.

"I'm looking for a more experienced woman, or shall I say women. I have in mind a little sport. What about that one?"

"Oh, Atata. A thoroughbred Egyptian from the upper reaches of the Nile. She is dirty and knows how to use her mouth. But I really would like you to try Zaida, I'm sure you would not be…"

"No. The Egyptian," he persisted. "And…" he turned, surveying the other assembled whores. "That black one. She looks a fine piece."

"Africanus. A new girl in my stable. She has already proved her worth and her arse will take a good whipping as she has already demonstrated."

"I'll take them both," he chuckled, leaning into Akara and whispering in her ear.

She listened intently and burst into a peal of high shrieked laughter. "No one's ever asked to see that before. But I'm sure they'll oblige such a distinguished visitor as yourself, Marius Aquinus. Atata, Africanus, go into the Hall of Entertainment."

The two whores got up and, flashing calculated smiles, trooped into the Hall.

"I wonder what the fuck he's got in mind," Hatentita sneered, giving the Roman an evil glance.

"The usual stuff," Africanus replied. "Thrashing our backsides and fucking us afterwards."

It seemed that in only the few minutes they had been together the two women were of a like mind. But it was too early to tell if the black woman would measure up to Hatentita's expectations.

The hall was already crowded with clients and their whores, and a naked slim dark girl was whirling around the vertical pole, keeping her legs wide open and flashing her sex as she spun. On the couches, couples were fondling and groping each other.

Akara disappeared into an antechamber and came back accompanied by a slave who carried a huge pitcher of stale, rancid wine and two goblets. She placed them on a table where Hatentita and Africanus were seated.

"Fill your bellies with this," she ordered, her tone brooking no argument.

Africanus took a hefty gulp and promptly heaved.

"Uurgh. What the hell is this?"

Hatentita followed and her face contorted into a distasteful grimace. "She's mixed it with lemon juice and cloves," she spat.

"Is that supposed to put us on heat?"

"No," Hatentita grated. "It's supposed to make us piss."

"Drink all of it, and then refill your goblets. I want to hear your bellies sloshing with wine," Akara said slyly.

The wine was so bitter that it was all they could do to take a mere sip, let alone drink the whole pitcher.

"I shall be sick if I drink this muck," Africanus shivered.

"You won't be sick," Hatentita assured, who knew a little of the art of poisoning. "But your bladder will give you hell."

They were left alone to drink the foul concoction that Akara had so expertly prepared, and no else in the room was permitted to approach them, apart from a burly male servant who stood over them ensuring they swallowed every drop.

Africanus, between heaving and coughing, took a longer look at the Roman. Dimly, she recalled seeing him at one of Lady Octavia's gatherings, and she shuddered at the remembrance of her earlier days when she had first encountered her, and the beating she had so joyously delivered.

But that was a long time ago, and she took another pull at the goblet.

When they had drained the pitcher, another was fetched equally as vile and potent.

"We can't drink all that!" Africanus protested. "Our bellies are already full."

"Do as you're told," the burly slave grumbled. "Or the mistress will have you as crocodile bait."

"Just drink it," Hatentita advised softly. "If you don't she'll have it poured down our throats. I know that bitch, and she's capable of anything."

It took a good half hour to drain the pitcher and already their guts were churning. They crossed their legs and squeezed their stomach muscles.

"I shall need to piss soon," Africanus winced, clutching her belly.

How much had she drunk? She guessed it to be at least somewhere close to a gallon, and her belly had visibly swollen. But strangely, she didn't feel drunk; neither was her head swimming or her fingers tingling.

"Take off your robes and get into the centre of the room," Akara chortled, barely containing the amusement creasing her face.

The women stood up and loosed the hasps, letting the robes drop from their shoulders. A hum of approval arose from the assembly at the sight of their nakedness. Walking tall and upright, the whores took long purposeful strides over the tiles, but despite their graceful posture, the holding of their heads and long, sensuous legs and full rounded breasts, there was no disguising the plump wobble of their bellies.

"Marius has devised an entertainment for you," Akara smiled, her rows of teeth gleaming. "Something I've never thought of, until now."

She put one arm around Africanus' shoulder and smoothed her palm over the rumbling belly. "Isn't she nice and fat? Enough wine in there to satisfy a whole legion. And take a long look at Atata; anyone would think she was with child."

47

The assembly laughed when she slapped their bellies and playfully punched them at the navel.

"Please, I need to piss," Africanus shuddered, feeling the wine working through her bladder.

"You will, all in good time," Akara placated. "Now fetch in the bowls."

A slave hurried across the floor and placed two earthenware bowls at an equal distance from where the two groaning women were standing.

"Your purpose now is to fill those bowls with piss. Do it anyway you like. The one who fills the most shall be rewarded. The one who fails, severely punished. Begin."

Hatentita had done some odd things in her time, but humiliating herself in front of a bunch of drunken Romans was too much.

"I'll fuck anyone you want me to," she choked, "but I'm not pissing in that bowl."

"Ah ha," Akara grinned. "I knew you'd need a little persuasion."

The whip she always carried lashed over Hatentita's belly with a hollow thump. She went behind her and lashed her buttocks.

"If you don't do as you're told, I'll have you dragged into the street, then the whole city will watch you piss."

She didn't know it, but that was one threat Hatentita couldn't risk. Her whole credibility as ruler would be destroyed, if anyone did recognize her when she ascended the throne.

Africanus merely shrugged. She had been forced to piss in public before and had got used to it, and her belly was wreaking havoc, grumbling and growling, not to mention the acute pain she was suffering.

Without waiting any further instructions, she got on her back and raised herself on her hands and feet, arching her spine and spreading her legs. Her bottom lifted high in the air, and for a few seconds nothing happened. Something inside had tightened, and try as she might she just couldn't perform. The assembly crowded forward, gazing into her winking sex, holding their breath, waiting to see her urine gushing from her cunt. It was Akara who came up with the solution. She fetched a large wooden spatula used for stirring the porridge pots and whacked it hard on the top of her belly. Africanus let out a harsh grunt and heaved her loins. Then, in a sudden rush, a stream of steaming water gushed from her sex. It was by accident that her aim was perfectly on target. The water drummed into the bowl and she emptied half her tortured bladder before the stream subsided into a trickle.

"You see," Akara, taunted the Egyptian. "She knows when to obey. Now do likewise."

And the whip cracked into her arse.

Hatentita got onto all fours, lowering her head and burying her face under the falling braids. She didn't want anyone to see the hot embarrassed flush colouring her cheeks. Resting on the palms of her hands, she dug her toes into the floor and raised her bottom as high as she could. Her legs spread and she thrust out her rump. Grunting, she strained her belly and emptied it in a flood.

"Rubbish!" the assembly roared, as her water sailed over the bowl and formed a steaming lake on the tiles.

Africanus gave another heave of her belly and sent another stream, not as fierce as the last, but a steady cascade directly over the bowl's rim. Three more heaves and grunts and she crashed to the floor, smiling like an idiot.

Hatentita braced her loins and emitted a few desultory squirts that splashed around her feet and then dripped sadly from her sex.

"What a miserable performance," Akara said with mock severity. "Now I shall have to punish you. I'll have your belly heaving with as much as you can take and have you whipped the whole length of the street."

"Leave her alone," Africanus intervened. "She did her best."

"Her best wasn't good enough. Now she'll be whipped, after she's filled her belly. Unless of course, you wish to administer the punishment, in which case I'll have her flogged now, over that pole."

If she thought that Africanus would baulk at that suggestion, she was mistaken.

"I'll flog her, if you'll forgo having her belly filled," she suggested.

Hatentita couldn't believe her ears. It took a lot of courage in defying Akara. She could easily turn and have her saviour sold into one of the gold mines, or pulling a plough under the searing heat. And she wondered why she had taken such a risk. She made a quick mental calculation. The black woman was tall, voluptuous, quick witted in saving her and was certainly brave, and her aim was good. But she wondered if she had the strength to use a whip. It wasn't everyone who could whip another's backside raw without flinching. If she could pass that test, she might well be the one she sought.

"Flog me," she said softly.

"Give the disobedient wretch twenty strokes," Akara commanded.

Hatentita stood upright, placing her hands on her head, keeping them out of harms way while Africanus took up her position.

All eyes were turned upon her and she wished now that she'd kept her mouth shut, after all the Egyptian was nothing to her, just another painted whore like all the rest she seemed fated to meet. But it wasn't so much the sympathy she had felt for the Egyptian as the dislike she harboured for the brothel mistress. If anything grated her nerves is was that silver smile and those teeth. Africanus didn't like women who displayed so many teeth when they smiled. She'd met too many like that and so far not one of them had done her any good.

"Get on with it," Akara chided. "Or don't you have the stomach for it."

And the teeth gleamed with malice.

"This is going to hurt," Africanus warned Hatentita in a low whisper.

Marius Aquinus moved to the front of the assembly and thought he had seen that black woman before. He was also sure that she had recognized him earlier on, and his face screwed in thought.

However, he was soon distracted by the sound of leather cracking onto bare flesh. Hatentita gritted her teeth and started recalling all the names of the people she intended to despatch into the underworld when she became queen. She had already put Akara at the top of her list as Africanus gathered the whip for the second lash.

It struck the small of her back, which was slim enough to allow the whip tail to coil around her waist. She sucked her breath and muttered the name of the Roman governor, the second who would make that fateful journey into darkness.

The whip landed diagonally from shoulder blade to buttock leaving a blazing welt in its wake. It seemed the black woman had no qualms about flogging her, much as she flogged her own slaves and, as the next lash came in an opposite diagonal, she realized that Africanus was no amateur.

Marius Aquinus studied the swinging ebony arm sailing through the air. Where in the name of all the Gods had he seen her before?

Hatentita ground her teeth and started breathing fast through her flaring nostrils. Tears salted her eyes and the assembly faded into an indistinct blur. Only the excited voices urging Africanus to greater efforts betrayed their presence.

"Whip her tits, let's see them jiggle," one of the whores bellowed.

Africanus moved to the left and the whip lashed over Hatentita's nipples. The shock was greater than she

51

anticipated and Hatentita's breasts wobbled and bounced and she doubled over in pain.

"Excellent!" Akara approved, genuinely surprised at Africanus' prowess.

Already she had designs on her. Women who could wield a whip with such devastating effect definitely had their uses, and there plenty of men who enjoyed being flogged by a woman, and were willing to pay handsomely for the privilege.

"Stay where you are and touch your toes," she yelled at Hatentita before the whipped woman could straighten up to her full height.

She bent lower, her fingertips just touching the floor. Africanus could see her trembling now as the pain sunk in. Her bottom was perfectly round and assumed the shape of a ripe pear as it swelled from her hips. She had a good body and Africanus found herself wondering why a woman as good looking as that had descended into whoredom. But women choose that profession for any number of reasons; some for money, others out of desperation, and some for the sheer joy at having so much cock, and she couldn't make up her mind which.

She brought her arm up in a swift uppercut, catching the Egyptian under her buttocks, then passed her arm across her chest and sent the whip downwards over the crown of the quivering cheeks. Without realizing it, she was going through the motions of swordplay, much as she had done in Quintus' training school, delivering each blow with studied precision, swinging the whip left and right, now in a forward thrust and then returning with what would have been the killing blow.

Marius Aquinus watched her through squinted eyes. It was coming back now; the place where he had seen her and, for several seconds, he stared agog. The Colosseum. He had seen her in the Colosseum. And he rubbed his eyes in disbelief. The bitch was a gladiatrix! No wonder she wielded that whip so accurately. Only a trained fighter could do that. He had also seen her before on a previous occasion, but couldn't remember where.

As the final stroke felled the Egyptian, he sidled up to Akara now flushed and flashing her teeth.

"I hope the display lived up to your expectations," she grovelled, sliding her arm around his waist.

"Wonderful," he acknowledged. "But where did you find her?"

"One of the agents bought her in Alexandria. Are you interested in buying her? Because if you are, she won't come cheap."

"I might have a use for her," he evaded. "Perhaps I could hire her for a night or two. I have visitors from Rome who might want to get between her thighs."

He was lying. Cellenius the governor would pay handsomely for a staged combat with a woman like that, and there was no shortage of slaves who would make ample sword fodder.

"I'll have to think about it," Akara hedged.

She also was fully aware that the black woman was worth a lot more wielding a whip than just lying on her back, and she wasn't going to take any chances in losing her.

"You did well, flogging that miserable wretch. She got what she deserved, and you are still entitled to your reward for filling that bowl. Please help yourself to the wine and meat, and if you choose to fuck any of the men you are free to do so." She looked at Hatentita struggling to her feet and wrinkled her nose in disgust. "This bitch isn't worth the ground she stands on. Have her flogged out of the house."

"I'd like her to wait on me," Africanus intervened, thinking that she had shown great fortitude in taking such a flogging, and she hadn't screamed once, not even a whimper.

"Very well, if that is your desire. She can wait on you

53

for the rest of the night and in the morning, I'll have her thrown in the gutter where she belongs. What a foul piece of shit," she muttered, going off to where Marius Aquinus was busy groping the tits of Zaida.

"I'm sorry I had to flog you so hard," Africanus apologized, as they made their way to a quiet alcove away from the rising hubbub.

"No need to feel sorry," Hatentita said unexpectedly, seating her welted rump on the luxury of a well-padded cushion.

She straightened her wig and wiped away the tears from her cheek, smudging black mascara all over her face. "I suppose you think I'm just a gutter whore," she said, lowering her voice.

"Aren't we all," Africanus replied, suddenly remembering how great she was once was.

"No, not all of us," Hatentita said calmly. "Does that cow own you, or do you live out?"

"One of her agents bought me from a Phoenician and had me shipped up here to this hell hole," Africanus informed, lifting a goblet.

"If you hate it so much, why don't you run?"

"Where is there to run to?"

"I know a place, not far from here where she would never find you. You would be well treated and could come and go as you pleased."

"You mean another brothel. What are you, a whore on the make?"

"I am not a whore," she said firmly. "Do you think I do this from choice?"

Africanus put down her goblet. "So why are you here?" she asked, intrigued.

"Let's just say I have a purpose and leave it at that for now. So are you interested in getting out of here, or do you want to spend the rest of your life at the beck and call of that bitch?"

Africanus twirled the stem of the goblet; thinking hard. If the whore was genuine it might be worth the risk, if anything just to see what might follow, and she couldn't fall much lower than fucking in this stinking dump.

"Where is this place you mentioned?" she asked.

"It is my home, in what was once a great temple. I promise you no harm will come to you. A woman like you is meant for better places than this. And I know a way out of here."

"I can come and go as I please," Africanus said casually.

"You wouldn't get far if you tried. The hovels at the end of the street have guards who watch this place day and night."

Africanus had not thought of that.

"So how will you get me out of here?" she said, warming more and more to the idea.

"Let me sleep with you tonight and I'll show you."

"Oh yeah," Africanus snorted derisively. "If women are to your liking why don't you fuck with that little Nubian, her cunt's well ridden I shouldn't wonder?"

"Listen, you stupid cow, I'm offering you the only chance you're ever likely to get, unless that Roman buys you and you know where you'll end up if he does."

Africanus looked at Marius whose furtive eyes had been riveted on her from the beginning. He was watching her now, but not in the way that men usually look at women, admiring their huge breasts and wishing they were between their splendid legs. There was something else going through his mind and she didn't like it.

"Let's go," she said suddenly, as Marius' attention was caught by the diminutive Nubian.

They slipped away unnoticed and made their way to Africanus' room. Hatentita went directly to the wash bowl and cleansed her face of paint and colouring. She threw off her robe and quite unashamedly squatted over the pot. The remains of the acrid wine discharged from her belly and she wiped herself clean. But she left her wig in place along with all the cheap and garish jewelry she wore.

Africanus had to admit that she did look stunning bereft of clothes, and the wig and twinkling gems seemed to emphasize the rest of her nakedness.

"Are we going to fuck?" Africanus asked, as a matter of course.

She assumed that having her was all part of the bargain in getting her out.

"We should save our strength and rest," Hatentita advised. "But that doesn't mean we can't rest together. You know, you're quite a good looking woman."

"You're not so bad yourself," Africanus replied truthfully.

And for a few moments they took time to appraise each other more closely, reaching out and gently fondling each others breasts, complimenting on their firmness and size of their now aroused nipples, sliding their arms around their hips and buttocks, patting the halves, and then finally placing their hands on their sex pouches and rubbing the lips softly back and forth. They kissed as naturally as they would a lover, hugging close and open mouthed, delving their tongues deep into their throats. Both sucked their breath as their breasts squashed and nipples collided. Their hands sought each other's buttocks and gripped firmly, pulling their hot bodies close until the pubic hair intermingled. They kissed again, but longer and more passionately. No words were needed as they clambered onto the bed, Africanus on her back, her magnificent long legs wide open, and Hatentita lying between them propping her weight on her elbows.

"You have a body like a panther," she whispered.

Africanus' lips broke into a snarl, biting Hatentita's shoulder. "And you're like a python."

"I am Nehebka, the Goddess," she said, but the allusion to the serpent headed deity was lost on the black woman.

They both began to move, slowly at first, snaking their hips and shoulders, encircling each other with long sinewy arms. Africanus raised her legs, throwing them wide, and then suddenly clamping them over Hatentita's back. She flexed her thighs almost crushing the smaller woman, making her fight for breath. The Egyptian opened her mouth, licking her lips in serpentine fashion then kissed the black woman, not holding back now, but pressing her hot mouth hard on the more voluptuous lips, her tongue searching from side to side. Africanus felt her heart quicken and took hold of Hatentita's ears rubbing them between her fingers, pinching the lobs and then stroking the back of her neck. Still moving slowly, their tongues swept over breasts and nipples, sucking in the teats and nibbling until their eyes misted.

Hatentita broke free and wriggled down Africanus' torso, licking into the breast cleft, sweeping her tongue over the plumper mound of her belly, not stopping until her face buried in the rich abundance of curls. Africanus released her grip and let her thighs fall open giving Hatentita free access to her sex. She wasted no time in sucking on the clit, taking it between pursed lips and teasing it with the tip of her tongue. Africanus' hands explored Hatentita's buttocks, smoothing and groping the firm, pert globes. She slapped her hard, not once, but many times until the skin turned scarlet. She eased open the blazing halves and inserted her forefinger into the tight puckered aperture, forcing it in and wiggling it fast. Hatentita purred, a deep warbling sound coming from the depths of her throat. Then she bit harder on Africanus' clit, grinding it between her teeth. The pain was excruciating yet delicious, sending tiny needle pricks through her belly and thighs. Hatentita kept up her teasing, breaking off to lick at the pouting labia, then forcing her face hard against the whole of Africanus' sex pouch, licking all around the sex walls until she could stand the torment no longer.

"Please make me come," she begged, scoring her nails over Hatentita's soft bottom.

"Not yet," she breathed, taking her head from between her legs, leaving the black woman teetering on the edge of a precipice, her orgasm desperate to release itself, half crazed and sobbing from the sensations tingling her sweating thighs.

Then without warning, Hatentita threw herself over Africanus, placing her hips between her thighs, grinding her sex pouch against her, moving faster now, her arms under Africanus' shoulders hugging her tight. She was like a man, thumping her pelvis, slamming her sex up and down, then slowing into a serpentine motion, writhing her whole body, flattening her breasts and belly. But when she felt her own orgasm rising she stopped, prolonging the agony of them both. Africanus took in Hatentita's nipples sucking until her lips ached. She snarled and bit the teats and Hatentita cried in pain. She slapped Africanus' face, and then kissed her, smothering her cheeks and throat with hot blasting breath.

Then suddenly, as if on a preconceived signal, they stopped and gazed at each other, not moving or kissing, but staring into the deep fathomless pools of their eyes. They put out their tongues and playfully licked each other, turning their heads away and then coming back catching one another off guard. Africanus licked Hatentita's throat tasting the sweet smell of her sweat, and her lover returned the compliment, licking into the well then sweeping outwards to her shoulder blades. Soon they were coated in saliva, their faces and necks drenched.

"Fuck me now," Africanus whispered.

Hatentita did not need telling twice and lifted her hips clear of Africanus' sex. She returned with a thump, smacking her sex pouch onto the quivering labia and riding harder now, letting her flowing sex juice mingle in the soaking curls of her lover. Gradually a strong smell arose from the sweating cunts, and they sniffed the fetid, heavily laden air, relishing the odour of their own aroused bodies.

Despite the open window and the ingress of cool night air, the room was stifling and their limbs drenched in perspiration. Africanus lifted her bottom from the bed and began a series of fast hip jerking movements. It was all Hatentita could do to stay mounted on the thrashing black woman. They were all legs and arms, tongues and hair, a confused tangle of bodies, panting, gasping, and snarling.

It was the sound of the snarls that drove them both to greater exertions. They had metamorphosed into cats; Africanus the sleek Black Panther, and Hatentita the paler skinned lioness, tearing and scratching and kissing until they both suddenly erupted a torrent of juice. Hatentita froze, her body trembling from head to foot and for one terrible moment, Africanus thought she was in a seizure, but then she fell quiet, her sex juice weeping gently from her lips.

She collapsed over the black woman and now limp and exhausted they drifted into slumber, disturbed only by the bright light of dawn lighting on their chilled bodies, and the sound of Akara crashing into the room.

"Get up, get dressed and get downstairs," she raged, lashing her whip over Africanus' bottom. "I have just hired you both to Marius Aquinus. It seems he was quite impressed with the way you flogged this thing," she said, turning to Hatentita with a look of disgust. "And you are to repeat the performance. I wish I was going to be there to see you thrash the skin of this dung beetle."

Ignoring her insults, they both scrambled into their robes and went downstairs where a cart was waiting to take them to the quay.

"So much for your plan of escape," Africanus remarked bitterly.

"There's plenty of time yet," Hatentita said with surprising calm.

The cart wound its way through the fetid streets, besieged on all sides by beggars and at the quay, they disembarked and got into a boat. The four oarsmen dipped their oars and the craft headed into midstream going down river.

Neither women were chained or manacled, but were seated in the prow side by side protected from the glaring sun by an awning. Hatentita, far from showing any signs of fear at what awaited her at the Roman's villa displayed an untoward calm and was smiling happily to herself, pointing out the vast temples of Thebes and waxing lyrical about their former splendour. They dined on fresh bread, olives and wine that tasted a good deal more palatable than the evil brew that Akara had forced them to swallow. Africanus reclined in her seat and let her hand trail in the water. Life it seemed had taken a turn for the better and she had escaped the brothel, well, for a short time anyway.

The city of Thebes grew fainter in the glaring haze and the boatmen headed for a quay to rest before embarking on the longer haul to Abydos. They allowed the women to stretch their legs and attend to their private functions before the craft set off.

It was when they emerged from the reeds that Hatentita put her plan into action.

She took off her jeweled collar and armlets, and laid them across the seat admitting their beauty and telling Africanus in loud tones how much they were all worth.

"Are you crazy," Africanus whispered, noticing the attention of the boatmen.

Nevertheless, she prattled on saying in louder tones how much she hated the life of a whore and would give anything to be free of it. She held the collar against Africanus' chest and told her how splendid she looked. One of the men squinted in the sun and leaned closer. Hatentita was holding up an armlet studded with rubies and emeralds, all of them not worth a brass penny. But the boatmen were not to know that. It would be easy to slit the throats of both whores and make off into the desert, but that they knew was tempting fate. Better to strike a deal with the woman and stay alive.

A breeze caught Hatentita's robe, blowing it open and revealing the whole length of her gorgeous thighs and the tiniest glimpse of her black pubic triangle. She made no attempt to hide it, but continued to finger her jewels.

"You want to get away from 'ere," the boatman said, moving closer. "Give us yor jewels then."

"My jewels!" she said aghast. "Have you any idea what they're worth?"

"A small price to pay for yor freedom," he said darkly.

"I'll give the armlets, if you let us head into the reeds," she offered.

"Not enough, it's the lot or nothing."

The other boatmen cast swift eyes up and down the river. It was a dangerous game their comrade was playing, but if he could pull it off...

"I suppose you're right," Hatentita said sadly. "The jewels are worth our freedom."

"I didn't say anything about the black slave," the boatman said.

"It's both of us or nothing," Hatentita said firmly, taking one hell of a gamble.

"I could throw in a bonus," Africanus interjected, sensing where all this was heading.

She had been thinking quickly. She had escaped the brothel but well knew it was only temporary and would be soon back again. If the Egyptian was speaking the truth and her home was not far away, it would be worth the risk until she could formulate a plan to get back to her real homeland.

"Fuck," thought Hatentita, getting on her back with these peasants was not what she had in mind, but if needs must...

The men moved swiftly, dragging the women into the reeds and mounting them, sweating like pigs and blasting foul breath into their faces. Africanus didn't even come, but went through the motions of gasping and panting at the right moments. She could have saved herself the trouble

61

for in no time the men were back at the boat heading down river gloating over Hatentita's worthless jewelry, leaving the women sluicing themselves at the water's edge.

"That was short and sweet," she laughed.

"But what happens when we don't turn up?" Africanus asked warily. "Someone is sure to come looking for us."

"Oh, you're so dumb," Hatentita chided with a tired sigh. "Those boatmen will vanish into the desert and we will make our way to my home and, as I told you, no one will ever find you there,"

"Then what?" Africanus asked suspiciously.

Hatentita didn't reply but set off through the reeds with Africanus in tow.

Now she had her in her grasp she wasn't going to ruin it by letting her know what really lay ahead. The most important thing now was getting her into the harem of Cellenius, and that would take very careful planning, that and persuading her to do as she was told.

But there was always the threat of handing her over to Akara and she wouldn't like that one little bit.

CHAPTER THREE

From a distance, the Temple of Anubis appeared as a wrecked ship marooned in a sea of wavering reeds. A well-trodden path brought the two women in to a wide piazza flanked on three sides with a colonnade. Abandoned since time immemorial, weeds sprouted between the flagstones and all around were signs of neglect and decay.

Africanus was used to seeing images of various Gods and Goddesses; in the Roman Empire, they took on human form and in Britannia that of animals, but here it was a sinister combination of both. They entered what had been the Great Hall and rearing up into the darkness was a wondrously carved statue of Hathor, the Goddess of love, beauty and fertility; an ample breasted woman with a cow's head, which alarmingly had distinctive feminine features. There were others, with the heads of rams, vultures, lions, and every species of animal that dwelt on and around the Nile. The largest and most spectacular was of Anubis, the jackal-headed God, the guardian of the underworld and littered on his plinth were the remains of devotional offerings.

Adorning the walls were thousands of hieroglyphs, the written language of the ancient Egyptians, which few people nowadays understood. It was the same on the columns; around the circumferences were more hieroglyphs and images, and Africanus paused to admire the skill and ingenuity that had created them.

Despite the dazzling array of frescos and carvings there was a dark foreboding about the place, and the silence was oppressive in its ghoulishness. She shivered and walked on, following Hatentita through a massive doorway and up a flight of stone steps, then suddenly found herself in a brightly lit chamber, the sun streaming through the windows.

"My slave will see to your comforts while I get out of

these rags," Hatentita informed, going through a lower doorway.

The girl slave bowed low and motioned the black woman to a couch. She was a living image of one of the frescos; a beautiful naked girl, hardly out of adolescence, wearing only a bejewelled waistband and a huge plaited wig reaching to her firm, pert breasts.

For a whole hour, Africanus waited and began to wonder if all this was a dream and she would awake in the brothel freshly whipped and her cunt sore from so many clients. When Hatentita finally appeared the black woman thought she was imagining things.

"You thought I was Atata, a common street whore," she smiled. "But I am Queen Hatentita, direct descendant of Hatshepsut and Tuthmosis, rightful heir to the throne of Egypt, on whom the sun never sets."

She stood tall and proud, aware of the stunning effect she made. Africanus stared agog at the flowing robe floating around her curvaceous body. One arm and breast had been left uncovered asymmetrically, her pale brown skin highlighted by the dazzling white linen. Around her neck, she wore a wide collar sparkling with jewels, not the cheap costume rubbish she had fobbed off on the boatmen, but the real thing. It was impossible to gauge its worth. On her head was a wig of different design than when Africanus had seen her in the brothel. The fine plaits were of real human hair and not tarred rope. She walked with a long, slow measured tread, swinging her magnificent hips and rolling her buttocks. She looked every inch a Queen with her face now finely powdered, black mascara darkening her eyes and trailing around her temples in a fine vanishing line. Her lips were of vermillion and the eyelids a dove blue, and Africanus felt decidedly uncomfortable in her bland, near nakedness.

"I'm sorry, Hatentita apologized, "I ought to have had my slave bathe and clothe you."

Africanus had a feeling that had been deliberately omitted to emphasize her own stunning beauty, but she did order it now, and the black woman trailed after the slave into an adjoining bathhouse. She washed and perfumed her body, unbraided and combed her hair, then tied it in a tail behind her head. A transparent dress she slipped around her shoulders was held in place with a gleaming golden hasp.

"Now you look beautiful," Hatentita greeted, when she joined her in the chamber.

They seated themselves in richly carved chairs, and the slave fetched wine and a bowl of fruit, and for a fleeting moment, Africanus thought she had died and gone to paradise.

"I want you to tell me all about yourself," Hatentita said, raising her goblet. "Leave nothing out, I shall know if you do," and her smile left the black woman in no doubt that she probably would.

She listened intently whilst Africanus related her history; her induction into Quintus' ludus, her training as a gladiatrix, her flight to Britannia and her sufferings at the hands of the mad priestess.

Hatentita never interrupted once, but her eyes growing wide, and then squinting into deep thought, betrayed that she taken it all in.

"You have suffered much at the hands of the Romans," Hatentita observed. "Have you ever considered getting your own back? I mean, given the opportunity you could be well rewarded and live in a fine palace with many slaves and all the wine you can drink."

"That would be nice, your majesty" she said stupidly, and glanced quickly out of the window.

She had heard of people who went mad because they had been under the sun for too long, and this one must have stripped naked and lain under it for weeks. She was probably some thieving concubine who had managed to make off with her mistress' jewelry and wardrobe, and had camped in this ruin, living out a life of phantasy, and got her jollies by whoring.

"And of course," Hatentita added with a smirk, "you would have your choice of men. Not these unwashed brutes you've been used to, but princes and fine warriors."

"I'd like that, your majesty," she said, digging her nails in her palms to stop herself laughing.

And she wondered how she was going to get out of this madhouse.

"You have heard of Cellenius, the Roman governor. In order to affect an uprising, I need to know the movements of the Roman legions and, most importantly, his movements. All you have to do is get into his harem, keep your eyes and ears open, listen to all the harem gossip, and report to my spies who will deliver that information to me. And when the time is ripe, I will destroy him, ascend my rightful throne, and reign as Queen. Of course, you will be expected to fulfil your duties as concubine, but from what I've seen of you, that will not present any problems. I think you could out fuck any woman living, and I happen to know that the governor has a penchant for beautiful black women, so you are well suited for my purpose."

"Right," Africanus said, her lips drooping at the corners. "So how do I get into this harem?"

"I have already taken care of that. You will be taken down river and presented to the harem mistress who will readily accept you. I think I can safely say that Cellenius will be riding you ere nightfall, and you in turn will fuck like a goat. Get those splendid thighs around him and work your bottom hard. Prove your worth and you will be in a position to learn everything. Understood?"

"Yes, it's understood," she said, thinking that as soon as she reached the governor's palace she would be running so fast that not even a galloping stallion would catch her. She thought she might be able to loot at least some of Hatentita's jewelry before she quit this dreary temple.

But Hatentita was not as gullible as she thought, and if instead of thinking she was deranged by the heat, had Africanus taken a closer look at her face she would have recognized a woman of great energy; clever, vindictive and thoroughly unscrupulous in getting her way. She never believed anything until she saw it.

"You said that you were a gladiatrix," she recounted. "And you were successful in the arenas."

"That is so your majesty."

"Then, if you speak truth, you would have no hesitation in proving it to me now. Would you?"

"If I had all the armour and weapons, indeed I could." Africanus evaded at this sudden and unexpected observation.

Hatentita turned to a man just entering the chamber whom she addressed as Nefru.

"Go and fetch Olassa, and bring her to me, and also a length of chain and a couple of wands."

The man bowed and departed, leaving Africanus smiling weakly at the Queen who in turn regarded her with a contorted smile as if to say, "Now I shall see if you are as good as you say you are."

"She is the most troublesome slave in my retinue," Hatentita informed, when Nefru reappeared towing a naked woman.

He threw her at Hatentita's feet and the woman knelt not daring to raise her eyes.

"Kiss my feet," she commanded, putting out her right foot and baring the sole.

In all her life, Africanus had never been asked to debase herself in such a way. Not even the Romans or Britons had ever asked her to humiliate herself like that, and she was beginning to realize just how vindictive Hatentita could be.

The naked slave lifted Hatentita's foot level with her chin and licked up and down the sole, wetting the heel with saliva and not stopping until the skin was licked clean.

"Now suck my toes," Hatentita sneered.

The slave took in each toe in turn, sucking them deep in her mouth and fanning her cheeks in and out. When she had finished she laid the foot gently on the tiles and remained with head bowed.

"Now suck Nefru's cock," she commanded, delighting in humiliating her slave.

Nefru loosed his tunic and the slave put her hand around the shaft, guiding the plum into her mouth. She angled her head and let the whole length slide into her throat. Her head bobbed up and down and Africanus saw her face flush with embarrassment.

"She would fuck with a hyena, if I commanded it," Hatentita boasted. "Isn't that right, Nefru?"

"It is your majesty," he agreed, relishing the woman's hot breath wafting over his throbbing organ.

Then without warning Hatentita marched over to the slave and seized a clump of her hair, tearing her head from Nefru's cock and hurling her to the floor.

"Have them both chained and armed," she commanded. "And clear the floor."

More naked young slaves appeared hurriedly moving all the furniture, creating a space where Africanus and Olassa would fight. One of them helped Africanus out of her robe and neatly folded it over a chair. A length of chain was manacled to the wrists of the combatants and stout ebony wands placed in their hands.

"Now show me how you fought in the arena," Hatentita said, folding her arms under her breasts.

Nefru had up until now not set eyes on the black gladiatrix, and he watched her closely, ogling at her long powerful thighs and rippling stomach. His queen had done well in finding her it seemed, and much quicker than he had anticipated, and he wondered whether the Gods really were on her side after all.

Olassa was clearly terror stricken at the sight of the

towering black woman, swinging the wand deftly in her hand. But Africanus knew that terror also spawns quick thinking and speed of limb. She also had an uncanny feeling that if by some slim chance she were beaten, Hatentita would have no hesitation in killing her. The Romans would pay handsomely for learning Hatentita's whereabouts and her intentions of overthrowing them.

The two manacled women stood about six feet apart, and for a few moments appraised each other's strength and probable speed.

Africanus struck first, pulling on the chain and catching Olassa off guard. She tumbled into the black gladiatrix and the wand sailed at full strength into her buttocks. Dazed from the sudden shock, Olassa reeled into a circle tangling her arm in the chain. Another swinging blow lashed across her belly, quickly followed by another striking hard on her nipples.

"She's good," Nefru remarked, paying more attention to her swinging breasts than the bruised slave.

Hatentita said nothing, but watched ever closer as Africanus moved in for a fresh strike.

Olassa went into a counter spin and untangled the chain. Her bottom jerked throwing her back into an arc and the wand missed her by a fraction. She raised her arm and sent her wand cracking over Africanus' shoulder blades. Then, more by chance than experience, she delivered another blow, striking as hard as she could and smacking the wand on Africanus' rump.

Hatentita's eyebrows lifted. She had assumed that her troublesome slave would soon be reduced to a blubbering pulp, but the wretch was putting up a good fight, which just went to show that one never knew what people are capable of until needs must.

Gradually, the skills that Africanus had learned returned, and she slowed her pace, keeping out of reach whilst she planned her next move. She swung the wand over her head, twirling it so fast it blurred, and whilst she caught Olassa's attention, suddenly sent it in a downward arc, smacking it on Olassa's naked thighs, another upper cut caught her under the legs and she screamed with pain. Even the hard faced Hatentita winced at that.

Olassa doubled up and Africanus' wand landed on the small of her back, and then on her rump. The naked slave quickly straightened and received four blows on her back and buttocks.

"She'll be finished soon," Nefru remarked, watching huge bruises beginning to blotch Olassa's skin.

But he spoke too quickly and, leading her assailant into a sense of false security, she stayed out of harm's way, gathering her strength, trying to gauge what the black woman would do next. The instant her arm moved, Olassa was there at once, skilfully parrying the blow and returning her wand onto Africanus' flank. As she turned, Olassa whipped the wand on her buttocks with all the strength she could muster, and for the first time Africanus wavered from the shock.

If Olassa had kept up her assault she just might have got the better of her, but she hesitated, watching the black woman going into a semi circle, gritting her teeth from the pain, and in that fateful interlude, her wand went whistling onto the flat of Olassa's stomach, striking with a peculiar hollow smack. She tugged on the chain and Olassa went onto one leg, careering over like a drunk, and it was then that Africanus delivered her killing blow. The wand lashed into the side of her right breast and she went into a demented spin tightening the chain between them and hopelessly entangling her arm. Africanus lashed with the fury of a demon, smacking her wand into Olassa's arse crease, and then, as she reeled from the pain, struck between her shoulder blades, and she fell in a heap, curling into a ball and grabbing her bruised arse cheeks.

"Finish her off," Hatentita said drily, as if the sobbing slave were of no more value than her fake jewelry.

"She fought well", Africanus grated, licking her parched lips and tossing away the wand. "Give her credit where it is due."

Hatentita permitted a wry smile. It was not the first time that she had intervened to save the life of another, and if anything, that might prove to be her downfall. In the struggle for power, there was no room for weakness or compassion.

"Very well. Unchain them and send the wretch back to her quarters."

After Olassa had quitted the chamber, Africanus was treated to a flagon of wine and her wounds bathed in oil and grease.

"So you weren't lying after all," Hatentita acknowledged. "It seems that you really were a gladiatrix and, when the situations arise, quite adept at making an escape, and I'm sure you've already thought of it, and you probably think I'm just a whore who's had too much sun and cock, eh?"

"I did think that, yes," she admitted, no longer so sure that that was really the case.

Hatentita looked at her long and hard with eyes that brooked no argument. "You are a slave," she reminded her, crossing her magnificent legs. "And you will always be one. Even if you did manage to escape from Cellenius' harem, where would you go? Sooner or later, you would be found and probably crucified. I'm offering you the chance of a lifetime. After you have served your purpose, you will be free to go wherever you like, unless of course, you choose to remain here in Egypt and take up my earlier offer. Now follow me."

Africanus was almost won over as they descended the stairs and left the temple and entered another piazza. It was larger than the first one and lined with a row of sphinxes. At the end of the piazza were the remains of a palace, much of it now in ruin.

"This is how my ancestors lived," she informed with a

sweep of her arm, going through a doorway and into a vast hall.

A statue of Queen Hatshepsut stood resplendent, carved from red and black marble, and Africanus saw at once the likeness between the two women.

"Now will you believe me?" she said softly.

Africanus nodded at the undeniable evidence of her own eyes. The woman of flesh and blood was indeed the very image of the one set in stone.

"You said I would be free to go wherever I chose," she reminded her.

Hatentita nodded and slipped her arm around the black woman's waist, and kissed her full on the lips. Their breasts met and squashed, and they clutched each other's buttocks.

"All right, I'll do as you ask," Africanus finally agreed truthfully. "But when you have got what you want, I'm gone."

They kissed long and hard and made their way back to Hatentita's bed chamber where the shutters were already closed against the glaring sun.

Nefru peering through the doorway saw his sovereign undressing the black woman and smiled as she clambered into bed.

It had cost a lot of money having that statue carved, Hatentita posing as a long dead queen, sitting still for hours on end whilst the sculptors did their work.

Chuckling, he went off to find Olassa who he knew would be in sore need of consoling and in greater need of his cock.

Why were women always gagging for cock after a good sound whipping?

"Well?" Marius Aquinus asked gazing with glazed hatred at Akara, standing naked before him, her hands shackled behind her back.

He had arranged a combat between Africanus and a host

72

of beautiful naked slaves, lightly armed and useless against her, but the thrill of watching them whipped and dancing naked was enthralling in itself. The governor had invited all the local dignitaries, men whom Marius Aquinus needed to finance his latest project of unearthing ancient tombs reputedly laden with treasure.

But Africanus was nowhere to be seen.

"Recognise this?" he said, tossing a battered and worthless headband to the floor. A couple of faked glass emeralds went rolling under the couch.

Akara looked at the trinket and swallowed.

"We found it on one of the boatmen you hired to transport the black woman and that Theban tart to my villa," he informed. "Drunk up to his eyeballs and trying to barter with a whore in exchange for her carnal favours. I should say it belonged to the tart, wouldn't you."

Akara was thinking fast. "The boatmen must have robbed and killed them," she said, going pale.

Marius Aquinus regarded her with supreme contempt. "He was boasting how he'd fucked her for her jewels. This worthless trash," he spat, kicking the band across the floor. "Now that has caused me a great deal of inconvenience and I hold you directly responsible. It was down to you to see they arrived at my villa, and they might've done, if you hadn't penny pinched by hiring a bunch of tramps to get them there."

There was nothing she could say to that.

"When the Lady Octavia hears of this, as surely she will, you'll be flogged from here to the sea, but first I have a little punishment of my own to inflict on that bare arse of yours. And your tits," he added malevolently

"It wasn't my fault," she shrieked. "How was I to know that Atata would exchange her…Aaoow!"

A whip sailing into her bottom abruptly silenced her.

"Ever seen this before?" he said, as a slave held up a leather harness.

She shook her head, but had a horrible feeling it was going to cause her a great deal of pain.

"Unshackle her," Marius Aquinus grunted. "And then fit the harness."

It had two huge cups, which easily fitted her breasts, and thin straps that went over her shoulders and around her back. A male slave positioned the cups and eased each breast into the hollow. When they were well cradled, he went behind her and buckled the back strap into place. Akara knitted her brow. Apart from the cold, rough interior of the cups, she felt nothing untoward, except perhaps for a slight tingling over the tops of her nipples.

Behind her, the slave slipped a long wooden rod between the back strap and her spine. Already the whores and slaves assembled in the brothel were crowding to see what would happen next. Many of the whores who had felt her hand slapping their faces, or had been soundly whipped at her command were eyeing her with glinting, expectant eyes. She looked venomously back but saw no sympathy, just retribution.

"Go ahead," Marius Aquinus said, now going to her front and standing only arm's length from her clouding face.

The slave gave the rod a half turn and Akara felt something sharp prick into her nipples. He turned it full circle, moving his hands slowly, twisting the back strap tighter and tighter. The pricking increased to a sharper pain and she sucked her breath. Another duller pain started up at the sides and under her breasts, but not nearly as painful as the one piercing her nipples.

The slave twisted the rod, his face grimacing as the back strap pulled tighter. He could see the strap digging into her shoulders and back. Akara let out a cry and clutched the leather cups, desperately trying to ease them away.

"Get your hands away from there," Marius Aquinus laughed, flicking a plaited whip across her wrists. Her hands flew to her sides and she winced as the slave gave another half turn.

The whores and brothel slaves had already guessed that the cups were fitted with needles projecting at points guaranteed to cause the maximum discomfort as the strap wound tight.

Now the needles fitted over the nipples dug deeper, piercing each teat, going right into the centre of each pulsating bud, almost spearing it to breast level. But that wasn't the only pain Akara was suffering. A smaller ring of needles now began to pierce each areola, digging into the pimples and sending fierce darts of pain throughout her whole breasts.

She sucked her breath and involuntarily arched her back, unwittingly increasing the pain as her breasts thrust outward and upward. Then the whip wielded by her own burly brothel guard lashed into her bottom. He had no fear of punishing his mistress, nor did the whores fear jeering her, for they all knew that after this she would be banished from the city or, on the express orders of the Lady Octavia, sent to labour in the gold mines as an unpaid whore.

"Stop," she hissed, spitting between her teeth and flaring her nostrils.

"Not until your arse is whipped raw and your tits stuck full of barbs," Marius Aquinus announced, nodding to the slave with the rod.

Grunting, he sent it into a full turn and Akara screamed so loudly the drunks reeling in the street suddenly stopped and peered through the doorway.

"Yes, come in," Marius Aquinus invited, adding to her humiliation.

It was bad enough that the brothel inmates should witness her punishment, let alone half the ne'er do wells that slumped outside the brothel walls. By morning, tarts and brothel keepers would be killing themselves laughing at what had taken place.

Her face flushed an angry scarlet, cursing that Theban tart and the black woman.

The slave gave a final turn of the rod and Akara's breasts went into spasms. The pain was coming from everywhere at once, all around and under the stinging globes, darting into her areolas, but most of all deep into her nipples.

"Now flog the bitch," Marius Aquinus said satisfactorily. "Start with the backs of her knees and work your way up to her big, fat arse."

The assembly went into wild guffaws. No one had ever dared address her in those terms.

There was method in the additional flogging the whores soon realized, and they pushed forward to watch the first lashes descend with unerring accuracy.

"See how the cow dances!" a whore bravely bawled, as the whip found its mark.

Akara's knees buckled and she bent backwards, straining the straps tighter. The next lash coming a little above the other had her straightening up again and the cups gripped into her breasts.

Now she too understood. Even the slightest twitch of her body had the needles going deeper and every time the whip sailed into the back of her legs she jolted this way and that, unable to hold still from the burning pain. The whip had reached mid thigh and at last, her will broke.

"Please, Marius," she begged, tears flowing down her cheeks. "Make this stop and I'll get those whore's back. I promise."

"You should've thought of that before you hired those duds to take them there," he said unsympathetically.

He was also thinking of how to explain to Cellenius that the gladiatorial display would now be cancelled because of her incompetence and his lack of foresight in ensuring their safe passage.

"Give her another twenty lashes, and make her lift those knees," he said, sliding his arm around a pretty young whore.

The whip whistled under her buttocks and she leaped in the air, throwing out her arms like a windmill. Her breasts and nipples were stinging so much that they had started to enlarge from the inrush of blood, and she clutched desperately at the shoulder straps.

The whip had reached her arse crease and the brothel guard, well used to beating her whores, brought his skill into play. The whip landed in a fast horizontal, embedding its plaits between her cheeks, then pulled out again and whistled under her open legs.

"Aaagh, aagh," she howled, jerking her hips and buttocks.

"She'd make a fortune if she fucked like that," one of the whores observed seriously.

Akara was breathing like a mare on heat, harsh snorts and grunts, punctuated with shrill shrieks of pain echoed through the thin partitions of the brothel. She bared her gleaming teeth in a snarl revealing more of them that anyone had ever seen. Her eyes were wide and glowing with pain and hatred. Her hair was standing on end and her face almost black with rage. Even Marius Aquinus baulked at her appearance and, for one moment, thought she had been driven out of her mind.

The last lash sliced into her buttocks and she collapsed with a grunt, falling to her knees and sobbing like a child.

"Take off the breast cups," he said flatly.

The slave removed the rod and the straps and cups suddenly went slack. A sigh of relief whooshed from Akara's lungs at the cessation of the pain. He unbuckled the strap and the cups fell forward hanging inoffensively under her breasts. Each globe was a mass of livid red pricks, but her nipples had swelled to an enormous size, almost as large as the tips of her thumbs. The areolas had spread over half her breasts and the pimples stood out like miniature versions of her throbbing nipples. Marius Aquinus had to admit, if only to himself that she did have a good pair of tits and even better after being so ardently pricked. Her arse looked good too, each half still quivering and shaking from the multitude of welts now blazing into each buttock. Bare, hot and throbbing, her bottom wobbled as she struggled to her feet, rubbing her breasts and wiping the tears from her face.

"You will now go to your room," he said dully. "I'll have a slave oil and salve you."

"Thank you, master," she said, pricked and whipped into total submission.

"Then whosoever wants to fuck you is free to do so. Your tits will be all the better for being sucked and squeezed after the punishment you've taken. I imagine that the Lady Octavia might well have you whoring from one end of the city to the other to make up for the loss of those other whores," he added, now fondling a little tart's breasts.

He playfully threw her over his shoulder and carried her upstairs to her room. She would at least provide a pleasant distraction from the mess Akara had created.

Akara was promptly seized and carried bodily to her room, and a stampede of men crashed upstairs eager to fuck her splendid arse and suck on those swollen tits. But as the first hardened cock thrust brutally into her slit, her mind was elsewhere.

When she eventually found that Theban tart and that black mare she would make much better use of that harness. It wouldn't be difficult having a similar one fashioned to fit around their backsides. See how they would cope with dozens of needles spearing buttocks and private parts.

She closed her eyes and started grunting and moaning. It seemed the right thing to do.

"You will invent a story that you were sold by Akara to a dealer in Abydos, were waylaid by river pirates, stripped, robbed and fucked, leaving me for dead and taking you into slavery. One of my henchmen will deliver you to Cellenius' palace and offer you for sale into his harem. Now have you got all that?"

Africanus nodded. It seemed simple enough, and one of the golden rules about lying is keeping the story simple and not embellishing it with unnecessary details. She would have to deliver her account in an off hand way without appearing hesitant or furtive. On no account must she mention the whereabouts of Hatentita's temple. As far as the world was concerned Atata the whore was dead and it would be pointless looking for her. Of course, neither Africanus nor Hatentita had any idea that Marius Aquinus had arranged a combat at the Governor's palace. As far as they and Akara knew, it was no more than a show in his own villa of the black woman flogging the pert buttocks of a Theban tart called Atata.

"One of my spies will contact you all in good time," Hatentita went on as the boat made its way serenely down river.

They passed a Roman legion encamped at the water's edge, and saw the legionaries languishing under canvas and a whole host of dark slaves scurrying to and fro.

"You see how my people are enslaved by these bastards," Hatentita observed, her face reddening.

But slavery comes in many guises, and there was nothing subservient in the way the girls were openly coupling with their supposed oppressors. And Africanus had done well as a slave gladiatrix. But she kept those thoughts to herself.

She was almost naked, except for a loincloth, and her hair left loose as befitted a slave. When they arrived at the Governor's palace, a pair of shackles would be fitted around her wrists and ankles. They travelled all day and reached the palace at sunset. The architecture was a curious mixture of Roman and Egyptian, but pleasing to the eye, set back from the river and surrounded with olive groves.

The henchman fitted the shackles and lifted Africanus out of the boat.

"May all the gods protect you," Hatentita whispered, kissing her cheek.

"I'm going to need them," Africanus thought, trudging behind the man and listening to the sounds of wild shrieks coming from the harem.

They passed along its outer walls and came to a low door, guarded by a fully armed soldier. There was nothing unusual about a slave brought to the harem and offered for sale. He knocked at the door and a small hatch opened. A pair of dark eyes surveyed the black woman, and after a few moments, the door creaked open.

They passed over the threshold and into a vestibule. It was some time before the slave master arrived, angry at being disturbed at that time of the day when he ought to have been resting.

"She's in good shape," he acknowledged, running his eyes over the near naked Africanus.

She stood perfectly still whilst he made the usual inspection, prodding and poking her thighs and breasts, slapping her buttocks, and then ripping off her loin cloth and ordering her to bend over whilst he checked her sex and anus for anything untoward. She seemed clean enough and he had to admit that she was tall and athletic with good legs and a flat belly. She opened her mouth and he checked her teeth. All good and firm.

"I'll offer five gold pieces," he said drily.

"She's worth at least twenty," the henchman choked, playing the part of dealer.

It had to look convincing. If he had just accepted the lowest price, the slave master would probably assume the woman had been rejected elsewhere and might start asking awkward questions.

He walked around her, eyeing her body more closely for any blemishes. He pinched her nipples watching to see how they responded, and his eyes widened as the teats went suddenly erect. She opened her legs and he rubbed his hand under them, and then sniffed his palm. He could tell a lot about a woman from the way her cunt smelled. This one had a powerful, musky aroma, and her sex juice was rich and creamy.

"I'll give seven," he said, slapping her buttocks.

The henchman looked cheated and crestfallen. "I couldn't go lower than twelve. Have you ever seen such a fine, strong body, and she fucks well. Just look at her legs. Did you ever see such splendid thighs, and her arse…!"

The slave master knew well that Africanus was worth every gold piece the dealer wanted, and as far as he could tell she was in good condition, and that his master had told him to keep an eye out for any black woman who fulfilled the harem's expectations.

This one had passed with flying colours.

"Ten. And that's my final offer," he said.

No mention of where she had been bought her or anything of her previous owners, which saved a lot of time and wasted explanation. The slave master would question her later if he deemed it necessary.

"Ten it is, and she's a bargain," the henchman said.

"I'll be the judge of that," he said brusquely, counting out the coins. "Have you ever been whipped, girl?"

"Not much, master," she said cleverly.

An admission of having been well flogged would indicate a troublemaker, and she might incur a flogging just to show her where she stood.

The slave master slapped her shoulder and drove her out of the vestibule and across the harem courtyard, and the outer door slammed shut.

The henchmen pocketed the money and went to the wharf where Hatentita was patiently waiting.

"I've sold her," he said triumphantly. "For six gold pieces."

The anxiety in her face evaporated. Getting through that door was one hurdle crossed. "You can keep one gold piece for yourself," Hatentita generously allowed, and he handed over five and thought he'd done well, all things considered.

The boat was rowed midstream and set off on its journey to the temple.

At the same time as it embarked, another boat, larger and a good deal more splendid set off from Thebes with Marius Aquinus seated in the cabin wondering again how in hell he was going to explain to Cellenius that the sword and bottom wiggling display he had promised would no longer take place.

And he cursed for not having Akara promptly executed.

CHAPTER FOUR

"Have her scrubbed, and then shave her head," the Harem mistress snapped, eyeing the new arrival with contempt.

"Don't mind her," a young concubine called Dorla consoled, leading Africanus along a maze of passages and into a bath house. "She used to be the Governor's principle woman, now she's just one of us, except that she rules the place. Messalina's the one you've got to watch." She helped Africanus into a bath and filled a huge copper jug. "She's the principle woman now and the Gods help you if you fall foul of her. She's as jealous as hell of any new arrival, especially a black woman with legs like you've got. And those big tits," the girl laughed, almost drowning Africanus under a sudden deluge of water.

The bath house was not dissimilar to those Africanus had bathed in at Rome; lots of polished marble and burning incense, and girl slaves running hither and thither filling the place with excited laughter.

Her assistant scrubbed her with a coarse flannel and then rubbed oil into her skin. "Now I must shave your head," she announced, leading the black woman to a wooden chair.

Her own head had been shaved, except for a side lock of braids that hung almost to her waist.

"Why does everyone have to have their heads shaved?" Africanus asked, looking mournfully at the cascade of thick tresses, tumbling sadly around her.

"For one thing, if you do happen to run from here, you'd be a lot easier to spot; secondly, the Governor likes our hair that way; and thirdly, if you misbehave it's useful for stringing you up."

"Oh," said Africanus, blinking as a lock went into her eyes.

"Mind you, one or two women have been thrown out for failing to measure up. They usually end up in brothels with all the other dirty tarts crawling this earth."

"Yes," said Africanus blankly, closing her eyes, not daring to look as Dorla passed a razor over her scalp.

She shaved the black woman's head as smooth as ebony, going expertly around the hair she had left in place, and then rubbing oil onto her bald head. Her slim fingers moved with amazing speed as she braided the side lock, twisting the lengths over one another into long thin plaits.

"Now I'll take you to the jeweller and have you fitted out," she chirped gaily, smiling at her own dexterous handiwork.

Naked, Africanus followed Dorla along more passages and into a room where another woman was busy sorting through a pile of gold and silver ornaments. As Mistress of the Jewels, her nipples were pierced with fine golden rings, and when she stood up Africanus could see that her sex lips had been similarly adorned.

"Good arms and legs, the mistress remarked, running her hands over Africanus' calves."

She went to the pile and selected superbly embossed bracelets, long and silver which she fitted to the black woman's left calf, and then to her right lower arm. A wide, silver collar went around her neck and fastened tight.

"These nipples will have to be ringed at some stage, if the master wills it," she mused, rolling the teats between her forefingers and thumbs. "Now get along and see the Mistress of the Robes."

Africanus had already formed a correct assumption that not only were the concubines expected to pleasure the Governor and his guests, but had also been allocated various offices within the Harem. Trust the Romans to be that enterprising.

The Mistress of the Robes greeted Africanus in a similar fashion, complimenting her on her fine figure and splendid buttocks. She couldn't resist patting them and smoothing her palm under the globes.

"Open your legs," she said kindly, snatching a long piece of white linen.

It was just wide enough to cover the new arrival's sex mound and the Mistress of the Robes held it in place while she passed one end under her legs and then deftly knotted it over the small of her back. For all the use it was, Africanus may as well have been naked. Her sex was covered, but the trailing piece pulled tight into her bottom crease and then wound under the pit of her belly leaving ample areas of naked skin.

"Is this all I get to wear?" she asked, suddenly feeling very vulnerable in her new surroundings.

"Until the master decides otherwise," the mistress informed, running her eyes over the whole length of Africanus' body.

She had also formed another correct assumption that the Mistress of the Robes was a rampant Lesbian and had already taken a fancy to the shimmering black limbs and breasts.

"We change partners a lot," Dorla informed, as they made their way to an upper floor. "It's nothing to worry about. Half the harem will have fucked you before the master even gets a look in."

"Oh thanks," Africanus said, following her into a dormitory.

The women slept on rugs side by side with barely enough room to move, it didn't take much imagination to see how convenient it was to change partners on a regular basis, and a cold sweat broke out under her arms.

"This is your bed," Dorla told her, pointing to a rug. "The harem mistress will allocate your duties. I expect you'll start as Messalina's personal slave. She likes to break in the new girls."

"Great," thought Africanus, "a slave to the one woman I need to avoid."

They went onto a roof where some of the concubines were languishing under an awning, sipping fruit drinks and idly chatting. Below she saw more of them splashing naked in a bath and indulging in friendly horseplay. A delicious smell of cooking food drifted from the kitchens, and beyond she could just glimpse the magnificent quarters of the Governor. Colonnades bordered on fishponds and well attended gardens blossoming with a variety of flowers and shrubs. The whole place was much larger than could be guessed from its outer walls and was well guarded with its own private garrison.

It would not be an easy place from which to escape.

But she couldn't even think about that until she had gathered the information Hatentita needed to affect her uprising.

As principle concubine, Messalina had her own quarters complete with bath and private garden, and a room where she could entertain the governor if he chose to visit her there.

She was standing at the edge of a small pool eating from a plate of honeyed fish when Dorla introduced Africanus.

For a fleeting moment, she experienced a rush of terror. It was in such surroundings that she had first encountered Quintus' wife, the Lady Octavia, and this woman had all her characteristics; cool beauty, a body any man would kill for, and a cold calculating mind.

She also had a penchant for humiliating the other concubines leaving them in no doubt who was Cellenius' favourite.

"Get on all fours," she said to Dorla, who dutifully dropped to her knees.

Then, without twitching a hair, she seated herself on the girl's back, using her as a bench. Africanus saw Dorla's spine bend under her weight and her knees digging painfully into the flags.

"Your first duty here," Messalina began, getting straight to the point, "is to learn your place within the Harem. You have the authority to beat any slave in the lower ranks. Those set in authority above you can beat you for any transgression. Twenty lashes are the normal amount allowed, although the Mistresses can give you up to forty if they so choose. Both the Harem Mistress and I can deliver up to a hundred and administer any other punishment we deem fit, within reason. The Governor can do whatever he pleases."

A sinking feeling went through Africanus' stomach. It seemed the whole Harem could beat her on the slightest pretext, and it was not a good feeling.

"Soon, you will be prepared for Cellenius who likes black women," she sneered, and already Africanus knew that she would have to be on her guard, and that Messalina regarded her as a dangerous rival.

She shifted her bottom over Dorla's back and slapped her rump.

"Do you think she's pretty?" she asked, smoothing her pert buttocks.

"I think she's very pretty," Africanus replied truthfully.

"And her bottom? Would it give you pleasure to lash those gorgeous halves?"

"Only if she deserved it," Africanus said, tactfully taking the middle ground.

Messalina smiled like a she wolf, and turned to Dorla, grunting under her weight.

"Do you think you deserve a good beating?" she taunted.

"I have been disobedient," Dorla whispered, tensing her buttocks. "And I need beating."

Africanus' throat went dry. The girl had obviously done nothing wrong but had offered no protest at having her bottom whipped.

"Fetch a switch," Messalina rasped, her dark eyes flashing with relish.

She got up and Dorla went off into the building.

"This is cruel," Africanus said, watching her slim figure disappear under an arch.

"But it's great entertainment, all the same," Messalina chortled.

Dorla came back and offered Africanus a long cane, smooth and supple. Then, without further ado, she bent over and touched her toes.

"Give her a modest ten strokes and lay them on hard. I want to see how good you are," Messalina told her.

Africanus knew this was a test of her obedience and if she failed, could expect at least four times that amount.

She flexed her arm and sent the cane whistling into Dorla's rump. The girl grunted, bucking her bottom from the shock. Another three lashes sailed onto her cheeks coming from the full strength of the black woman's arm. Long, scarlet welts appeared in their wake, and Africanus watched as they turned a livid purple. The girl was sobbing and clenching her fists from the pain seeping through her blazing rump.

"Well go on then," Messalina tested. "Give her another six; three on her thighs and the rest on her back."

What a fucking bitch, Africanus thought, forcing her to beat a defenceless girl who had done no harm. She delivered the rest in quick succession, landing three lashes on the backs of her slim thighs, and the remainder on her back just above the base of her spine.

"Now thank her for beating you so well," Messalina ordered.

Dorla knelt at Africanus' feet and looked up with wide, tear-filled eyes.

"Thank you, mistress," she sobbed, bowing her head in submission.

She got up rubbing her welted bottom, but Messalina ordered her back on all fours and seated herself on her back ensuring her weight rested over the freshly whipped flesh.

Africanus couldn't believe what had taken place. Not only had Dorla welcomed the cane thrashing her thighs, bottom and back, but had actually thanked her afterwards, even though she was entirely innocent of any crime. She made up her mind there and then that when she got out of this fearful place, Dorla would be coming with her.

Much to her surprise, Africanus was left unmolested and allowed, along with the other concubines to wander at will within the harem precincts. She had to admit that all the women and girls were well fed and cared for, and life was pleasant. She bathed in the pool and languished under the colonnades and dined off well-prepared dishes. Messalina generally kept to her own quarters and the shrieks and sound of cane on bare flesh went ignored as if were part of the daily routine. So far, Cellenius had not made an appearance apart from visiting Messalina and summoning a few of the younger Egyptian slaves into his bedchamber. Visitors came and went and the concubines left the harem temporarily to fulfil their duty. Some were even rewarded with trinkets. But it was the night that Africanus dreaded. Huddled like bees in a hive, the girls slept naked, and every night she heard them moving about as silently as shadows, wriggling beside one another, and then going through the grunting and panting motions of lovemaking. In the moonlight, she saw the silhouettes of long legs pointing to the ceiling, and heaving buttocks bouncing joyfully over the grunting woman beneath. Yet strangely, no one bothered her. Only Dorla dared approach, wriggling her lithe body alongside the more mature and fuller figure of Africanus.

"I'm sorry I had to whip you," the black woman whispered, as the younger girl settled between her thighs.

"Oh, that was only Messalina. She gets really hot when she sees us whipped."

"Yes, I guessed as much," Africanus said, resting her hands on the girl's bottom and kneading the soft, wobbling buttocks.

Dorla bent her head and sucked on the erect nipples, teasing them with pursed lips. Her slim legs opened and Africanus, uninvited, reached under her belly and slipped her fingers inside her sex. She was already wet and in heat.

88

"Make me come," she whispered softly.

Africanus worked her fingers faster and faster, and Dorla came quickly, stuffing her tiny fist in her mouth to stifle the groans rising in her throat. They lay until dawn; Dorla on her side with her thigh draped over Africanus' middle, and the black woman holding her close, watched by one of the concubines consumed with jealousy.

It was after Messalina had had her flogged and she was desperate to assuage the unrequited orgasm trembling in her the depths of her belly that the concubine finely summed up the courage to lie alongside her.

The black woman stirred in her sleep. She had got so used to hearing the nocturnal comings and goings that now she paid them little heed, until a hand slipped between her legs and hot, urgent breath wafted in her ear.

Africanus stirred at the touch and involuntarily shifted her thighs. The body of a woman rolled deftly on top of her and she put her hands on the buttocks, not soft or pert, but firm and round. Neither were the breasts small, but large and full.

"Dorla?" Africanus whispered. "Is that you?"

"It's Magenta," a voice whispered. "And I want fucking."

Before Africanus could utter another word, the woman's lips pressed hard on her own, forcing open her mouth and wriggling her tongue to the back of her throat. Fumbling hands groped clumsily in the dark, finding her breasts, cupping and squeezing them. Her hips began a slow rotation, bearing down hard and grinding her pubic mound hard onto Africanus sex.

"Get off me!" Africanus hissed, in no mood for sex with a woman she barely knew.

But Magenta was more persistent than she anticipated, and strong. Her hands flew to Africanus' shoulders, pinning her to the rug. If Africanus had but realised that struggling against her only heightened her desire to make love to the sleek, dark woman beneath her, she might have just submitted and got it over and done with. But Africanus was not one to give in lightly.

"Get the fuck off me," she snapped, bucking her hips.

Magenta thrilled to this unexpected opposition and started teasing her nipples, flicking her hot tongue over the swelling buds, and nibbling the tender, wrinkling areolas. Between Africanus' thighs, a warm dampness started to seep from her sex.

Magenta bit harder, grinding the teats between her sharp teeth, and Africanus' belly throbbed like a drum. Her heart beat faster, and somewhere in the pit of her stomach, an icy chill churned. She sucked her breath and moaned, trying to raise her shoulders from the rug. But Magenta held her rigid.

"Just...get...the fuck...off...me," she groaned, feeling her strength rapidly waning.

"Not until you let me have you," Magenta whispered, lifting her head from Africanus' breasts

The black woman made a final desperate heave of her hips, but Magenta merely slammed her bottom harder. She tentatively took away one hand from Africanus' shoulder and reached under her belly. She found the hot cavern of the black woman's sex and plunged her fingers into the knuckle.

"Ohh!" Africanus grunted at the sudden shock.

Her bottom squirming from Magenta's searching hand, she arched her back and threw open her legs.

"I knew you'd give in," Magenta purred, rubbing her breasts across Africanus' chest.

"You artful bitch," was all she could reply, as she felt Magenta's other hand slip from her shoulder and go straight to her flanks, smoothing up and down, and then reaching under her buttocks and grasping each half in turn, pinching until her eyes misted.

"Keep still," Magenta whispered. "I'm going to make you come."

In the sweating heat of the dormitory her tone seemed almost hypnotic; her voice deep and husky. Africanus lay still surrendering to the wetted fingers teasing the swelling and pulsating lips of her sex. She bore down with her elbows, lifting her back into an arc. Her heels dug into the rug and Magenta's body lifted over the black woman's hips. But she kept her fingers well inside, wiggling them fast against the soaking vaginal walls.

Africanus, hardly aware of what she was doing arched her head against Magenta's chest and started sucking on the aroused nipples. She bit hard and heard a sharp cry of pain. One or two of the other concubines sat up to watch Magenta now riding the black woman with magnificent undulations of her hips. But it was Africanus' straining thighs that held their attention. Hard, black and sweating, the muscles hollowed and hardened from Magenta's weight. Her hips jerked and twisted and it was all Magenta could do to stay between her thighs.

Drenched in sweat, their bodies slithered like eels, their breasts and bellies slapping and wobbling, incurring the curiosity of more awakened spectators. Magenta found Africanus' weak spot and concentrated on her breasts, her lips closing over each erect nipple, sucking and nibbling until the black woman cried out for her to make her come. Magenta eased her soaking fingers from Africanus' sex and smeared the juice-slicked tips over the throbbing nipples. She bent her head and sucked at the musky cream running into the breast cleft. Her tongue swept up through it and licked all around Africanus' neck, deliberately delaying her own orgasm whilst increasing that of her lover.

One of the concubines crawled over the rugs like a predatory cat and leaned over Magenta's back, sweeping her tongue up the length of her spine, and then all the way back down again and into her bottom crease. She was on all fours, her legs open, and breasts swinging beneath her like bells. It was too much for the concubine's lover who came up behind her and rubbed her hand hard over her sex pouch. Soon, the woman on all fours was panting and dripping, and the concubine swiftly laid herself under her and buried her head in the soaking slit. More concubines gathered around the four women filling the room with their raucous grunts and sighs.

The woman at Magenta's rear began biting the proffered buttocks and felt, at the same time a hot searching tongue inside her own sex.

Magenta flicked her tongue over the black woman's nipples, licking them clean and then returning to kiss her full on the lips.

Africanus let out her long, throaty pre-orgasmic groans and gave a mighty shove of her loins.

"I'm coming now," she wailed, crashing her back and buttocks on the rug.

Her whole body went into spasm and then Magenta bore down on her with all her weight, holding her trapped to the floor while she climaxed, not allowing her even the slightest movement, except for her powerful legs which locked rapidly over Magenta's back. The concubine who had been biting and licking Magenta's bottom now turned her attention to Africanus' thighs. She licked them from knee to hip, tasting the acrid smell of sweat oozing from the hot pores. Then suddenly the fourth concubine left off sucking her lover's cunt and dived over the black woman's chest sucking and teasing her breasts.

Africanus felt as if she were drowning under a welter of sweating writhing bodies. Legs, arms and buttocks were twisting and thrashing in all directions, much to the amusement and fascination of the other concubines who had rarely witnessed such a spontaneous display of so many women in orgasm.

The concubine who had been licking Africanus' thighs wrestled herself free from the tangle and stood up over Magenta's back, her legs wide open and cunt dripping. She reached for her breasts and flicked the nipples, then, with a mighty heave of her belly came in full flood, dripping her copious juice over Magenta's back. Her lover who had been feasting on Africanus' nipples broke free and licked the hot juice flooding into Magenta's bottom crease.

Magenta suddenly reached her orgasm and let out a harsh groan, loud enough to wake the dead, and attract the attention of Messalina coming furtively from the guards' barracks.

But Magenta had not yet finished and kept thumping her pelvis over Africanus' hips, trying vainly to reach a second climax. The other two concubines, their lust slaked crept back to their rugs and lay staring calmly at the ceiling, listening to the sucking noises coming from Magenta's cunt.

Africanus, caught in the maelstrom of her second orgasm clenched her thighs, crushing Magenta's ribs and halting her manic thumping.

"Please let me come," she rasped, clawing at the rug.

She was so close that only a few more jerks of her hips would have her sex streaming, but the black woman's thighs were too well locked and she spent with an apologetic wriggle and collapsed exhausted.

Africanus squeezed her belly and buttocks and came with one colossal thrust of her hips. Suddenly, what remained of her strength ebbed away and she lay still, her breast heaving. Magenta rolled off her and lay on her side in a pool of sex juice, her tongue hanging from her mouth.

Messalina had come quietly up the staircase and listened to all the noise coming from within. Everyone knew and accepted that love making between the concubines was rife, but according to the harem rules, it was strictly forbidden that they should pleasure themselves. That privilege was supposed to be reserved for the Governor and his guests.

She poked her head around the corner and saw Africanus sprawled naked on her rug, legs wide apart and the rug still wet. Magenta was fast asleep on her side, snoring like a horse.

The punishment for disobeying the harem rules was severe, and Africanus, innocently sleeping had no idea just how severe.

But she was soon going to find out.

CHAPTER FIVE

"Who is this woman, Akara?" Cellenius asked, after Marius Aquinus informed him that the black gladiatrix and the Theban whore had vanished.

"She runs one of Lady Octavia's brothels in Thebes," Marius Aquinus replied.

"I will accept that she was indirectly responsible for the gladaitrix' escape, but you ought to have supervised the voyage yourself. I think it's safe to assume that both of those whores are far away by now, which just goes to show that you can't trust a woman."

They were in Cellenius' palace, and he had been informed that a new black slave had arrived and had settled in well.

But there were other things on his mind than enjoying the charms of a new concubine. The guests were due to arrive and there had not been time to inform them that the show they were coming to see was cancelled. Cellenius was not a man who could cope well with loss of face and, more importantly, Marius' incompetence in failing to come up with the goods would reflect on him, and badly.

"If the Lady Octavia is here," Marius Aquinus suggested, "she may be able to come up with a solution."

"With over a hundred slaves, concubines and whores in this place, I'm sure I can come up with a solution myself," Cellenius snapped.

He immediately sent a slave to find Messalina who seemed to know everything that went on in the harem, and as principle concubine, it was her duty to keep him abreast of things. On the whole, he preferred Egyptian woman and Nubians to the paler skinned Romans, but after the recent uprising at Semna, he wasn't sure if they could be trusted and, as he well knew, the harem was a hot bed of gossip and dissention. Why, only a short time ago, the Governor in Assyria had had his throat cut by a concubine, and now Cellenius was beginning to see assassins around every corner.

"What's she like, this new black slave?" he asked.

"Tall, a good body, and not afraid to use a whip when necessary. I had her flog one of the junior slaves just for the pleasure of it."

Cellenius nodded, a vague idea forming in his mind. "Where did she come from?"

In truth, Messalina had not troubled herself to ask. It wasn't her job to know such things. She shrugged. "A dealer from somewhere in Thebes or Luxor," she hazarded.

Her eyes squinted in thought. She had heard of the forthcoming banquet and rumours that the gladiatrix had not appeared, and she had been looking forward to watching some of the new slave women flogged raw.

"I think I could arrange another form of entertainment," she suggested slyly, seemingly reading his thoughts. "The black woman has been caught red handed sleeping and fucking with the other women in the dormitory. I was going to have her punished, but if you prefer, I could delay it until the guests arrive. I'm sure they would enjoy watching her whipped."

Cellenius had to think about that. It was not what they had come to see, but having a new slave flogged for their pleasure was better than nothing at all.

"Have it arranged," he said suddenly. "And see that the choicest wines are served and the concubines well oiled. I want plenty of naked slaves in attendance."

He hoped that would ease things. It was quite remarkable, the effect a naked and willing woman had on a man, especially if he had a belly full of wine into the bargain.

Messalina did not see assassins around every corner, but she did regard any new arrival as a potential threat to her own position. She was well aware of Cellenius' preference for darker skinned beauties, and Africanus was very dark, and beautiful. Having her trussed like an animal and flogged at a banquet would be a wonderful way of humiliating her and, if she could be reduced to a sorry looking heap of whipped flesh, then so much the better, especially if it were the principle concubine delivering the punishment.

She wasted no time in having an apparatus prepared. Carpenters and metal smiths hurried into the banqueting hall, hammering and sawing, building a peculiar wooden frame with ropes and chains slung beneath it. When they had finished it stood tall and sinister, quite out of keeping with the ornate and lavish furnishings. The banquet was not an extravagant affair, more of an informal gathering with just the right amount of naked concubines to pleasure the guests. The dignitaries sprawled on divans waited upon by a bevy of well-oiled and perfumed slaves especially selected for their beauty and nubile figures. Cellenius had invented an elaborate excuse that the gladiatrix had gone down with river fever, a malady not uncommon in that hot and uncompromising climate. To his immense relief the dignitaries accepted it with good grace and the fawning concubines provided more than adequate distraction. It was when the guests heady with wine and mesmerized with such an abundance of naked, gleaming flesh that Messalina announced the entertainment, clapping her hands as the curtain hiding the apparatus was withdrawn. At the same time Africanus appeared naked, led into the hall by a male slave,

"A splendid piece of fucking flesh," Cellenius breathed, totally unprepared for what he saw halting before the apparatus.

Marius Aquinus rubbed his eyes and quickly took another gulp from his goblet. Either he was drunk or his mind was playing tricks.

Lady Octavia looked over the shoulder of a man busy burying his head between her breasts. Her chest heaved and the man uttered a satisfied groan. She wasn't drunk and neither was her mind deranged.

Both she and Marius Aquinus unwittingly looked at each

other silently mouthing the word, 'Africanus' the shock on their faces lost amid the gawping guests. Marius Aquinus moved first, making his way to Lady Octavia, edging politely through the guests and coming within earshot. Lady Octavia with equal politeness gently took the man's head from her bosom and quickly signalled another girl. Happily, he was too drunk to notice the difference.

"Where the fuck did she spring from?" Marius Aquinus muttered, as Africanus drew closer to the apparatus.

Lady Octavia shook her head, her mind in turmoil. If that black bitch was here, her husband was certain to be in the near vicinity. And that had her racing for the toilet.

The apparatus was a sturdy wooden frame about twelve feet in height with chains hanging from either side. On the end of the chains, thick leather slings now draped harmlessly over the mosaic floor. Africanus laid herself full length over the slings; one passing neatly under her breasts, the other under the pit of her stomach. A slave knelt at her side and taking her arms bent them behind her. Another slave grabbed her ankles and bent them over her buttocks. Swiftly and expertly, the slaves manacled them together and she let out a painful groan, her spine forcing into an arc. Overhead the frame creaked as the slings and chains took her weight lifting her very slowly upwards. Her head hung down and she saw the floor falling away. Her huge breasts hanging from their own weight wobbled deliciously beneath her and her body now at man height went into a slow spin. Marius Aquinus, still in a state of shock gazed at her widely spread thighs flexing hard under the strain. Her rounded, firm buttocks hollowed at the sides and there was nothing he could do to halt the erection throbbing madly under his toga. But he was still at a loss as to how she had entered Cellenius' palace as nothing more significant than a mere concubine.

Lady Octavia returned from the toilet and having squatted over the rim for a good ten minutes was now much clearer in her mind. Either there had been some confusion as to Africanus' identity, or she had arrived there from her own volition quite unknown to either Cellenius or Marius Aquinus. As Messalina gathered a three-tailed whip in her hand Lady Octavia had joyfully concluded that her husband must have sold his prize gladiatrix for nothing more than a scrap of whipping meat, which meant that he must have gone bankrupt. And that made her happy. A thought suddenly occurred and a wolfish smile creased her lips as the whip descended full force over Africanus' naked rump.

The black woman's body shuddered and went into a faster spin, her body whirling around displaying first her swaying breasts hanging like ripe melons, then a magnificent view of her profile, arms and legs firmly bent and manacled. A second later, as she completed full circle, an uninterrupted view of her naked sex glistening between outstretched thighs bared itself to the audience.

"Messalina has excelled herself." Cellenius approved, noticing the stunned look on the guests' faces.

All activity ceased and the assembly watched in a heavily laden sexual silence as Messalina's whip cracked over Africanus' arched back. Her body rocked back and forth suspended in the slings making her breasts wobble and shake and her legs and belly tremor into painful spasms. Hanging manacled and defenceless there was nothing she could do to prevent her tormentor from delivering the next carefully planned assault. The audience watched spellbound as Messalina's arm sailed in a beautiful sweeping arc sending the tails directly between the black slave's open legs. A heart-rending howl broke from Africanus' lips and her whole torso lifted from the slings. For several moments, it seemed that the world had stopped and she was only dimly aware of the room going in circles. A fiery pain spread rapidly through her loins and belly and upwards through her spine and breasts. Her nipples had gone into hard points throbbing with pain and it was there that Messalina struck the next blow. She had whipped scores of female slaves and knew exactly the effect the whip was having and where. The tails whistled under the slings lashing with an ear-piercing crack on the throbbing globes, striking with perfect precision, cutting into the hardened nipples and over the ample breast flesh.

"Uh, where did you find this gorgeous specimen?" Marius Aquinus asked tentatively.

Cellenius not taking his eyes from Africanus' spinning body merely shrugged.

"One of Messalina's acquisitions," he replied vaguely, already riding Africanus in his mind.

Marius Aquinus was thinking fast. Would it be best now to tell Cellenius who Africanus really was, or keep silent and let things take their natural course? Unless the girl told him, he was unlikely to find out and concubines came and went through the harem faster than whores in the Theban brothels. As and when Cellenius tired of her she would be put up for sale and Marius Aquinus could buy her and hire her out for his own lucrative purposes. He too was also aware that Roman governors were constantly under threat of assassination and it wasn't too fanciful that he just might, with sufficient bribes step right into Cellenius' sandals.

"She's a good find," he said absently, and permitted his lips a thoughtful smile.

The harsh rhythmic grunts coming deep from Africanus' parched throat already had the guests in heat. Some were already coupling with the concubines, and one or two had discreetly retired to the rooms taking a slave or two to wile away the night. Messalina had stopped whipping Africanus' sex and waited patiently for the slings to stop spinning. When Africanus' body finally glided to a halt, she reached up under her legs and blatantly fondled the dripping sex lips.

"I want to hear you come," she whispered harshly,

looking at the remaining guests still ogling the sweating black woman.

It was the final humiliation that Africanus feared, trussed like an animal, whipped and now forced into a public orgasm. Her new master it seemed had little inclination in having her unchained and taken to his quarters. One of the concubines was sitting astride him and her lithe body going through the motions of bringing him off. Messalina's hand plopped over Africanus' sex mound gently squeezing the plump and quivering flesh. Listening to her ecstatic moans, Lady Octavia also had designs on her not too dissimilar from those of Marius Aquinus, but first she needed to talk to her, find out where she had been and with whom since the collapse of her husband's ludus. After that, she would work on Cellenius, inform him of Africanus' identity and offer to sponsor her in combat, but not in this backward dump. Her real ambition was to return to Rome, buy off the authorities who might prosecute her and begin again her dream of owning her own ludus. Cellenius, she knew was fickle as far as women were concerned and she was certain that another black concubine could be easily found to replace her.

"The girl certainly has a large cunt," Cellenius remarked, breaking in on her thoughts.

Messalina had slipped four fingers into Africanus' sex and had closed her thumb into her palm in preparation for working her whole fist into the black woman's sex tunnel.

"I know of one larger," Lady Octavia rejoined, watching Africanus' face screwed in sexual torment.

Cellenius suddenly looked around. "Impossible," he blurted. "No woman could possibly be larger. An equal perhaps, but not wider than that."

"Care to make a wager?" Lady Octavia offered, now seated alongside him.

"Name your price," he laughed, finding her salacious grin irresistible.

"A night with the black slave," she said boldly.

"Done. If you can come up with a woman whose cunt is larger than that I'll allow you to sleep with her for one night."

Lady Octavia had bluffed, but was certain that somewhere in one of her brothels there had to be at least one whore with a cunt like a mare. She turned back just in time to witness Messalina's fist thrusting madly into the soaking depths of Africanus' sex and the feel of a hand diving into her own cleavage.

"Oh piss off Crixus," she said laughing, roughly taking the hand groping her breast.

"After watching that display I'm as horny as a goat," Crixus said, returning his hand.

"I admit it was good," Lady Octavia agreed, letting the hand roam freely. "And if your hand goes lower than my naval you'd better open your purse."

"I'd much rather open your cunt."

"You can't have one without the other, so pay up or piss off."

"Once a whore always a whore," he said bitterly, but smiled when he spoke.

He opened his purse and tipped three gold pieces into her lap. As a matter of course, she put each coin between her teeth testing and tasting the metal.

"You remind me of that fat lump of lard you've got working for you in Alexandria," he laughed. "She tests every single coin. No wonder your coffers are full."

Lady Octavia's lips twitched at the corners as they always did when a thought suddenly sprang into her mind.

"Have you fucked her, Crixus?"

"Yes," he admitted after a couple of seconds delay. "But who hasn't?"

"Did she measure up to this?" she asked, squeezing his throbbing cock. "I know your reputation for being hung like a mule."

"She has a cunt that could take....my whole arm," he grunted, trying to think of a suitable comparison. "And tits like a cow's udders and her nipples…"

To his immense surprise, she handed back the gold coins and gripped his cock tightly.

"I'll give it you for free if you'll ride to Alexandria and bring her to me at my villa by tomorrow sunset."

It was an offer he couldn't refuse but one that could not be easily fulfilled.

"Agreed," he said, lifting her dress high over her thighs. "But Alexandria is a long way, so on your back right now."

"What! Here in Cellenius' hall, I think we'd be better in…aaagh!"

He gave one vigorous shove on her chest toppling her straight onto her back. Her long silky legs flew open and Crixus was between them faster than she could blink.

"This is where you get fucked hard," he rasped, grabbing her wrists and throwing her arms wide.

Crixus was a tall man, standing six feet four on his bare feet and as with all tall men, his limbs were long, much longer than those of the grunting woman struggling under him.

"Crixus you'll rip my arms off," she shrieked, feeling the sockets straining as he raised her arms over her head.

Her chest heaved and her slim back went into a bridge. He kept her arms together pointing above her body as straight as spear shafts. Her buttocks twitched and tossed when he slammed his legendary organ hard into her quivering cunt.

"Please, Crixus, my arms…" she sobbed, but finding the pain racking at her shoulders and chest ecstatic.

Like all women worth their stunning bodies, Lady Octavia welcomed the hurt that had her juices flowing, and Crixus did not intend to spare her. Keeping her arms pinioned, he gathered his pelvic strength and slowly withdrew until the tip of his cock hovered at her quaking sex lips.

"Keep your back arched," he told her, watching her aching biceps quiver in pain.

She nodded, gritting her teeth knowing what was to follow. Eyes closed into tight slits she held her breath and waited. A passing concubine, her face flushed from a recent fucking stopped at the sound of a high-pitched shriek coming from a nearby divan. She looked just in time to catch Crixus' muscular buttocks giving a massive heave and her hand flew to her mouth. Crixus had not yet fucked his way through all the available concubines, but the girl had heard of his reputation and now saw the evidence before her very eyes. His cock was as thick as her wrist and about three quarters the length of her forearm. With one manic thrust, his throbbing length sank into the shrieking woman and so hard and fast, his balls slapped against her cunt. The concubine saw Lady Octavia's back and buttocks lift from the couch, her legs bent from the weight as she bore the man above her now pumping like a maniac.

"It's too long," she uttered, tears welling in her eyes. "Please, Crixus, take it out."

But Crixus had a reputation to maintain and the writhing tart wasn't going to compromise it. But he could feel his strength waning and called to the concubine.

"Fetch a pine cone!" he barked.

Bemused at the command she tore off to where a pile of huge pine cones lay stacked ready for burning and sweetening the air with their fragrance. She plucked the largest she could find and came speedily back.

"Put it under her," he grunted. "At the small of her back."

The girl slipped the cone under Lady Octavia and stood back awaiting the result. The cone's hard and pointed barbs were only a fingers' breath from the ridged spine. Crixus withdrew his cock as before but still kept Lady Octavia's body fully stretched. He bent his head and sucked on her aroused nipples, tickling the teats with the tip of his tongue and gently rubbing all around the areola. A deep throaty purr warbled from Lady Octavia's throat as the tingling sensation in her nipples spread rapidly through her breasts.

"By all the Gods," she sighed.

Then Crixus' massive cock rammed full length into her belly. Her bottom, supported by flexing thighs lifted, hovered for a second and crashed to the divan. The scream was deafening, so loud that more than one interested guest had ceased his own coupling and had gathered to witness the mighty Crixus fucking the life out of the beautiful Lady Octavia.

"What the fuck is under my arse," she swore, forgetting that she was supposed to maintain the dignity of a highborn lady.

"A pine cone," he told her, grinding his pelvis hard into the fork of her thighs.

"You bastard," she hissed, lifting her bottom, for the sudden thrust had moved her up the divan and the sharp edges of the cone barbs now rolled under her soft buttock cheeks bruising and digging into them at every fresh pelvic shudder.

Her arms still pinioned above her head but the pressure had ceased and the shoulder sockets no longer wrenched and tore, but there was no denying the stabbing pain in her bottom. Lady Octavia's legs took the strain, the muscles hard and flexing as she kept her bottom raised. Crixus maintained a steady penetration riding her with long even insertions, a smile creasing his lips as he felt her tender vaginal walls embracing his length. He also liked the look of agony on her face, the squinting eyes and bared teeth struggling against a mounting orgasm, and the cone only a finger's width from her hitherto unblemished arse cheeks. Lady Octavia was proud of her firm rounded buttocks, pale and velvet smooth which she liked displaying at every opportunity. If those pine barbs kept crunching into her skin, she would be scarred for weeks. But Crixus didn't give a fuck about that. As far as he was rightly concerned, a woman's arse was built for punishing and he slammed into her belly with all the force his loins could muster.

The soles of Lady Octavia's feet lost their grip and shot forward and the cone barbs crackled into her bare, wobbling bottom. She tried to raise herself but her assailant was bearing down with his full weight and all she could do was writhe and squirm like an eel caught in a net. For Crixus the pleasure was immense. Her bottom cheeks squeezed from the numbing pain as the cone barbs embedded in her buttocks making her cunt tighten and her sex lips slaver around the root of his cock.

"Hurry up and come," she winced. "Remember your mission."

I'm on a mission now, he thought, releasing her wrists and making an instant play for her breasts. Lady Octavia grunted, vainly trying to wriggle her bottom away from the cone whilst Crixus rolled and groped her breasts, then biting on the nipples until she screamed.

"By all that is sacred," she moaned, feeling sharp darts of pain piercing through her arse and sex. "Please, Crixus, come or I shall I die."

He laughed at that. It would take a hell of a lot more than a pine cone splitting her arse and having a rock hard cock pounding inside her to send her splendid body into the underworld.

"Make your arse dance and I'll come," he said brusquely, thoughtfully taking his weight on his elbows.

"You're such a shit," she hissed, and then began jerking her hips in time with his thrusting.

For a good fifteen minutes, the assembled onlookers were treated to a cock hardening display of Lady Octavia's bottom bouncing on and off the upholstery and the sound of splintering pine barbs. Her hips seemed to break into wonderful rolling undulations, then suddenly her arse lifted and the feminine strength in her thighs and calves came into play, throwing wide and heaving her whole body in wild convulsions. Crixus always critical of women and their artful trickery just had to give credit where it was rightfully due. A rich stream of spunk shot uncontrollably up his cock and flooded Lady Octavia's cunt. Groaning like tortured animals, they collapsed and rolled from the divan reeking of sex and sweat.

Remarkable, thought Crixus, when he later embarked to Alexandria how an innocent thing like a pinecone could produce such climactic results and he wished he had thought of it earlier.

"Oh what the fuck does she want?" the foul-mouthed Calla swore when Crixus informed her of his mission to bring her to Lady Octavia's villa.

He shrugged truthfully. Lady Octavia had not actually told him the reason.

"Just come with me," he said flatly, already exhausted from the frantic dash to Alexandria and not looking forward to the return journey either.

Calla went off swearing and cursing. Although she was the most successful of Lady Octavia's procuresses, she had also made a tidy sum for herself, buying and selling boatloads of female slaves and now, just as a ship full of Libyan slaves had arrived she had to pack her bag and head all the way up river on some pointless errand or other.

"I've come all the way up here just for this!" she gasped, after her mistress informed her that the governor of the province wished to see her cunt.

"All of Alexandria has seen it and half of Upper Egypt so why miss him out?" Lady Octavia retorted drily.

But she had to be careful. Calla was a free agent contracted to Lady Octavia and was quite within her legal rights to refuse such a request if she so desired.

"All right, I'll do it," Calla smirked. "But not for less than twenty gold pieces."

Lady Octavia reddened but knew that the procuress was a skilled negotiator and it would take hours to knock even one piece off the price.

"He will probably want to fuck you into the bargain," Lady Octavia informed, running her eyes over Calla's massive thighs.

She showed no surprise but merely asked when all this was going to take place as she had pressing business waiting in Alexandria.

"Immediately after you've washed and perfumed," Lady Octavia told her, just as eager to conclude the business.

The sooner she was with Africanus the better. It wasn't too wild a leap of the imagination to guess that Marius Aquinus would move just as fast for reasons of his own.

Cellenius was in a black mood when Lady Octavia arrived at his palace with Calla. Again, there were rumours, as yet unsubstantiated that some mad woman believing herself Queen of Egypt was plotting an uprising and not one of his spies had been able to locate her whereabouts.

And that troubled him.

"Who's this hippo," he asked rudely, when Lady Octavia introduced Calla and reminded him of their bargain.

Calla had been called many things and accepted most of them with good humour, but compared with a hippopotamus was not something she took lightly.

"If you want to see my cunt, it'll cost you a hundred marks," she said without hesitation.

Lady Octavia almost fouled her underskirt. No one spoke to the governor in that tone, and least of all some insignificant slave dealer from the back streets of Alexandria.

"Guard," Cellenius called with surprising calm. "Have this tub of lard put in the sling and flogged and then starve her for a month. The new concubine can administer the punishment. If the hippo measures up I'll grant you your side of the bargain," he said to Lady Octavia. He turned to

107

go but halted as if something had suddenly struck him. "Does the name, Queen Hatentita mean anything to you?"

"No, it doesn't," Lady Octavia replied, wondering what had prompted such a strange question.

And they trooped into the hall, the palace guards dragging Calla's bulk before the wooden frame.

"Strip the fat bitch!" Messalina rasped, angry at been caught unawares.

When Cellenius summoned her to his bed the sex was magic, but during the intervals when she was not required, she suffered agonies of frustration and was now slaking her lust with one of the palace guards. It was not only being fucked continuously for hours on end which thrilled her, but the intrigue and the thought of getting away with it added spice to the dish, but on this occasion she had nearly been caught with her long creamy thighs spread wide and his buttocks pounding between them. The guard had just managed to get dressed and dive through a window before a messenger burst unceremoniously into her room catching her stark naked and breathless.

"You will flog the fat from her bones," she hissed at Africanus who had been dragged from her cot naked and still aching from her previous bout at the frame.

The shock of seeing Calla's voluptuous body trussed in the slings almost had the whip falling from her hand, but the sight of her former mistress had her even more wide eyed and gaping like an imbecile.

"Get on with it!" Messalina snapped, her eyes impatient and venomous.

Africanus gathered the whip and sent it full force over Calla's broad back. Her body shuddered, the abundant flesh rippling from the sudden pain. Unlike Africanus who, when she was being flogged, went into a spin, Calla's bulk remained still, her weight creaking in the straps. Africanus could see her lips visibly cursing as the whip smacked into her buttocks. She could also see her new master Cellenius who watched the proceedings with a curious lack of interest, his eyes seemed to be staring past her at some unseen event. Even the loud hollow smack of the whip thudding onto Calla's meaty thighs failed to distract him, but he did glance at her breasts occasionally, hanging full weight beneath her, and swaying ponderously from every fresh lash.

Calla didn't scream or howl as the whip tails cut their welts over her buttocks and thighs, but protected as she was by so much corpulent flesh merely grunted and sneered at the onlookers. Most of her anger was directed at Lady Octavia who, she was sure had engineered the whole episode, and as the tails flicked painfully between her open thighs already made up her mind that one way or another the painted bitch was going to taste the wrong end of her fist.

Flogging Calla was no light task and Africanus had broken into sheen of sweat that lent her body a shimmering gleam. It ran in tiny rivulets from her shaven scalp and through the deep sensuous clefts of her breasts and buttocks. Cellenius had stopped gazing into infinity and was now eyeing his new concubine with renewed interest. Messalina had proved herself right; the black woman certainly knew how to handle a whip. The fat woman's buttocks and thighs were crossed with welts and her glimmering assailant must have delivered at least forty lashes and showed no signs of exhaustion.

Then he remembered his wager with Lady Octavia.

"Drop that whip and let's see if the hippo can take your arm," he said, lips flickering.

Africanus let the whip fall and stood directly behind Calla whose sex lips still quivered from the aftershock. Lady Octavia's eyes were full on her and filled with glazed urgency and Africanus instinctively knew that her former mistress had struck some deal or other, probably for money.

She crossed her fingers at the tips and slipped them into

Calla's soaking sex, and then slowly bunched them into a fist.

"By all the Gods," Cellenius muttered.

"By the grace of Jupiter," Lady Octavia blurted.

"Fuck me," Africanus whispered.

"You bunch of bastards," Calla snorted, feeling Africanus' fist revolving into her sex tunnel.

Africanus' wrist had disappeared into Calla's slavering cunt and it seemed her sex was still begging for more. The vaginal walls made a sucking sound and then emitted a cunt fart loud enough for the assembly to gawp in amazement.

"The hippo wins," Cellenius conceded. "The black woman's yours until sunrise."

Lady Octavia blinked in disbelief as Africanus worked her elbow so fast sweat dripped from her temples. Calla snorted and groaned as her orgasm reached its climax. The juices flooded over Africanus' arm and soaked the tiles beneath. It was possible even from where the assembly were standing to smell her deep, rich sexual aroma.

"Have her released and present her to the guards," Cellenius offered graciously, as Africanus' fist slurped from Calla's cunt. Lady Octavia wasted no time in taking Africanus' hand and almost dragging her to her room.

The two women sat opposite each other; one magnificent in her fine robe, legs shaved and shapely, pubic hair finely clipped and smelling of rose water; the other naked and streaked with stale sweat, her head shaved apart from her side locks and skin still bearing the traces of whip welts.

For a few moments, they stared into their eyes, and then at last Lady Octavia broke the brittle silence.

"You have lost none of your beauty and your body is in good shape even though you look and smell like a dung heap."

"Thank you, mistress," Africanus replied, still unable to think of herself as anything but a slave.

At Lady Octavia's bidding, she stood up letting soft palms roam over her body, cupping her breasts, weighing their fullness, pinching the nipples and seeing her nod satisfactorily at the hardened response. She patted her belly murmuring it was still nice and flat, then smoothed the long ebony thighs and rounded bottom, fingers manipulated the tight hard buttocks, but most of all she inspected her arms still strong and capable of wielding a gladius, and bearing a heavy shield. That told her what she most wanted to know and she ordered a slave to bring wine and food. There was only one more thing she needed to know.

"Quintus drowned in the ship wreck," Africanus told her, and then gave a brief outline of her life in Britannia, and then sailing to Egypt, telling Lady Octavia everything she thought she wanted to hear.

"I didn't know you were in one of my brothels," Lady Octavia said, raising her eyebrows, wondering how she had missed such an opportunity, and she went on hearing about how Africanus had come into Cellenius' harem as a concubine. The more she listened the more Lady Octavia decided that Africanus had to be got to Rome as fast as possible, with or without Cellenius permission.

"Yes mistress, I would like that very much," Africanus informed, thrilled at becoming a gladiatrix again, perhaps even meeting up with Fortuna.

"She has her own ludus now," Lady Octavia informed, "and speaks of you often."

I shall return to Rome, Africanus thought, and fight in the Colosseum alongside Fortuna, but on my own terms. Fuck you, Lady Octavia.

First, she had to fulfill her obligation to Hatentita and get out of this prison.

"I'm surprised my new master hasn't fucked me," she said, emptying her goblet, deliberately changing the subject.

"He will all in good time, but now, as we have the rest of

the night together I would like to see if you still posses all your fighting skills."

"You saw me flog your fat procuress," she replied wearily.

"Any fool could've done that and Cellenius wouldn't know a gladiatrix in action if he saw her. It is I who wants to see you fight. In the absence of suitable armour, you can combat naked and use a flail. I'll match, you against three of Cellenius' house slaves. Use any tactics you wish."

She stalked off leaving Africanus dumbstruck. Would she never rid herself of this scheming harridan? She would probably even follow her into the underworld. Lady Octavia came back leading the house slaves, surely looking creatures with eyes like serpents and who had a grudge against just about everything. They were armed with crudely improvised weapons; lengths of knotted rope weighted at the ends with lumps of lead cast into the rope itself.

"Five silver coins to the last one on her feet," Lady Octavia announced as an incentive to the three slaves, whose eyes already glinted with greed. A slave could do a lot with five silver coins. They were worth battling over and all three moved cautiously towards the tall black woman, keeping a level gaze, wondering where and whom she would strike first. The flail in Africanus' hand was fearful in itself; a long stout wooden handle with four lengths of thick plaited leather interwoven with bronze studs, enough to inflict serious damage on naked skin. But in the eyes of the slaves, Africanus recognized grim purpose. Lady Octavia had let it be known that the winner, if it were one of the three might be granted her freedom and after twenty years of slavery it seemed like a gift from the Gods. All they had to do was defeat the tall, naked black slave.

Simple.

Africanus took up the classical pose of attack, knees

slightly bent, back bending forward, heels ready to spring. The three slaves were ordered to attack individually which would help to avoid confusion if Africanus fell. The first, driven by Lady Octavia's silver tongue, attacked like a mad woman, slashing and whipping in all directions. Africanus took a couple of painful smacks on the rump and one on her left flank, but she had not forgotten her training and moved swiftly out of reach making the woman more exasperated and careless as her manic lashing brought no results. Africanus could see her tiring and, when she judged the moment was right, moved in rapidly. The flail swung in so fast that the onlookers only saw the slave buckle under its connection; four whip tails equally spread lashed across her upper buttocks and thighs. Africanus span in a circle keeping her balance on one foot as she lashed at the slave full frontal, this time sending the tails thudding over her belly and breasts. The woman screamed and bent double and howled again as her assailant lashed the flail full strength over her back and onto the rounded rump of her buttocks. Caught up in the heady whirlwind of combat she gave another two furious lashes over the woman's shoulders and backs of her thighs, then stood back panting as the woman groaned and rolled into a somersault, face crunching to the floor. She was still conscious and Africanus was about to deliver a swift kick to her stomach but remembered her training at Quintus' ludus; if an opponent is finished why expend any more energy, and she smiled grimly at the remaining two slaves.

"Next!" she bawled, her harsh voice echoing around the room.

There was an uneasy tension as the two remaining slaves shuffled their feet. It had taken less than seven minutes for the black woman to destroy her opponent and now she stood tall and upright, her silky skin gleaming with sweat. Lady Octavia had forgotten how magnificent Africanus appeared naked in combat, her full breasts high and firm,

113

nipples fully erect and throbbing, her splendid thighs hard and stunningly beautiful in their strength. She would earn her a fortune back in the Colosseum, and she smacked her foot into the nearest slaves' buttocks, propelling her forward into the gladiatrix' awaiting flail. But to her surprise she deftly side stepped the swinging tails and Africanus went into a spin thrashing the flail through the air. The slave already knew she had lost and could only hope to keep out of range until the gladiatrix was exhausted.

Now a deadly game began, each opponent going in wider circles, their long legs moving in sweeps, eyes riveted on each other. Africanus had already worked out her tactics and skilfully drove her opponent away from the centre of the floor towards a wall from which there would be no escape. Lady Octavia watched closely as the slave was trapped like a sheep in a pen and couldn't disguise the admiration on her face. Africanus had lost none of her skills and in one single lash disarmed the terrified slave sending her crashing into the wall. She stood against the painted plaster, legs together and buttocks closed tight.

"Open your legs!" Africanus demanded, her eyes gone into slits.

If this miserable display just might be her ticket back into the Colosseum and her mistress was awaiting the final onslaught, then Africanus would not disappoint her. The slave spread her legs wide, flexing her thighs and calves.

"Spread your cheeks!" Africanus ordered, gripping the flail handle.

The woman reached behind and placed her hands on her buttocks, fingertips embedded deeply into the arse crease. Curling her fingers, she prized open the cleft and Africanus could visibly see her trembling with terror.

"Keep your fingers where they are," the gladiatrix, told her, gathering the plaited tails.

In one long, upward sweep the tails whistled under the slaves' parted legs. Two of the plaits sailed into her sex;

114

the other two caught her arse cheeks and wrists. Her slender body juddered against the wall, squashing her breasts and flattening her stomach. Her hands flew from her bottom and with clenched fists, she beat the air in agony.

"I told you to spread your arse," Africanus barked, snapping the tails.

The slave woman sobbed and slowly put her hands behind her, sinking the fingertips into the crease.

"Wider," Africanus said huskily. "Spread your cheeks until they split."

The poor, defenceless woman had no choice but to obey. She buried her fingers into the crease as deep as she could and pulled the halves apart, groaning from the pain.

"Not far enough," Africanus whispered, moving closer. "I want to see your dirt hole."

The woman sobbed again and wrenched at her bottom exposing the dark aperture of her anus and Africanus suddenly laughed.

"This wretch has got hairs all around her dirt hole, so let's see if I can shave them, leave her nice and clean."

She saw the slave's back and buttocks twitch in anticipation as she moved in, adopting a stance a little to the left and lifting her arm, letting the tails slowly swing back and forth, deliberately prolonging the agony. Then, quicker than lightning, the tails whipped under the woman's legs. The angle was perfect and as Africanus withdrew the tails they raked up through her victim's arse crease, each bronze stud tearing at the fine silky cluster of hair encircling her anus. Her shrieks echoed around the wall as the hairs ripped from her skin leaving her writhing with pain.

"Spread!" Africanus rasped, allowing enough time for the pain to sink in.

Again, the woman's curling fingers tugged at her cheeks and again Africanus whistled the tails into her sex and arse crease. Now the woman was up on her toes, back arched and head rolling dementedly from side to side.

"I'll give you another twelve, and then I'll let you go," Africanus announced, lashing the whip directly over her bottom.

Whilst the slave dutifully kept her hands in place Africanus whipped with steady, measured strokes, keeping each lash close together, working her way upwards, her strength increasing as the tails left their deadly wake. But Africanus had to give the naked slave credit, throughout the whipping she did as she was told, hands remaining on her cheeks, fingers frozen into the cleft. Her slim back laddered with lash welts and she leaned against the wall, emitting harsh grunts, her tongue hanging limply from her lips. Africanus placed the sole of her right foot on the woman's flank and gave a gentle shove. Without a whimper, she keeled over and fell flat on her back, eyes staring vacantly at the ceiling.

The third slave gripped the end of her rope and walked slowly into the centre of the room. Keeping her eyes fixed rigidly on Africanus; she bowed and then raised her rope in salutation, a perfect imitation of how real gladiatrix greeted each other before combat. Africanus' lips tightened. Either she had actually witnessed the procedure, or was poking fun and Africanus felt a sudden blood rush. The snarl curling her lips was real and like a cat, she bared her claws and rushed at the slave swinging the whip at buttock height. At the same time, the slave executed a fast spin to her left and sent her rope in an upward arc to meet the whistling tails. In a second, both tails and rope intertwined and the combatants stumbled and tugged trying to regain their weapons. But it was useless, the more they pulled the tighter the knot, and the closer they came until Africanus dropped her handle and thudded her fist into the slave's head.

"Aaroogh!" she grunted, dropping the rope.

But she quickly responded with a vicious kick into the black woman's rump.

Lady Octavia's eyes lifted, wrinkling her fine brow. What ought to have been another skilful display of gladiatorial combat had suddenly degenerated into a bitch fight and both antagonists it seemed were on equal terms. She seated herself, crossing her magnificent legs and summoning a girl slave for wine and sweetmeats, much as she might if she were attending a garden party, but this contest now increasing in ferocity was proving a lot more interesting. She smiled a self-satisfied smile and congratulated herself for both combatants had reason to fight like demons, one on the promise of her freedom, and the other desperate to get back to the Colosseum.

She sipped her wine and crunched on a grape just as Africanus grabbed the slave between her legs, squeezing her hand with all the strength she could muster.

"You howling bitch," the slave screamed, her eyes watering from the crushing fingers.

Using her free arm, she swung in a wide sweep, delivering a resounding slap at the side of Africanus' head. Then, quicker than Lady Octavia thought possible, she grabbed one of the gladiatrix' side locks and gave it a heart-rending tug.

"Fuck!" Africanus bawled, and dropped the slave to her feet.

But the girl hung on like grim death, almost ripping the braid from her opponent's scalp. Africanus brought up her knee and slammed it into the girl's sex bending her double. A swift upper cut rammed under her chin and she somersaulted backwards, rolling uncontrollably to Lady Octavia's painted toenails. Africanus was there at once, seizing the girl by the hair and dragging her across the floor. But her opponent was quicker than she thought and her hand went out and gripped Africanus' left ankle. A sharp wrench had the black woman tumbling into a table, knocking over the contents and smashing glass in all directions. The slave picked up a bottle and would have disfigured the black woman's face for life had she not slipped and fallen head first into a column. Dazed, she looked up just as a clenched fist slammed into her stomach, winding her and leaving her doubling up with pain. Africanus' killing blow was a hefty punch on her jaw and, uttering a slow groan, she passed out.

"Well done," Lady Octavia complimented unconvincingly. "The slave proved more resilient than you imagined, eh?"

"She fought well, mistress," Africanus magnanimously allowed.

"I'll give her a silver piece for her efforts. Would you like her as a companion? I can arrange it."

"I am a slave just like her," Africanus said, on a note of bitterness. "Why would she want to be my companion?"

"Because I order it. Cellenius won't mind. She can wait on you. A slave to a slave," she laughed, handing Africanus her goblet.

Africanus swallowed and would have liked to send the liquid hissing through her teeth directly into Lady Octavia's powdered face, but thought better of it and swallowed deeply.

"I'll take her," Africanus said dully, watching the girl struggling to her feet.

"Ustane, take your new mistress to my bath and see she is well scrubbed and perfumed, and then show her to my bed. And afterwards scrub yourself, you stink."

"Yes, mistress," she bowed, surprised at this sudden turn of events.

And both combatants trooped off to the baths leaving Lady Octavia in deep thought.

CHAPTER SIX

Seeing them bathing together no one would ever have believed that only a short time before they had beating each other senseless. Africanus, foregoing being washed and perfumed, invited Ustane to join her in the bath. They sat opposite one another, resting their ankles on each other's shoulders, coolly appraising their ample breasts and playfully stroking their silky thighs.

"I like it up my bum three times a week," Ustane laughed, tossing back her hair. "Especially if the cock's long and rock hard and he's giving it me like a real stallion."

"I like being tied up," Africanus said, rolling one of her nipples in her fingers. "Then he gives me a mild beating and fucks me hard whilst I'm begging him to stop."

Ustane laughed aloud and licked Africanus' calf. There was no hatred now, just the two of them indulging in feminine dalliance. They both knew they were slaves forced to fight each other and were at the beck and call of anyone who wanted them. Here, for a short while at least was freedom of sorts.

"I like men shooting their loads over my face and tits, after I've sucked 'em," Ustane continued. "Then they lick it off while I'm fingering myself to orgasm."

"I once tossed two men at once with their cocks aimed into my open mouth, and two more were rubbing their balls into my tits. That was a real thrill when they all came at once. I was covered in the stuff. It was dribbling off my nipples and they sucked my teats, then I fucked all four of them, one straight after the other, two in my cunt and two up my arse," Africanus confessed, tweaking Ustane's nipple with her toes.

"What if you don't want it? I mean how do you get him to finish quickly?"

"Just fuck him fast and get it over and done with. Sometimes I flog their logs and when their spunk hits the ceiling, they're finished."

"I know of a better way than that," Ustane grinned, running a hand up Africanus' thigh. "Ever met Halalia? She works in the infirmary, knows everything about medicine, made up a concoction that you paint on your nipples and all around your cunt, smells of almonds. When the man is sucking your tits and licking your cunt, it knocks him out cold. He just thinks he's fallen asleep."

Africanus abruptly ceased licking Ustane's thigh. "You mean a drug?"

"That's what it is all right."

"Could you get me some?"

She shrugged. "Yeah, I suppose so."

Africanus sat up and leaned forward, kissing Ustane full on the lips, working her tongue deep into her throat.

"How soon can you get it?"

"Whenever you like," she said, returning Africanus' lips and worming her tongue into the black woman's mouth.

They knelt up, embraced, hands smoothing backs and buttocks, and would have made love there and then were it not for an infuriating girl concubine coming unannounced into the bath chamber, saying that the Lady Octavia was growing impatient, and for how much longer were those two whores going to be?

Ustane on a fit of temper reached out and grabbed the girl's hair, dragging her into the bath.

"You insolent little bitch. I ought to drown you for that," she raged, angry at the destruction of such a beautiful moment.

"Just beat her and let her go," Africanus said dully, swinging a long leg over the rim.

"You 'card," Ustane muttered savagely. "Put your arse over that woman's knee."

Africanus was seated on a stone bench towelling her body when the girl threw herself over her knees baring her bottom to Ustane.

"Hold her still while I give 'er a walloping," Ustane

ordered, her dark eyes flashing with sudden rage.

Africanus, stunned at the transformation, merely obeyed, placing the flat of her hand between the girl's shoulder blades and bearing down hard.

Ustane grabbed a towel, soaked it in the bath and wound it into a rope, deftly knotting the wetted end.

"I'll give her ten lashes, then perhaps she'll learn not to come bursting in here like that," Ustane announced, winging the towel into the girl's proffered rump.

She swung at her with full strength and Africanus seized her own towel and stuffed it into the girl's mouth, instantly stifling her agonizing cries. A belting from Ustane was no light thing and she whipped the knotted end hard onto the crown of the girl's bottom, making her legs fly open and jolting her whole body over Africanus'knees.

"Let's see if I can hit her sweet little cunt," Ustane grinned nastily.

"That's cruel," Africanus whispered, but secretly delighting in feeling the girl's slim body squirming over her thighs.

Her budding breasts squashed over her knees and she felt her tiny, pointed nipples stiffen with fright. Africanus put her arm around the girl's trim waist and held her rigid as the knotted end whipped between her open legs.

It was not only the sound of the knot lashing into the squelching sex, but also the muffled sounds of pain coming from the girl's gagged mouth that sent Africanus' chest heaving. Already the juice was oozing from her sex.

"Lash her buttocks," she encouraged, watching the girl's bottom suddenly tighten.

Ustane wasted no time in lashing her, delivering stroke after stroke hard onto each buttock until they blazed a deeper hue of brown. The girl was audibly sobbing, and clenching her tiny fists in agony.

Africanus removed the gag and hauled her upright, wiping away a tear with her towel.

121

"Now you can go," she said softly, patting the girl's bruised cheeks.

"She's not going anywhere!" Ustane broke in, her tone harsh and unforgiving. "When did you last have a cock up your arse?" she asked, a question that left Africanus astounded

"I've never done that," the girl sobbed, rubbing her throbbing cheeks.

"You filthy little liar. I know you've had it up your arse, I can tell by the size of your bottom hole that you're no stranger to bum fucking. So tell me the truth, when did you last have it up your pretty little bum?"

The girl hesitated, not knowing how to answer. Was she to go on truthfully denying, or tell her terrifying tormentor what she wanted to hear?

She swallowed hard and looked pleadingly at the black woman. But Africanus kept silent. She needed Ustane's help in getting hold of that drug and it would be unwise to rob her of her sport.

"I had it yesterday," the girl whispered, and bowed her head in shame at her own false and degrading confession.

"I knew it!" Ustane exclaimed triumphantly, her eyes glinting. "How many men did you have? Tell me the truth or I'll give you another ten strokes on your cunt."

Again, she looked imploring at the black woman who avoided her gaze. "I had six cocks up my bum," she wept, and Africanus saw her slim legs turn rigid with fright.

"And you liked it?" Ustane taunted.

"Yes, I liked it," she said, sniffing back a tear.

"In that case you wouldn't mind 'aving another one now would you? I mean, there's a guard standing out there with a cock like a horse, and he'll just love you."

This was too much and Africanus broke in tactfully reminding Ustane that the Lady Octavia was expecting her presence in her bedchamber forthwith and perhaps the girl could be bum fucked another time.

"She's going to have it now!" Ustane retorted. "Guard!"

He came into the bath chamber; a tall, swarthy Nubian, solid muscle and bored out of his skull guarding nothing more precious than a bath chamber.

"What the fuck do you want?" he said rudely, not being obliged to obey the instructions of a mere house slave.

"Tell the guard what you want," Ustane said to the girl, folding her arms under her breasts.

"I want your cock up my bottom," she whispered through trembling lips.

"You want what?" he said, looking askance at the naked girl, and then at the tall black woman who gave a barely perceptible nod.

"You heard her," Ustane said in a husky whisper. "Give it to her. You can see she's just begging for it."

The guard looked at the girl suspiciously. She certainly didn't give the impression of begging for an enormous cock rammed tightly up her bottom.

"Aren't you capable, or are you afraid you won't measure up," Ustane dangerously taunted.

Africanus took an involuntary step backwards, well out of striking range. He was powerfully built and one swing of his fist could leave either of the two women unconscious.

"I'd rather have her," he murmured, indicating Africanus.

"She's already taken," Ustane told him. "It's that little tart or nothing. Up to you, so take what's offered or get back to where you came from."

"I ought to beat you for that," he snapped.

"But you won't, coz you know that it's forbidden for any palace guards to beat a female slave without permission from the chief concubine."

Africanus just had to admire her guts. Fearless and straight to the point. She would make a good gladiatrix.

"I'll take her," he said, cornered by the skilful Ustane who smiled insolently at his dilemma. If he did not rise to the challenge it would be all over the harem by morning, and Nubians had a reputation to uphold.

He unbuckled his tunic and let it fall revealing an organ that had Africanus gasping.

The girl opened her mouth but no sound came she was so stunned at his size.

"Please, I can't take that," she pleaded, putting her hands behind her and covering her bottom hole.

"Bend over the bench and spread your legs," Ustane said in a cold measured tone.

Her voice had a strange hypnotic timbre that had the girl dumbly doing as she was told, and she put her belly over the bench seat and dutifully spread her legs.

"Hold her head and gag the little slut," Ustane ordered to Africanus, who in turn dutifully obeyed.

She wound her towel around the girl's head and then held it rigid, and had an uncanny feeling that all of this was somehow against the harem rules, but kept her peace and watched the guard kneel up behind the girl, cock in hand and aiming ominously at her anus.

"Put your hands behind you and open your arse," Ustane said, standing to the left of the girl's bottom where she could witness her penetration.

Her tiny hands pressed hard on her cheeks and eased them apart. The guard chuckled and nudged his plum against the girl's bottom hole.

"She's tight," he observed. "I think she's a virgin."

"She's had more cock than you've had whores," Ustane corrected, knowing full well the poor girl had never been bum fucked in her life.

The guard gripped her slender hips and pulled her gently backwards, keeping his plum aimed into her bottom. At the first touch, the girl's arse suddenly jolted and a muffled cry came from her gagged mouth. Africanus gripped her head wishing she were in Lady Octavia's bed, anywhere but having to participate in this sickening spectacle.

"Go on, give it to her!" Ustane screamed venomously.

The guard, galvanized into action, slammed the girl's

cheeks against his pelvis but penetrated her only by an inch.

"She's too tight, I tell you," he snapped.

Ustane was there at once, thumping her clenched fist onto the base of the girl's spine. "Now open up you sorry little shit," she hissed.

Grunting, the guard gave a thrust of his loins and to his surprise, his cock glided effortlessly into her anus. It took one more thrust and his balls buried in her cleft. A cheerful grin creased his lips as he rode easily in and out of her, his hands on the sides of her pert buttocks keeping them spread. Africanus stole a swift glance at the girl's wincing face, the eyes screwed with pain, her teeth chewing voraciously on the towel. The guard, warming to the comfort of her bottom increased his tempo, riding her faster and faster, then angling his hips to widen the tight aperture of her bottom hole. Then, laughing at the girl's obvious discomfort, he wriggled his hips from side to side, breaking into a dance, clenching his buttocks and thrusting deeper with every insertion.

Africanus' nipples stiffened at the sight of his splendid physique. His chest, rippling with muscle had broken into a sweat and his body shone like polished ebony, a sight not lost on Ustane who crept behind him and rubbed her ample naked breasts into his back. Then she reached under his parted legs and gripped his balls, manipulating them in her palm.

The girl's head twisted madly from side to side at the sudden increase in his length. She was sure he had gained another inch and was definitely a lot harder. Africanus cautiously let go of her head and cupped her own breasts, unashamedly pinching her puckered nipples and flicking her thumbs over the aroused teats.

"Slap her thighs," Ustane whispered. "Hurt the bitch."

The guard lifted his hand and delivered a resounding slap on the girl's thigh. She bucked her bottom and inside her anal muscles went tight. It was a strange, yet curious sensation he felt going all around his cock, her anal muscles enveloping his length with a peculiar sort of warmth. Now he was riding harder, oblivious to the muffled torments coming from behind the towel. He withdrew until his reddened plum was at the very entrance to her bottom and then slammed into her full force. Africanus actually saw her bottom cheeks involuntarily spread from the shock, and then flex hard at the sides. The guard noticed the effect his cock was having and gave her cheeks a playful pinch, digging his nails into the soft flesh of her cheeks and twisting it until she bit clean through the gag.

He slapped her again, this time all down her slim back, hitting hard enough to leave an imprint of his hand. Africanus swiftly grabbed the towel and forced it back into her mouth. At this time of night, her screams would awaken the whole harem. The girl squirmed like a weasel in a trap, dancing her hips and wriggling her bottom, thrusting her arse against the pounding cock, jerking faster and panting through her gag.

"See how she likes it!" Ustane said victoriously, squashing her breasts into his back.

But Africanus could see the girl was trying to bring him off. Inside it felt as if her bottom was splitting in half and when he angled into her anal walls, the pain was unbearable. Her bottom hole stretched to the limit, forced wider by his twisting pelvis, and at every fresh insertion, her stomach heaved.

"She'll shit like a cow after this," Ustane laughed, and even Africanus thought that was funny.

Her slim legs thrashed in all directions, bending at the knees and then going rigid, thrown as wide as she could take them. The guard rammed tight against her bottom, juddering inside her with all the strength his rippling torso could summon. He leaned over and seized her shoulders, digging his fingers into her collarbones and arching her back. Beneath his massive frame, her slender body looked so tiny and almost disappeared under the broad expanse of his chest and arms. Ustane had lifted her thigh, crooked it around his waist, and was clinging to his side like grim death. Her mouth opened gulping for air and Africanus could plainly see the hot flush spreading across her face. Her breasts jiggled into his rib cage and the unmistakable groans of orgasm slowly filled the chamber. Only Africanus remained passive amongst this welter of gyrating and twisting bodies, the guard bum fucking the young girl slave rocking and humping over the bench, and Ustane working her hips fast and furious. The black woman, caught up in the heady maelstrom of sex, reached under her legs and calmly stroked her sex, letting her fingertips gently coax her love bud to erection. Her free hand thumbed and tweaked each nipple now hard and throbbing. The guard erupted into the girl with a groan like a wounded ox, whilst Ustane emitted a series of harsh porcine grunts. Only the girl remained dumb, uttering muffled pants behind her gag. Africanus came with her head thrown back and a long, satisfied moan. She took her soaking fingers from her sex and, wrenching the gag from the girl's mouth, thrust her fingers into her parched throat. The slave girl sucked on them like a baby desperate to assuage its thirst. She swallowed and lifted her tear streaked face, then dropped her head with a deep sigh. The guard pulled back and wiped his punished cock in the girl's trailing hair, roughly pushing Ustane from his side who staggered back, hands between her legs, sex rubbed raw.

"Get up," she muttered to the girl.

But she was lifeless, worn out from such a pounding. Africanus helped her to her feet, putting her strong arms under the hollows of her armpits and hauling her upright. She noticed how her bottom cheeks had not yet returned to their normal rounded shape and her bum hole still stretched open.

"Now you are no longer a virgin," she whispered kindly. "Run along and tell no one what has happened here."

The girl could barely take one step forward, let alone run along. She hobbled across the tiles and slipped noiselessly away, followed by the guard taking manly strides and guffawing like a buffoon.

"I came like a volcano," Ustane grinned, licking her lips and leaping back into the bath.

"That was nasty," Africanus said, taking her towel and rubbing the drying streams of juice from her sex.

Ustane leaned against the bath edge and clasped her hands behind her head. "But you must admit, it was funny, watching her lose her virginity to that beast. Her sweet little arse will ache for a month," and she ducked under the water leaving Africanus heading slowly towards Lady Octavia's private bedroom, her face screwed in thought.

"You've been a hell of a long time," Lady Octavia said coldly. "What were you both doing in there, fucking each other?"

"We were interrupted," she answered vaguely, "by one of the…"

"Never mind that," Lady Octavia snapped. "Pour me some wine and sit down and listen carefully."

Africanus obeyed and after handing her mistress a goblet, seated her self on a couch, crossing her splendid legs and folding her arms, wondering what fresh trickery her former mistress was cooking up now.

"I have news that Cellenius is planning a journey up the river and then into the desert where he intends to camp for a while and this is a good opportunity…are you listening?"

Africanus' eyes had taken on a vacant stare. Here at last was what she had been waiting to know, and could hardly believe her ears.

"Yes, mistress," she simpered, looking hard at her with exaggerated attention.

"As I said, before you drifted off, Cellenius is planning an expedition into the desert, which of course is as we all know just an excuse to take along a gaggle of concubines and whores and spend the whole time fucking, which just happens to suit my purpose, although he isn't aware of it. Are you with me so far?"

"Yes mistress," Africanus replied, now listening intently.

"I have decided to leave this flea infested hole and we are finally going back to where we belong; Rome and the Colosseum, and have great adventures and you will take your rightful place amongst your own kind, fighting and winning glory in the arena."

She concluded her speech with a beaming smile that left Africanus cold, and she wondered how long it had taken her mistress to memorize it all. She also knew that sending her back into the Colosseum was to fill her own coffers. She also rightly guessed that spiriting her away was probably tantamount to high treason, making off with the governor's property. But then, where money was concerned the Lady Octavia would do almost anything.

"When's the governor making this expedition?" Africanus inquired casually.

"As soon as all the preparations are in hand. My guess it will be in about a week or even less. Have you ever heard of someone called, 'Queen Hatentita'?"

Africanus nearly wetted all over the seat. "No," she said blankly, raising a goblet to her lips.

"The reason I ask is that there is some wild rumour that this woman is planning a rebellion. The harem's buzzing with it, which might, I suppose, have something to do with Cellenius making off into the desert."

Africanus kept tactfully silent, but her heart was racing. It wouldn't take long to find out the exact date the governor intended to leave because the Lady Octavia would be amongst the first to know. Once that information passed to Hatentita's spies, she could leave the harem on her own terms, and be amply rewarded by the Queen. She might even make her own way to Rome. There would be little her former mistress could do about it, especially if she joined Fortuna's ludus.

"What's the matter with you, girl? Are you sickening for something?" Lady Octavia asked, noticing an involuntary smile creasing the black woman's lips.

"I'm tired," she said, and made a show of yawning.

"Too much romping in that bath with that other worthless piece of shit," she observed nastily. "Are you in need of a man, or do you now only prefer women?" she said slyly.

"I'd like Dorla," she said firmly.

"Who in the name of all the Gods is Dorla?"

"She shaved my head, and I happen to like her," she replied.

"I like you."

"Do you intend to have me?"

"I can have you any time I like, but as I'm in conciliatory mood, I'll allow you this…Dorla. You can even have my bed as I shall be sleeping elsewhere tonight."

And she laughed out loud.

"Africanus!" Dorla exclaimed, beaming widely. She came into the bedchamber and Africanus noticed that her nipples were pierced and ornamented with huge golden rings. Her ears sported rings of the same dimensions and an enamel brooch fitted snugly into her navel. Around her head, she wore a band of gold studded with jewels.

"You look magnificent," Africanus complimented truthfully. "What did you do to earn all that stuff?"

"I fucked the governor," she said proudly.

"I'm going to fuck you," Africanus said without hesitation.

"That's what Lady Octavia said, you're going to fuck me, and I said I wanted to fuck you."

"And what did she say to that."

"Nothing, she just laughed and said mind I oiled my cunt first, coz you've got long bony fingers."

Africanus couldn't help but laugh and moved forward hugging her. "Now go and fetch over that jar and do as the Lady Octavia suggested, then join me on the bed."

Dorla, happy to be with the tall, statuesque black women went cheerfully about her task. To Africanus' amusement, she did not merely oil her fingers and slip them inside her sex, but laid herself on the bed, lifting her thighs and bending her knees, opening her legs and upending the bottle into her sex lips, holding it still until she emptied the entire contents.

"I can see you mean business," Africanus smiled, feeling nothing but warm affection for the girl slave now slowly returning her legs to the mattress. "I don't have a cock to use in you," she said, "but my fingers will bring you off just as well."

"I bet the Lady Octavia has got one lying around," Dorla chuckled. "You know what she's like."

Africanus hadn't thought of that. She went straight away to a cabinet, and rummaged in the drawers. She found what she was looking for concealed in an ornamental wooden box; a long, thick dildo fashioned from cedar wood and carved to perfection.

"Do you think you can take all this?" Africanus asked seriously, running its length through her fingers. "I mean, it's huge."

Dorla studied it closely, her eyes twinkling. "If you wear it, I'll take it."

Africanus strapped the weapon to her pubic mound, passing the thin leather straps under her legs and tightly through her bottom crease. It rose from the under pit of her belly like a phallus on one of the statues in Cellenius' harem.

"I've always wanted you to fuck me," Dorla confessed, eyeing the black woman with adoration. "You're so beautiful."

"You're silly," Africanus smiled lovingly, mounting the bed and climbing over Dorla. "Now take it in your hand and put it inside you, carefully mind you, let it go in an inch at a time and I'll see if you can really take it all."

She had one of the biggest shocks of her life. Dorla gripped the shaft and aimed it between her sex lips, easing in the polished head and raising her bottom from the bed. Before Africanus could even compliment her she threw open her legs and, giving a mighty heave of her belly, impaled her whole sex. Her calves went over Africanus' back and locked at the heels.

"See, I knew I could," she smiled, and put her thin arms around Africanus' shoulders.

"Peach blossom," the gladiatrix whispered, kissing her fondly.

"Fuck me hard," Dorla whispered.

It was rare for any gladiatrix to form attachments, life was cheap and short in harems and arenas, women slaves came and went, just faces like the whores' clients, but with Dorla, she felt a peculiar kinship. She was about the same age as she had been when sold into slavery, young, slender and willing, and easy meat to anyone who wanted her.

"I'll fuck you so hard you won't walk for a week," she laughed, putting her hands under Dorla's shoulder blades.

Dorla clung like a limpet, taking huge gulps pf air whilst the dildo rammed inside her. Africanus was true to her word and gave the girl what she desired. Although she loved her, she did not intend to show any mercy. If she wanted a hard fucking, she was going to get one. She rode her steadily to start with, getting the measure of her strokes, rocking easily over Dorla's pert breasts, and occasionally slowing the pace so she could suck and bite on the hardened nipples.

"Take your legs off my back," she rasped, and Dorla, ever eager to please her heroine, obeyed.

Africanus' eyes glazed with manic desire as she lifted the girl's slim legs over her shoulders, then in a single sweep she pinioned them over Dorla's head, bending them so far the soles of her feet touched the wall. Bent double, Dorla inhaled like one who has almost drowned, sucking in air as the powerful black woman slammed into her.

"It hurts," she wailed.

"You wanted it, so shut your gob," Africanus returned brusquely, supporting her weight on her hands and coming upright.

She pumped as if it were the last fuck she was ever going to get, and beneath her Dorla humped and bucked, reaching over her head and grabbing her ankles.

"You fuck like a stallion," she complimented, catching her breath.

Africanus just smiled and thumped the dildo into Dorla's belly, watching with grim satisfaction her squinting eyes and grinding teeth. At last, she rose to her orgasm, a darker flush spread over her face and her eyes suddenly opened staring at her lover with wide-eyed astonishment. Then they rolled in their sockets, the irises disappearing under the lids and then gazing with fierce demonic concentration. Her mouth opened even wider and, as she climaxed, Africanus clamped her mouth to Dorla's startled face. They kissed until their lips were sore and their tongues ached.

"Are you going to beat me?" Dorla asked softly, as they lay side by side locked in each other's arms.

"Do you want me to?" Africanus whispered.

She nodded and freed her limbs from Africanus' grasp and padded softly across the room. In the dim light, the gladiatrix saw her select one of Lady Octavia's sandals and come quietly back offering it in her outstretched hand.

"Put your belly over that chair," Africanus said her tone subdued and thoughtful. "Bottom up if you please. Do you want a gag, or can you hold your tongue?"

"I think you'd better gag me," Dorla requested, and handed the gladiatrix a thick leather belt.

Almost tenderly, Africanus passed it around her head and pulled the buckle tight, ensuring the leather was snugly between her teeth.

"How many?" she asked. Dorla spread the fingers of both hands. "Ten it is," the gladiatrix confirmed, and sent the sandal winging into Dorla's rump.

The girl grunted but kept her slim legs pressed together. Her buttocks remained soft and compliant, not flexing or straining under the reddening skin. Africanus beat her in slow succession, striking where she knew the pain would be greatest, under the fat of each buttock, hitting hard enough to lift the globe from the tops of her thighs, and then using all her strength to strike the wobbling sides. But still Dorla remained unflinching, not uttering a sound, just breathing heavily through the gag and clenching her fists.

"You show great fortitude," Africanus complimented, marvelling at the swelling halves.

She stepped forward and smacked the sandal on the base of Dorla's spine. Her head shook from the sudden pain and Africanus caught a whimper.

"I knew you'd break in the end. They all do," she said, smacking Dorla's rump dead centre across the crease.

Ignoring the request for ten strokes, the gladiatrix went all around the blazing cheeks, lashing with increased fury, turning the smacked skin from red to dark brown. It was even possible to see the imprint of the sole firmly etched on the pulsating skin. She finished with a singeing stroke into the crease and this time Dorla's legs shot open and she reached behind rubbing her throbbing bottom. Africanus loosed the buckle and lifted her off the chair seat.

"You did well," she said, hugging her. "But did you come?"

Dorla sadly shook her head. "Almost," she sobbed. "Another five and I would've done."

"Five it is," Africanus said. "Bend over and touch your toes."

Dorla turned and bent over, offering her bottom to the sandal. Africanus beat her without mercy, delivering the strokes hard and fast, and on the last one Dorla grunted, and then broke into a welter of groans, her slim body trembling from head to foot. Africanus was still wearing the phallus.

"Spread your legs," she said studiously.

Dorla knew what was coming and braced herself against

the chair back, opening her legs and looking over her shoulder at the black woman guiding the phallus head into her twitching sex lips. She embedded its length in a single thrust, gripping Dorla's hips and riding her with a steady rocking of her pelvis. As the phallus glided in and out of the sucking sex lips, Africanus silently renewed her pledge that wherever she was going she was taking Dorla with her. She would make a good slave and might eventually win her freedom.

"I'm coming," Dorla squeaked, and her arms and legs went rigid.

Africanus rode her arse so fast the sex juices squelched from the swollen lips, dripping to the floor and trickling down the insides of her thighs. Dorla emitted a high-pitched whine and slumped over the chair; exhausted. The pain from her recent beating still throbbed and spread through her sex and belly, and she gave a final sigh and uttered a barely audible, "thank you, mistress."

Africanus untied the dildo and let it fall. She knelt behind her young lover, showering the burning cheeks with kisses, and then pressed her whole face into the dripping sex lips. Her pouting lips found Dorla's love bud and sucked it greedily into her mouth, nibbling on the soft flesh and poking her tongue deep in the hot, soaking sex tunnel. Sex juice still flowed from the quivering depths and Africanus lapped at the vaginal walls like a hungry kitten.

"You're making me come again," Dorla heaved, reaching for her pert breasts.

She pinched her budding nipples until her eyes watered, and somewhere behind the black woman was sucking her dry.

"I came three times," Dorla announced cheerfully, when they lay on the bed, sweat chilling on their limbs.

Africanus kissed her on the cheek, and then bit her nipples. Her long fingers stroked into the warm sex of her lover and gently stroked around the lips.

"I suppose you know everything that goes on in this place,"

she said idly, letting her fingers slip inside her wetted cunt.

"Mostly," Dorla said, nestling her head into Africanus' ample breasts.

"You hear all the gossip?"

"You know what them women are like, never stop talking'"

"So you know all about the governor's intended journey into the desert?"

"I've heard something like that."

"You know where he's going, exactly?"

"Oh, that's a secret. No one knows. I only know he's takin' his favourite concubines and that big fat one what you flogged."

"You mean Carla?" Africanus asked agog, turning to face her.

"Some men like big fat women."

There wasn't much she could say to that. "And have you heard of Queen Hatentita?" her voice lowered.

She had to think for a moment. Thinking was always a problem for her. "Only what Tiye told me. Hatentita is a woman what owns a brothel in Thebes, that's where Tiye came from."

"Oh, you stupid half wit," Africanus snorted unkindly, after all the girl was only trying to be helpful.

She kissed Dorla on the forehead and saw the first rays of dawn lighting up the walls of the harem. Soon, Lady Octavia would return from one of her nocturnal copulations and send both slaves back where they belonged.

She rubbed her palm softly over Dorla's sex mound. The girl angled her head into Africanus' breasts and sucked on the erect nipple. The black woman reached out to where the phallus lay and just managed to retrieve it.

Dorla caught her breath as the full length glided into her sex.

"Relax," Africanus whispered. "There is time enough."

CHAPTER SEVEN

"I've been hunting this whole fucking harem for you," Messalina swore, eyeing Africanus with undisguised hatred. "You are always to be found when you are not wanted, and never when you are. What's your excuse this time?"

"The governor gave me as a present to Lady Octavia," she replied truthfully, omitting everything that had taken place and her sojourn with Dorla. There was no telling how she might react in that dangerous mood.

"I know that, but you were gone a hell of a long time. You weren't back at your duties until well after sunrise, and I happen to know that Lady Octavia wasn't with you all night. So who were you with?"

"Ustane," she lied, praying that she had no idea of the house slave's whereabouts.

"Oh, I see, and I suppose you were fucking each other. You should've returned here as soon as Lady Octavia finished with you. You have no business in any other part of the palace without my express permission. Go to the punishment room and tell that acid faced whore that you are to be strapped and whipped, forty strokes on your bare arse. Then perhaps you'll learn obedience."

"Yes, mistress," Africanus replied, turning on her heels.

Forty strokes on her bare arse was a high price to pay for silence, but she reckoned it was worth it, to find out that precious snippet of information about Cellenius, not to mention all the other bonuses that had come her way. Although it was common knowledge that he was intent on his journey into the desert, as yet the exact date had not been revealed and she would just have to be patient until Lady Octavia got wind of it, then inform Hatentita's spies, whoever they were, for as yet she had no idea.

"Neglecting your duties," the acid faced whore remarked drily, as the gladiatrix entered the punishment room. "You can thank the Gods you weren't executed."

"I'm thankful," she replied without any emotion whatever.

She handed the whore a note stating she was to be strapped and whipped who in return uttered a rueful grunt. She was tall and wiry with long sinewy limbs and an exaggerated bony frame. Only her breasts seemed out of proportion to the rest of her body and Africanus wondered how so narrow a frame could carry such a weight. Her head had not been shaved in accordance with harem custom, but hung down her back to almost buttock length and was held in place with a plain golden band. Her face was foxy but not unattractive with a wide mouth and long, pointed nose. The eyes were wide and lustrous set under finely arched brows. Her only attire was a thin linen robe tied at the waist.

"Forty strokes is a lot in one beating," she grunted. "I'll deliver half now, and the rest after I've rested. Now reach up and take hold of that bar."

Africanus raised her arms and gripped a horizontal iron bar spanning the whole width of the room. She clenched her teeth and awaited the first belt stroke to whip into her naked rump. But it never came. Instead, she heard the whore rummaging inside a coffer, and a moment later a pile of straps landed at her feet.

"Keep still whilst I strap you," she said, kneeling behind the black woman.

The first strap fitted around her ankles and pulled as tightly as the woman's strength allowed. Already Africanus had formed the opinion that she was a great deal stronger than her wiry frame betrayed. She passed one end of the strap through a buckle and then neatly slipped the end through a loop.

"Hmm, good legs," she complimented, taking the next strap and passing it around the black woman's knees. She buckled it at the backs and jerked it tight, looping it and humming quietly to herself.

"Strong thighs," she murmured, fitting the third strap at mid thigh. She buckled it and gave Africanus' thigh a friendly slap. "I suppose you've had your fair share of cock between these beautiful black pillars," she observed, patting both thighs.

Africanus said nothing. It was none of her fucking business.

The whore fetched a stool and mounted it, standing so close behind her that her breasts rubbed into Africanus' back.

"Put your arms together," she said kindly.

Again, three straps were fitted at her wrists, elbows and mid upper arm, pulled tightly and deftly buckled into place.

She got off the stool and stood back to admire the finished result. Africanus stood tall and straight, arms and legs firmly strapped, giving the impression that she was much taller than she really was. Her buttocks clenched firmly, strong and powerful, each half perfectly formed into the deep crease. Her back was as straight as a surveyor's pole, the deeply indented spine dividing the muscles and ribs. The whore walked to her front and nodded her satisfaction at the splendid length of shining thighs, the perfect pubic triangle, thick and glistening, the flat stomach and huge breasts now uplifted with erect and pointed nipples.

The woman didn't try to hide the glimmer in her eyes, but merely slipped the thin robe from her shoulders and stood naked in front of her.

"I've belted and whipped hundreds in here," she said in a gravely voice. "But you are one of the most magnificent pieces of whipping flesh I've ever had the pleasure to set eyes on. I'm only sorry that Messalina didn't order you a hundred."

There was a predatory look in her dark eyes that made Africanus shudder. Her manner was cold and calculating and she wondered how well she fucked, if at all.

"It said in the order that you are to receive forty on your bare arse, but given the sheer beauty of your legs and back,

|I think I'll whip every inch of you. I'm sure Messalina won't object. Would you prefer a cane or a whip? I'd choose the cane; it's more thorough and leaves lovely deep welts."

'She's mad,' thought Africanus. 'I'm in the hands of a lunatic,' and she wondered if she was actually going to get out the cell alive.

"Make your choice," the whore said, going behind her and patting her buttocks.

Whilst Africanus thought about it, she took off her headband and tied her hair in a huge knot, and then helped herself to a goblet of wine, which was understandable. Beating the black woman was going to be thirsty work. Africanus chose the cane and had the distinctive impression that the whore had already made up her mind to use it whatever the choice.

"Half now and half later," she reminded her, and swished a long supple cane through the still air.

The sound was enough to make Africanus' bottom twitch and she grabbed the bar and held her breath; waiting.

It was like being struck with a red hot iron, the pain was so intense, landing at full strength directly across her naked bottom. Now Africanus understood why she was so firmly bound. Try as she might she couldn't move, except for her hips and shoulders.

"You dance well," the acid faced one complimented, lips breaking into a broad, thin smile.

Another thing Africanus quickly grasped. This wasn't punishment for its own sake, but an erotic display of her sufferings, and the cane whistled over the tops of her thighs. It struck solid muscle unable to move or evade the scorching pain seeping deeper through the skin. Whoever this woman was, she was mistress of her craft and had a thorough understanding of how to inflict maximum pain with the minimum of effort.

Africanus gripped the iron bar and held her breath, wondering where the cane would strike next.

"Squeeze your arse," she said, tapping each buttock with the tip of her cane.

Africanus squeezed and the cane flicked sharply against the hollows. "Harder. I want to those pretty bum cheeks as tight as a walnut."

The buttock halves flexed and hollowed deeper, going hard and tight.

"Good. Now hold them there while I cane them. On the sides to begin with."

The cane whistled and bounced, leaving its deadly mark; a welt, long and dark, and Africanus uttered a harsh grunt. The whore paced back and forth like a caged tiger, audibly snarling as she whipped the cane in quick succession, passing from left to right, marking each buttock with measured strokes.

How many had Africanus taken now? She counted ten and gritted her teeth. The fiery pain slowly penetrated under her bottom and through her sex, but oddly, her orgasm, which usually followed a hard whipping, subsided into a dull ache. Her nipples tingled and throbbed as the pain gradually increased in ferocity. Then the whore struck fast and furious, caning under the buttocks where they creased into the thighs.

Africanus sucked her breath and clung to the bar. Involuntarily, the force from the upper cut had her on her toes, beautifully hardening her calf muscles. She heard the whore mutter her approval and for a couple of spine chilling moments the room fell silent. She knew the whore was somewhere behind her, moving stealthily in the half light, moving to her left.

"Thighs," the whore whispered. "I've never seen such magnificent thighs."

A long, wet tongue swept up the backs of each thigh, lapping at the sheen of sweat gathering on the skin. The cane came quicker than Africanus thought possible, landing just above the backs of her knees, and leaving a ladder of welts all the way up to her bottom. She counted five strokes on each thigh and the whore placed the cane neatly on a bench and picked up a bottle, half draining its contents. She belched, hiccoughed and went into an alcove. Her urine drummed into a pot and she came out again, taking up the cane and swishing it to and fro.

"The rest on your back, and perhaps a few across your breasts. What do you think?" the whore teased.

"You're only supposed to beat my bum," Africanus protested, blasting air and mucus from her nostrils.

"I told you, Messalina doesn't care where I beat you," she chuckled. "And a body like yours is made for beating, so shut up."

She began at the base of the spine, using wide sweeps of her arm, laying on the strokes with uncompromising accuracy. Africanus' hips rose and fell in accordance with the lashing cane; her back arced straining her shoulders and arms. Here at last, after being lashed on the softer globes of her bottom, the pain was most acute.

And the whore knew it.

"That made you dance, eh?" she chortled, winging the cane across the rib cage. "But wait 'til I cane your tits. Then you'll know it."

Africanus bit her lower lip. Normally she would be muttering silent curses, or giving vent to stentorian grunts and swearing like a trooper. Now she made not a sound, but breathed harshly through her dilated nostrils, and clung to the bar as if it were flotsam in a tossing sea.

The whore knitted her brows and came around to the black woman's front, gazing into her face. As a rule when the cane bit into the spine or shoulder blades, the slave would be screaming for mercy. But this one just curled her lips and breathed heavily, making no sound except for the air rushing from her nose. She flicked the tip of the cane over the erect nipples, teasing the sprouting teats, watching for any reaction on the slave's face. Then she poked the sides of breasts, digging the cane in sharply and twisting it. Africanus uttered a barely audible groan but held on. However great the pain burning through her body she was not going to give this bitch the satisfaction of hearing her beg. She wondered if the whore liked women, or hated them. She thought she had detected the tell tale signs of woman to woman; the teasing of her bottom and thighs, the fury of the cane whipping her to orgasm: now she wasn't so sure. There was no emotion on the whore's face that betrayed any sexual arousal, just the professional nonchalance that comes from the constant wielding of authority.

She placed the full length of the cane over Africanus' breasts, resting its polished surface on both nipples, testing where to strike.

"You're fortunate to have such full breasts," the whore complimented. "Some of these girl's have tits so small they're not even a handful. And your nipples, phew! Has Cellenius sucked on them?" Africanus shook her head. "Don't worry he will, all in good time," the woman assured.

She lifted the cane and swung it over her head. In a single stroke, it landed deftly over both nipples, crushing the teats into the areolas. The breasts globes visibly squashed from the force of the stroke and the whore broke into a wide smile.

"That made them wobble, eh?" she laughed, going wide-eyed at the jiggling breasts.

To her dismay, Africanus felt a cold tingle shoot through her sex. Her belly churned, stirring into life.

'Oh, shit,' she thought.

The last thing she wanted was to give the whore the satisfaction of seeing her come, let alone listen to all the accompanying groans and sighs. Her belted legs went rigid as she fought the rising chill in her loins. Strangely, the whore didn't seem to notice, and sent the cane whipping under the black woman's breasts. The globes, already stretched, bounced from her chest and wobbled back into place. The nipples rose up and hardened like young acorns and, for a fleeting moment, Africanus was reminded of the mad priestess she had met at the circle of stones. The whore tossed back her hair and wiped sweat from her brow.

"Another five and I'm done," she said, much as a washerwoman might say after working her way through a pile of dirty linen.

The cane landed not where Africanus thought it would, but on the flat of her stomach, making a peculiar hollow smack.

"I should've filled your belly with wine before I started," the whore observed. "Then I would've had the pleasure of watching you piss yourself."

"Bitch," Africanus surrendered, mouthing silent obscenities.

The cane whistled across her navel, creasing her stomach and making it heave. The whore smiled grimly at Africanus' distorted face and retuned the strokes, cutting into the flattened stomach and belly. Slowly the strokes descended, moving towards the undefended pubic mound. A scorching pain shot through Africanus' belly and sex, burning right into her womb, and the first faint weeps of sex juice trickled from her labia.

"I knew you'd come in the end," the whore said triumphantly, noticing the glistening juice on the sweating thighs.

She delivered the final strokes with full strength of her wiry arms, and then idly tossed the cane over her shoulder. It fell with an echoing clatter and the room went into dark silence.

"Drink?" the whore asked, fetching over a wine jar.

She raised it to Africanus' parched lips and lifted the end. The wine flowed like an amber river, most of it pouring over the black woman's chest and breasts. It flowed over her belly, gathered into her navel, and then soaked into her

144

pubic hair. Some even ran down the fronts of her thighs and dripped to the stone floor.

"You held up well," the whore said, taking away the jar.

Africanus said nothing.

The whore ran the tip of her forefinger up the length of Africanus front, licking the wine into her mouth.

"You taste sweet," she smiled, coming closer.

She bent her head and lapped at the wine-stained skin. Her sharpened teeth nibbled over the black woman's breasts, biting on the nipples, rolling and crushing the tender sprouts.

"Aaaagh!" Africanus yelled. "That hurt!"

"I seem to have found your weak spot," she said slyly.

Her mouth opened wide and broke into a snarl. From the depths of her throat, a husky purring echoed around the room. Her eyes widened and Africanus clenched her buttocks. The eyes twinkled and flashed, burning brightly, the same as she had seen in great cats before they moved in for the kill. Even the whore's movements were feline as she prowled around the fettered black woman, moving so softly her footsteps were inaudible. She pressed her head and sucked on the nipples, drawing them deep into her mouth. Her tongue lapped over the teats, flicking rapidly around the pimples discs. Africanus sighed. There was no pain now, just the delicious sensation of the whore's tongue working slowly around each nipple. Her head went to each breast in turn, and the vacant nipple was rolled and squeezed between pressing fingers. She took her head away and cupped both breasts, squeezing and manipulating the ample flesh. Her tongue swept up through the breast cleft and into the well of Africanus' throat.

"Shall I release you?" she whispered, licking under the her chin.

"By all the Gods, yes," Africanus breathed, her bottom and breasts throbbing so much they hurt.

The loosed belts dropped to the floor and Africanus

flexed her limbs and rubbed her bottom.

"Shall I oil you?" the whore asked softly, placing her hand on the welted cheeks.

Africanus readily agreed anything to avoid meeting Messalina again. She followed her through a curtain and into a small chamber comfortably furnished with the minimum of requirements. A couch stood against a wall and beside that a plain wooden cabinet where the occupant kept her things. A table with bottles of various sizes and shapes filled an alcove. Incense burned in a small bowl sweetening the air with its fragrance. She assumed the mat spread over the floor was where the whore slept, and had at once the impression that this small, half-lit chamber was her private world into which few ventured. Yet, there was a calming stillness about the place that bordered on the soporific.

"Lie on the couch, bottom upwards and I'll oil you," the whore spoke dreamily, moving towards the table.

Africanus laid herself out full length, resting her head on her arms and marvelling at this sudden change of mien. She was still uncertain as to the woman's state of mind, instantly changing from one mood to the next. She thought she could floor her if needs must. A quick glance around the chamber revealed no weapons of any kind.

"This will sooth away the ache," the whore said, tipping oil all over Africanus' back and buttocks.

She began at the ankles and calves, first rubbing in the oil and then squeezing and massaging the muscles, working in silence. At the thighs, she worked her hands in long, downward sweeps, all the way to the soles of the feet, applying a surprisingly gentle pressure, and Africanus closed her eyes feeling the pain evaporating.

"I don't normally do this," the whore confessed, placing both hands on Africanus' bottom. "But in your case I've made an exception. It's just that you've got such a lovely body, and so strong, but beautifully shaped."

"Thank you, mistress," Africanus replied, carried along with the ambience.

"I'm not your mistress. I'm a slave like you," the whore said, bringing her whole weight to bear on the rounded buttocks.

She pressed and squeezed, pulling the halves apart and worming her oiled fingers deep into the crease. Africanus bucked as a finger went into her bottom hole, massaging her anus, whilst the other started pummeling her bottom. She withdrew her finger and placed both hands under the curving buttocks, pushing them upwards and going in circles, murmuring her approval as each half rubbed against the other and then separated, opening the crease wider. She moved slowly up the back, pressing with full weight onto the spine and then forcing the muscles outwards towards the rib cage. She stopped and gained her breath before pummeling and slapping her way up and down the length of the black woman's body.

"Have you heard about this journey the governor is planning?" Africanus asked with deliberate casualness.

"I don't listen to harem gossip," she returned. "But I suppose I shall hear about it all in good time. He usually takes me along to keep the slaves and concubines in check. And he likes seeing them whipped, especially when they scream for mercy. Messalina had one of them tied up and pricked her body with a golden needle. You should've heard her screaming."

"I'm not surprised," Africanus muttered, hating the very name. "Have you always done this job, caning slaves?"

"Not always. I came here as a concubine, but when the governor got tired of fucking me I was given this job. I know how to cane a woman, and a man if I have to. It's good fun whipping them up to erection, then watching them come."

And she purred like a cat. "Turn over."

Africanus rolled over onto her back. The whore let down

her hair and it spread about her shoulders like a dark, silky cloak. Her eyes twinkled when they lighted on the black woman's breasts, and again she bent her head sucking on the distended nipples. Her body crouched as if ready to spring, and in an instant, she had transformed into a cat, purring and licking, raking her claws onto Africanus' chest.

"I want to fuck you," she rasped, easing open the black, shining thighs.

But something in the black woman's brain snapped. She didn't mind fucking with Dorla, and anyone else she liked, but not with an unpredictable maniac who could metamorphose into a cat, and even acted like one.

"I don't think so," she returned, clamping her thighs together.

The cat's eyes narrowed into long slits and the purring came in throaty, guttural sobs. "I'll be the best fuck you're ever likely to get," she rasped, placing her hands on the gladiatrix' knees and forcing them open.

"Get the fuck off me," Africanus grunted, trying to push her away.

"Have it your own way," she hissed, then picked up the cane and lashed her own thighs, leaving heavy welts in their wake.

Africanus lay dumbstruck, staring with the terror stricken eyes of one in sudden confrontation with a raving mad woman, unable to comprehend anything but the half conceived notion that she could quite easily kill with her bare hands.

"I'll report to Messalina that you attacked me, and you know what that means."

It meant instant death.

"All right," Africanus surrendered. "You can fuck me. But just keep your claws away from my bum."

It was over a lot faster than Africanus ever imagined. The cat merely lay over her, jerking her pelvis and rubbing her sex mound hard into the black woman's groin, hissing, spitting and snarling until she reached her orgasm with a long wailing sound.

Africanus stared blankly at the ceiling, nothing on her mind except she just had to escape. After this encounter, even the ravings of Messalina and the money grubbing machinations of Lady Octavia seemed normal.

The cat woman rolled off her lover and for a few brief moments, they kissed.

"Your punishment is over," the cat announced, as another sobbing girl slave entered the outer chamber.

She handed over her note for thirty lashes and stood trembling before her. How old was she, sixteen perhaps, not much more.

"What a pretty little kitten," the whore observed, patting the girl's boyish buttocks.

In a fleeting moment, she had completely forgotten Africanus who stole quietly from the chamber to the sounds of the lashing cane and high-pitched shrieks. Outside, she blinked in the bright sunlight and saw men and women rushing back and forth in all directions, barking orders and gathering pace

"What in the name of Jupiter is going on?" she asked Magenta hurrying by carrying a rug.

"The governor's going into the desert," she yelled back, unable to complete her sentence.

If Cellenius had intended to keep his journey a closely guarded secret it wasn't going to be easy with dozens of slaves scurrying about like ants. That in itself was not important. What Africanus needed to know was when and where he intended to go, and she headed for Lady Octavia's quarters, the purring of the whore still reverberating in her brain.

"I can see someone's been teaching you your manners," Lady Octavia observed, looking at Africanus' welted arse cheeks. "What have you done this time?"

"Late on duty," she replied flatly.

Lady Octavia clicked her tongue. "Serves you right for spending too much time with that girl. So what do you want now?"

She seemed irritated and had got into the habit of twirling her hair and biting her lip, the tell tale signs of sexual frustration. Obviously, her intended night of manic, unbridled sex had not gone according to plan. Her nipples were erect and poking through her linen dress, another sign of desperation.

"I've just come from the harem and seen the concubines running about like headless chickens. It seems that the governor is moving soon so I wondered what we are to do."

"Nothing for the present. We'll wait until he's well out of the way, then we'll move. I'll summon you when I'm ready."

'Fuck,' thought Africanus, not hearing what she wanted to know.

"Yes, mistress," she bowed, and made her way to the door.

"I didn't give you permission to leave," Lady Octavia bawled. Africanus came back and stood contrite, head bowed and hands clasped over her belly. "I'm in the mood for giving you the thrashing of your life," she hissed, her face clouding.

She moved closer until their nipples touched. Her hand reached up and stroked Africanus' cheek. She raised her right leg and rubbed her thigh against Africanus' flank. "I need a man between my thighs," she murmured. "Go and find Crixus and tell him I'm hot and throbbing. He'll understand. And if it's of any interest to you, Cellenius is moving tonight, up river as far as the Esnem Oasis. Keep out of the way until I send word where you are to join me. And take a bath, you smell like an alley cat. Now get out."

Africanus' long legs flew across the great courtyard and into the nobleman's quarters where she found Crixus.

"Hot and throbbing, eh?" he laughed, rising from his seat. "That means she's on heat and begging for it."

He strolled casually to Lady Octavia's room, unhurried. There were plenty of women in this place he could fuck anytime he chose. Lady Octavia was just another body.

Africanus watched him safely out of sight and went to the concubines' quarters, deserted now except for those who had been up all night pleasuring the governor's guests, worn out with so much sex and snoring contentedly. She lay on her mat and gazed idly at the ceiling wondering how to get in contact with Queen Hatentita's spies. The chances were that the time of the governor's departure was still a closely guarded secret, known only to the select few, and they would be sworn to secrecy. But as yet, Africanus had no idea who the spies were, let alone impart her information.

In the way of subterfuge all over the world, the spy contacted her. And it surprised her. But there was no doubting his validity. He knew everything about the black gladiatrix; how she met the Queen and where, their interlude at the temple, her mock combat, and the river boat trip. In fact, he seemed to know every detail.

He was not like the normal perception one has of a spy, but then again, a good spy does look totally nondescript.

He was an armourer, working in the palace barracks, sharpening swords and fashioning helmets. He looked quite ordinary. But he knew his job and was definitely not a man to upset. He introduced himself when Africanus was alone, doing nothing more offensive than filling huge amphorae with wine.

At first, she paid him little heed, just one of the palace servants trying to inveigle his way into her arse.

That was before he started talking.

"Yes, I know when Cellenius intends to depart, and where he's going," she muttered, lifting one of the amphorae and carrying it to where the others had been filled. He took it from her and, despite his apparent lack of build, lifted it easily.

She told him what he wanted to know.

"Her imperial majesty will reward you well for this," he told her, holding an amphora while she filled it. "My advice to you is get out of here and make your way to the place in the reeds where she took you. Just wait until it's all over, and when she returns victorious you will be wealthier than you could ever have imagined."

Well, that was worth considering. Being loaded with gold before she returned to Rome would be a great advantage. She might even start her own ludus.

"What does her majesty intend to do with Cellenius?" she asked, putting down her barrel.

"That's none of your business. But you'll hear of it soon enough. Let me just say that her majesty is most displeased with the Romans and none of them will survive the attack. Every man, woman and whore in that camp will taste her swords. She takes no prisoners. The Nile will run with blood for a hundred miles."

"Oh," she said stupidly, hoping that Dorla would not be one of the concubines the governor intended to take for entertainment.

The armourer carried the last of the amphora to the pile and without a word stalked off into the barracks. Before Cellenius even left the palace, he would be well on his way to Queen Hatentita, no doubt equally as well rewarded.

She left her place of work and wondered where Dorla might be at that moment. She had to find her and keep the girl well out of harm's way until the boats embarked, then together they would bolt. The idea that every living soul in Cellenius' entourage was to be despatched was not a happy one. But then that was no business of hers, just as long as she was far away when the slaughter began.

She headed for the concubines' dormitories and would have gained the stairwell had not Messalina blocked her path.

"Oh, Africanus, I've been looking for you," she said gaily, her face flushed as if she had recently been hard ridden.

The black woman stepped back nonplussed by this sudden change in the chief concubine's demeanor. Only a few hours ago she had ordered her severely flogged. Now she was almost on the point of embracing her.

"We're all going up river," she announced as if no one else in the palace was aware of that fact, although like all the other passengers she was unaware of the exact time of departure. "And Cellenius is taking his latest acquisition, the one concubine he has not yet had the pleasure of fucking."

"Oh, really, and who might that be?" Africanus replied with undisguised lack of interest.

Messalina kissed her on the cheek and smiled smugly.

"Why, you of course."

CHAPTER EIGHT

Africanus sat in Cellenius' barge still in a state of shock and deaf to the excited chatter going on all around her. The sun had not yet set and burned a bright red as it slowly dipped to the horizon. The governor seated himself under an awning where he could watch the rowers plying the oars. She recognized many of the other concubines and slaves resting idly over the oars. Magenta and Ustane sat side by side near the front, and like all the other female slaves were attired in fishnets, cut off at mid thigh and pulled tightly over their ample breasts, leaving their arms bare, and giving tantalizing glimpses of the naked flesh beneath. When they plied the oars, their muscles straining to move the heavy craft, the mesh would pull even tighter, the nipples would poke through and the nets ride up around their buttocks, which was just what Cellenius planned. Is there no more an erotic display on earth than a fine figured, beautiful woman so attired, heaving and sweating, bending backwards, thrusting out her fettered breasts, and then leaning forward letting them swing to and fro like temple bells, not to mention all their splendid legs flexing and stretching at every stroke?

Africanus swallowed hard when the barge overseer came marching along the centre plank, swinging her whip and shielding her eyes from the glow of the sun.

It had to be the cat woman. Who else could wield a whip with such feline ferocity?

Of Dorla, there was no sign, and Africanus muttered a silent prayer, thankful she had been spared this torment.

Other boats were moored astern alongside the jetty loaded with tents and supplies. There were a few armed men but nowhere near enough to ward off the impending attack.

Africanus shuddered at what she knew was coming and watched as the mooring ropes were cast off. Slowly the whole convoy moved into the greater depths of the river, and she couldn't help but admire the awesome sight. In perfect unison the rowers of no less than nine boats, now three abreast glided through the tranquil waters, each craft echoing to the steady rhythmic beat of a drum. Thankful that the boats had not set off under the glaring heat of the sun, the women slaves rocked back and forth, seated side by side, two abreast and grunting as the oars dipped and swung. A full moon was on the rise, and as the sun set its silvery rays lit up the convoy. Africanus looked heavenward and wondered at the star spangled sky. It seemed that the whole firmament was covered with them, and at the stern of the craft, she saw Cellenius eyeing the net clad slaves with wide-eyed wonder. Despite the cooling air, rowing was hot work and already sweat ran from their bodies, and the odorous smell of their shining skin drifted into his nostrils.

"Keep together," the cat woman bawled, prowling up and down the plank, and lashing at anyone within reach.

She wore only a narrow strip of white linen around her hips, just enough to cover her sex and deliberately passing tightly through her bottom crease. Her long, sinewy legs strode past the slaves with grim purpose, bare feet padding softly on the wooden walk way. Her hair, held in place with a golden band, not tied or knotted, flowed freely around her mobile buttocks.

Cellenius had his seat moved forward, less than an arm's length from the first line of rowers, and sat contentedly watching their straining limbs and heaving breasts. Even under the moonlight, he could see their thighs glistening with sweat, not to mention their erect nipples protruding through the mesh, and thought it a pleasant distraction having one of them flogged.

"You may choose, Tamara," he offered generously to the cat woman. "Have her strung up against the mast and see she is well whipped."

That was one offer she wasn't going to let slip. "You," she addressed a slender slave, "put your belly against the mast."

Dumbly and without the slightest murmur, the girl rose from her seat, cast aside her net, and walked naked amidships, dutifully doing as she was bid, raising her hands above her head whilst a male crewmember deftly roped her hands. He gave a sharp tug on a guide rope and the girl's feet lifted above the deck, toes only just touching the planks. Tamara gathered her whip and knew that the Governor's eyes were upon her, and exactly what he was expecting.

"The girl has fine buttocks," Cellenius remarked to Messalina. "You have chosen your slaves well. I intend to have all of them before the return journey. Where is the tall black one?" Following her directions, he made out Africanus close to the prow, her shapely arms dragging the oar back and forth. Every time she returned stroke her heavy breasts fell forward and swung ponderously under the mesh. When she straightened, they rose fully from her chest and almost burst the netting. "When we are camped, have her scrubbed and brought to my tent," he ordered, and sat back popping grapes into his mouth as the first lash descended onto the slave's naked bottom.

Much to Tamara's chagrin the girl hardly moved, giving no more than a twist of her hips. The second lash whipped around her buttocks, but again she hung immobile, just letting her body sway from her suspended arms.

"You disobedient bitch!" she hissed, winding the whip into a coil.

She stood back; giving plenty of room for her next manoeuver, then with a sharp flick of her arm sent the whip uncoiling into the small of the girl's back. A loud crack echoed to the mast top as the whip wrapped around her hips. A wrench from her tormentor's arm had her spinning above the deck. Now Tamara displayed all her skills, returning the next stroke with deadly precision, catching the girl's twitching bottom as it spun into view. A high-pitched howl reverberated through the night subsiding into a low moan when the whip caught her belly. She spun faster, angling and twisting her body away from the lashing tail. But Tamara was wise to that and waited until the momentum slowed before sending her whip in an upward arc, lashing under the girl's legs. Her knees bent in agony, lifting so high they almost touched her belly. Tamara had already anticipated the reaction and brought the whistling tail over the front of her thighs. The girl's legs went dead straight and she swung in a circle baring her bottom and back. Now the whip fell in steady, calculated strokes, lashing across her pert bottom and tops of her thighs, and then striking the backs of her knees. The girl howled like a she wolf, but there was nothing she could do to prevent her body spinning from the descending whip, and again she came full frontal, wobbling breasts inviting the next stoke. It struck across her nipples and shoulders, slamming her against the mast. Tamara's lips broke into a satisfied grin now that her victim was doing exactly what was required.

"Push out your bum," she said, folding the long whip tail in half.

Struggling in her bonds, the girl forced her bottom outwards, round and pert, the buttock halves squeezing into the cheeks. Tamara played the whip around her haunches, not lashing hard, but teasing her skin with short, painful flicks.

"What a bitch," Africanus muttered, lifting the oar. "Why doesn't she just get it over with and leave her be."

"She's playing up to the master," the woman beside her whispered. "Those short strokes will soon bring her on, then she'll be taken down and given to him."

Africanus listened to the soft moans coming from the girl's lips, not cries of agony but a woman close to her climax. Tamara was used to that and hesitated before flicking the folded whip into her bottom crease. The tail was just long enough to pass under her legs and lick against her sex lips. An orgiastic groan broke the still air and the girl's eyes rolled in their sockets. Tamara knew exactly what was happening inside the girl's belly, the chilling butterfly sensation sending tremors through her sex now longing for a stiff cock. She struck hard, spinning the girl until her breasts came again into view. Artfully, she left off teasing her arse crease and concentrated on her throbbing nipples, but the flicking tail was no less painful as it smacked around her teats. The girl's dark areolas spread in wider discs covering half her breasts. Cellenius could hardly disguise his longing to penetrate her now the sound of panting drifted into his ears. But then Tamara suddenly changed tack and sent the whip full length across the girl's ribs and belly. The pain scorched through her distracting her mind from the throbbing orgasm threatening to erupt at any second. Keeping a whipped slave on heat was what Tamara did best She knew just when and where to tease, almost bringing her off, and then moving artfully to another part of her body, increasing the pain, giving it time to sink in, then returning the whip in short, sharp flicks into her bottom and sex. The girl was suffering torments of agony, almost reaching her climax, breasts and nipples throbbing in desperation, only to feel the whip lashing hard onto her naked back and well clear from where she really wanted it. Her body, unable to withstand so much unrequited sexual torment broke into manic twitching. Her slender hips and buttocks twisted from left to right from the whip now lashing furiously over her thighs.

"Empty your bladder," Tamara hissed. "The master wants to see you piss."

Africanus and the other slaves could hardly believe their ears. Being whipped was one thing, in some ways it showed strength, but ordered to humiliate oneself in front of the entire crew was demeaning in the extreme. But Tamara was adamant.

She whipped the lash into the pit of the girl's stomach, then over her navel, encouraging the water filled bladder to empty itself. The girl gritted her teeth and squeezed her buttocks, hanging on against the terrible fluttering inside her belly. Tamara laughed at that. She knew it was only a matter of time before the girl broke and went on teasing her belly, occasionally flicking the whip end into her quivering sex lips, adding yet more pain to the girl's torments. Then Tamara grew impatient. Out of the corner of her eyes she saw her master eagerly awaiting the girl's soaking sex and lashed with her full strength, striking at random, letting the whip fall where it would; buttocks, breasts, nipples, hips, but most of all on her stomach. The slave went into a demented spin, driven in circles from the whip criss crossing her bottom and thighs.

"Have it your own way," Tamara rasped, metamorphosing into the creature that had had Africanus questioning the woman's sanity.

A throaty purr warbled in her throat and she bared her claws, gripping the whip handle so tightly her knuckles turned white. The whip lifted above her head and came cracking down on the girl's defenceless buttocks. But this time she remained still, not going into a spin but driven from the sheer force of the blow hard against the mast.

Snarling and spitting, Tamara came close, repeating her deadly aim and whipping into the girl's back, pressing her swollen belly against the trunk of the mast, bringing unrelenting pressure to bear on her churning bladder.

"I'd love to drown that bitch," Africanus muttered, looking into Tamara's demented eyes.

"We all would," her companion remarked. "But if you think this is bad, wait until we make camp. She'll be flogging every one of us."

Then the whipped girl's shrieks subsided into a soft whimpering. Each lash brought on a tightening in her belly, a spasmodic clenching of her fists and curling of her toes. Almost deadened to any further lashes, she let out a long groan and her will finally broke. A fast jet of steaming urine gushed from her sex, cascading to the deck and splattering over the nearest rowers.

Tamara lips broke into a wide grin, seemingly going half way around her narrow face. She had pleased her master and knew she would be suitable rewarded.

"She's ready now, master," she said, signaling the sailor to release the girl.

Looking over her shoulder, Cellenius was nowhere to be seen. Magenta had vacated her seat and had gone to offer up her services under the awning. Her long legs, fully illuminated by the silvery rays of the moon, pointed to the velvet sky. Her harsh groans rose from behind a pile of cushions as Cellenius pumped her belly.

"What a wasted effort," Tamara hissed, and sent her foot flying into the girl's rump.

Then she marched up and down the gangway, lashing into every bare back she could strike, assuaging her anger and the persistent tingling in her sex.

"She's desperate for it," the slave remarked.

"A good stiff cock would sort her out," Africanus grunted, swinging the oar clear of the water.

"I wonder if she's ever had one," she replied. "Perhaps she mates with cats, you know, like lions and such."

"If she does, she'd make a fortune in the Colosseum. I don't think that's ever been done."

The whip crashing into their backs caught them unawares and both women suddenly straightened feeling its burning heat scorching their skin.

"I heard every word of that, you sewer rats," Tamara hissed. "When we make camp I'll punish the pair of you day in and day out. You can be sure of that."

She gave each another four lashes just for the pleasure of it.

"She definitely needs it," the slave whispered, prudently waiting until Tamara was well out of earshot.

"Oh, she'll get it all right, but not where she wants it," Africanus promised.

And she fell in with the slave and together they worked the oar in time with the monotonous beating of the drum.

All through the night the boats made their way up river, the silence broken only by the continual creaking of the oars and the occasional titter of laughter coming from the cabins. Unseen on the bank, a horseman kept pace with the convoy, then as dawn broke and the boats made for the shore; he galloped off across the desert to report to his sovereign.

The rowers disembarked and were set to work unloading the boats. All the supplies were loaded onto camels and mules. That done each slave was fitted with a neck collar and chained fore and aft to her companions. There were at least two hundred women fettered together, still wearing their nets and their bodies stinking of sweat. In a long column, they set off for the Esnem Oasis, seared by the heat of the sun and the constant lashings from Tamara's eager whip.

They reached their destination at sunset and Africanus thought she was seeing things. Rising from the barren waste were groves of palm trees with birds fluttering joyfully in the branches. A lake lay partially hidden in a dip, its waters cool and clear. It was the animals that were allowed to drink first, then the male members of the crew and finally the parched slave women who, still yet unchained, rushed to the water's edge and slaked their burning tongues.

"Let them rest for an hour and then have the tents erected," Cellenius ordered, settling on a rug under the welcoming shade of a palm tree. "Then have the bitches washed and painted. I'm planning a little party tonight and that black one will be the first to have my cock."

"Of course," Messalina bowed, striding across the grass and ordering the collars to be removed from their necks.

The tents were grouped at one side of the lake and a

small boat, which had been dragged all the way there was launched into the water. Later a few of the more voluptuous female slaves would be set to work, dressed in their nets to row the Governor around the perimeter whilst he feasted his eyes on their straining bodies, but Africanus was not one of them.

"Wash yourself in the lake and report to my tent," Messalina told her, returning to her usual spiteful self.

While Africanus cooled her blazing skin in the water slaves rushed hither and thither, carrying furniture into the Governor's tent, spreading rugs and setting up cooking fires. All thoughts of their previous sufferings were forgotten now as they excitedly prepared themselves for the forthcoming feast. Even Tamara seemed joyful as she put up her hair and oiled her lithe, sinuous body.

"I am to prepare you for the Governor," Messalina told Africanus, and she clapped her hands.

A young naked slave still wearing her enormous nipple and ear rings came into the tent.

"Dorla, see she is well oiled and painted. She is to wear only her loincloth and jewelry. See that her head is freshly shaved, and her cunt. I want her gleaming. Understood?"

"Yes, mistress," she bowed, keeping her back bent until Messalina had gone.

"Oh, what the fuck are you doing here?" Africanus asked wearily.

"I got to prepare you," Dorla replied, surprised at such an obvious question.

"Tch, I didn't mean that, you thick little tart. I meant why you are here at all. I thought you'd been left behind at the palace."

"I asked to come when I heard you was goin'", she beamed.

"Oh, Dorla, if only you knew. But never mind that now. Get on with what you have to do, and go careful with that razor."

Africanus seated herself cross-legged on the floor whilst Dorla lathered her scalp. It was quite possible that when the camp came under attack, she could escape the melee, but now she had Dorla to take care of and that bothered her. She would be sure to panic and that was the last thing she wanted.

The razor scraped over her scalp expertly removing the stubble of hair that had grown since the girl's last shaving. She left the side locks in place and then oiled the skin.

"What's that?" Africanus asked, a sweet perfume drifting into her nostrils.

"Frankincense and myrtle berry," she chirped, rubbing more furiously into Africanus' skull.

The black woman didn't notice the artful smile creasing her lips as she upended the bottle and tipped the contents into her tiny palm.

She rubbed it all over Africanus' back and arms, and then started on her breasts, taking great care to ensure that every inch of skin was covered. She paid particular attention to the dark areolas and nipples, rubbing it well into the pimpled discs and teats. Her hand flattened on the chest, going in slow circles, down through the breast cleft and all over the stomach. She tipped a generous amount into the navel and let it settle.

"Shall I shave your cunt now, mistress," she warbled, obviously enjoying her task.

Africanus lay on her back, raising her bottom as the young slave slipped a cushion beneath it. She opened her thighs and propped her ankles on Dorla's shoulders. She was sure she felt a slight tingling in her skin, but dismissed it and closed her eyes as the razor gently did its work. The young slave left not a hair in place, even shaving right under her legs and just stopping at her bottom hole.

"You look ever so sexy," she smiled, looking at Africanus' shaven mound.

"Just get on with it, you," she laughed, clicking her tongue.

Dorla tipped a generous helping of oil onto her palm and rubbed it firmly over the sex mound, using the tips of her fingers to oil the labia and clitoris. Then she oiled the whole length of her legs until they shone like glossed ebony.

Africanus rolled over and the bottle tipped over her buttocks, oil pouring into her bottom crease. Tiny hands went in circles, rubbing as hard as they could into each buttock and going deep into the crease. It wasn't Africanus' imagination, the tingling sensation was becoming more ardent and a slight throbbing started in her nipples. Perhaps it was just the effects of the oil and would subside eventually. Dorla moved to the fronts of her thighs and knees, again rubbing well into the skin and not stopping until she had reached the soles of her feet.

"All done, mistress," she said gaily, reaching for the loincloth.

It was of transparent linen and reached to mid thigh, tight enough to suck into the bum crease and hug her hips. Deft movements of her fingers slipped it around the shining black woman.

"Now I've got to paint your face," Dorla announced, bringing over a tray of bottles and brushes.

Africanus shifted uneasily. That persistent tingling had returned, but greater than before and a faint stirring started in her belly.

Her eyes were outlined in turquoise, the lids a darker hue of the same, and her lips a subdued scarlet. Powder was puffed onto her cheeks then highlighted in red. More perfume sprinkled onto her neck, chest and breasts. Dorla refashioned the side locks into braids then weighted the ends with golden pendants. Huge circular earrings were fitted to the lobes, and a huge bejewelled collar fitted over her chest. Golden armlets closed around her fore and upper arms then carefully wiped clean of finger marks. The final touch was an ornamental belt fitted snugly around her waist.

She looked stunningly beautiful.

"What in hell is all this in aid of?" Africanus asked, admiring her beauty in a polished mirror.

"The Governor is holding a party and everyone's got to look like ancient Egyptian princesses," Dorla trilled, admiring her handiwork.

'How ironic,' she thought, 'got up to look like the very people coming to destroy us.'

She walked to Cellenius' tent, tall and proud, swinging her arms and hips, holding her head high. If by any chance the attack came tonight, she might as well perish looking her best. She was beginning to have second thoughts whether anyone would survive.

The interior of the tent was packed with naked women of all professions, not only concubines and whores, but musicians, dancers, jugglers and one or two famed for their erotic contortions. All were naked except for a narrow belt fitted under the pits of their stomachs. Only the favoured were attired in fine robes, and Africanus had to admit they looked dazzling.

Messalina was seated at a table wearing a long, transparent orange dress, slit to the hip, one breast and arm bare, the others covered. On her head, she wore an enormous scented wig, the plaits reaching to her shoulder blades, not too dissimilar to the one worn by Hatentita when she went disguised into the brothels and cathouses of Thebes. The place was in uproar, the din rising in volume by the second. Above the mass of naked breasts and bottoms, gleaming thighs and sinewy arms arose the heady, intoxicating smell of perfumes and sweat. The air was so thick it took a couple of minutes before Africanus' eyes adjusted to the atmosphere. She took her place at the end of the table as Cellenius' favoured concubine and liberally helped herself from a bowl of fruit.

Yet there was order in this chaos. First, the musicians struck up their chords; a troupe of girls from Assyria, naked apart from their wigs and squatting in a semi circle, tuned up their instruments, and when they commenced playing

165

in unison the whole babble suddenly ceased. Flautists, percussionists banging on tambourines and cymbals, an oboe and harp providing the bass notes while a drummer kept a steady beat. Then the dancers took to the floor; Nubians this time, selected for the length of their arms and legs, ample breast size and of course, their splendid buttocks. They too were mistresses of their craft, beginning with slow, serpentine movements, twisting their hips and revolving their buttocks, then as the tempo increased breaking into pirouettes backwards and forwards, cartwheels, the splits and backward flips. Some performed in pairs, one of the dancers standing full height and the other on her back with her head between the legs of the first girl, licking exaggeratedly into her sex. Cellenius watched open mouthed as the tallest, at least six feet in height leapt through the air, turned a somersault and crashed to the floor opening her long, gleaming legs as wide as possible.

"They are summoning Hathor, the Goddess of love, happiness and long life," a concubine seated next to Africanus informed.

They were also summoning the hardened cocks of the male guests, but she thought it prudent not to mention that.

In the middle of this exotic display, an acrobatic contortionist displayed her skills, and Africanus, along with all the other assembled guests stared agog. It just didn't seem possible the human body could twist into such bizarre shapes. She knelt with her knees wide apart, bent backwards until her face appeared between her thighs, and then, after licking her sex, put both arms behind her, reached over her shoulders and played with her breasts, cupping and lifting, teasing the nipples to erection.

"I'll bet she fucks like a stoat," a male guest proclaimed, now watching spellbound as she contorted her lithe body into an S shape, then bent so far backwards her tongue licked the whole length of her arse crease.

166

"True," his friend replied. "But I'd come too quickly with that bouncing over my cock."

A couple of acrobats leapt onto the rug leaping and jumping in all directions; one standing upright whilst the other climbed onto her front, facing her upside down. She wriggled her groin into the first girl's face and while her sex was tongue-flicked, buried her head between the open legs of the standing girl.

Already the male guests were feeling up the concubines, forcing them to their knees, opening their mouths and burying their hard cocks deep into their throats. And all the while the musicians and dancers kept up their din and mind-boggling contortions.

In the distance, Africanus saw Carla looking surprisingly beautiful in a long plaited wig, stuffing her mouth with everything kind of food within reach.

Dorla flitted back and forth, waiting upon the male guests with wine and sweetmeats, giggling and chirruping, her eyes wide and lustrous. Only Ustane remained passive, seated on a cushion watching the goings on through dark, brooding eyes. Then Africanus remembered the drug she'd promised and made a mental note to get hold of it. Later it just might prove to be her saviour.

Of Tamara, there was no sign.

Neither was there any sign of Marius Aquinus, who was also strangely absent.

Messalina stood up clapping her hands, and as always revelling in her own self-importance. The music became more subdued, a solitary flute and tambourine beat time as a girl slave was led chained into the centre of the tent.

"Your Excellency," she fawned, turning her head to face Cellenius. "Would you care to choose her partner?"

He cast his eyes around the dozens of naked concubines and selected Dorla.

She put down her tray of drinks and joined the slave on the rug.

167

"What's that bitch Messalina up to now?" Africanus asked the girl seated next to her.

"Another one of her punishments," she whispered.

But to be fair to Messalina, in ancient Egypt it was not uncommon for a young, nubile slave girl to be stripped naked and whipped for the edification of the guests. She was only following a time-honoured custom, but with a few added distractions of her own.

A male slave came into the tent carrying a basket and placed it between the girls. He lifted the lid and the flautist began playing solitary, plaintive notes. The look on their faces was one of abject horror as a snake slowly arose, its head appearing first, then the rest of its body, moving from side to side, its dark beady eyes gleaming.

"By all the Gods," Africanus breathed, as the python's tongue flicked from its jaws.

It made first for Dorla, curling around her calf and going between her open legs. She trembled so much the golden rings through her nipples shook and rattled. It worked its way around her slender thigh and aimed its head into her sex, the long forked tongue teasing her sex lips.

"Open wider!" Messalina bawled.

But she was frozen in horror unable to move a muscle. It was Ustane who came towards her, wielding a short single tailed whip, which she lashed across Dorla's bare rump. A titter of laughter went up as the guests, whores and concubines crowded closer.

Another lash sliced into her buttocks and she shuffled her feet over the rug, opening her slim legs as wide as she could. She took a deep breath and closed her eyes, feeling the long tongue lapping at her sex lips.

"You," Messalina barked at the other terror-stricken slave. "Put your back against her."

She went behind Dorla and stood buttock to buttock, pressing her trembling frame against her companion. Involuntarily they caught hold of each other's hands and

168

stood rigid as the serpent went under the other slave's open legs. Its tongue went into her sex, but its long body was still coiling around Dorla's thighs and calves. Slowly it came to the front of the girl, gliding around her hips and moving towards her pert breasts. Her nipples had gone stiff with fright and almost twitched when the forked tongue lapped at the teats. By now, its tail was between Dorla's legs and sliding slowly through her sex. Her lips parted and she swallowed hard, her chest heaving as she sucked her breath.

"By Jupiter, the slut's coming," a voice uttered in disbelief.

"You have excelled yourself," Cellenius said, patting Messalina's bottom. "I shall see you are showered with gold."

"Oh, thank you, master," she smiled, putting her arm around his shoulder.

"And give my congratulations to the serpent's trainer. He has done well."

The flautist's fingers played up and down her instrument, artfully dancing over the holes as she encouraged the serpent to move its head between the girl's breasts. It snaked around her neck and passed easily over her shoulder and around Dorla's throat, upside down now and moving stealthily towards her nipples. Her breasts visibly wobbled as its cold scales went under her breasts tongue darting over her nipples. Sheens of glistening sweat broke out all over body and she went rigid with fear. One false movement and the reptile would strike. Its tail was gliding noiselessly over the other slave's belly, its body still wrapped around her. She too had gone rigid with fear and both slaves stood as frozen as marble statues.

"Whip them!" Messalina bawled. "Welt their thighs."

Ustane bowed and sent the whip whistling into Dorla's bare thighs. She gave her four strokes, hard and fast, each lash hot and painful and she couldn't help but jolt her buttocks against her trembling companion. The serpent alarmed at this sudden disturbance, opened its jaws and made to swallow Dorla's left breast. Her head rolled on her shoulders and she choked back a sob, certain its fangs would sink deep into her breasts. But oddly, it went on flicking her nipples, curiously delighting in the scented teats. When it had taken its fill, it continued downward, heading over her belly and again aiming its tongue into her quivering sex lips.

"Give the wretches another dozen lashes," Messalina ordered.

Ustane dutifully obeyed, lashing the whip over the slave's haunches and flanks. It was impossible to resist the pain blazing through their skin and both girls writhed and twisted as Ustane piled on the strokes. Now the whole orchestra joined in, the tambourines beating time, the cymbals banging and clashing, drums thumping out the bass. The serpent was obviously trained to move in accordance with the notes and rhythms and now moved quicker, going under the legs of both slaves and coiling around their thighs. Having little knowledge of snakes the girls were terrified of being bitten, not realizing that a python is not a poisonous snake and its bite would cause pain but not death. They were not to know it but the real danger to them was of being crushed.

The python slithered off them and made its way back to the basket and went into a harmless coil. But Messalina had not yet finished. Giving the serpent time to rest, she ordered both slaves to kneel on all fours, side by side, baring their naked buttocks to the audience, knees well parted.

Africanus stole a furtive glance at the assembly who by now were beginning to suffer from the effects of copious amounts of wine and beer. Men and slaves were unashamedly coupling on the rugs and divans. Two of the female contortionists were performing outrageous sex, twisting their lithe bodies into impossible positions, sucking each other to orgasm and watched by gaping eyes.

Magenta was on all fours taking one cock into her bottom whilst another filled her throat. As soon as the man at her rear delivered his spunk, another speedily took his place. Idly, she wondered where the demented cat woman had disappeared. But dismissed it as of no real importance and turned back to where the reptile was again rising from its basket.

It slithered towards the heady and powerful aroma of sex juice dripping from Dorla and her companion, going over Dorla's bottom crease and up her naked, shining back. Pausing for a moment as if to collect its thoughts, it went under her chest over her breasts, keeping its body firmly anchored around her slender hips. One movement brought its long body slithering over the other slave's breasts and nipples, then around her ribs so that its length now encompassed both girls' bodies. It moved on under the slave's legs and lapped into her sex, then into her bottom crease.

Messalina was beside herself with laughter, drunk now and losing control.

"Spread your cheeks," she fumbled. "Let the creature have a taste of your arse."

Both Dorla and the slave looked at each other in disbelief, but knew not to argue and placed their hands on their buttocks, pulling open the halves. The serpent glided through the girl's crease flicking its tongue left and right into the open cheeks. She visibly shuddered as it went up her back and returned to her hanging breasts, feasting its tongue on her nipples. Then the orchestra ceased its cacophony and the reptile having delighted the assembly by terrifying the kneeling slaves out of their wits returned to its basket and promptly fell into a contented slumber.

"Anyone who wants them can fuck their arses," Messalina announced drunkenly, and in a trice two men rushed forward, the first sinking his exited cock into Dorla's cunt, the other brutally penetrating the girl's anus.

The girls were still in a state of shock, mistakenly believing that they had narrowly escaped death and offered no resistance to the men pounding into their tunnels. Two more came forward and forced their throbbing lengths into their mouths. While they sucked, bobbing their heads up and down, another two came forward and joyfully fondled their breasts.

"It's high time you were fucked," Messalina slurred, wafting her alcoholic breath into Africanus' face. But Cellenius was already preoccupied with a concubine and had temporarily forgotten about the black woman. "If you're discreet, I'll allow you to fuck with one of the guards," she generously permitted.

And she staggered over to one of the guards and whispered in his ear. He glanced at the black woman, then at Messalina and burst out laughing.

"Join him outside," she said, "and try not to make too much noise."

Africanus got up and padded from the tent, exchanging the stifling atmosphere for the refreshing coolness of the desert night. He took her hand and led her to the remaining piles of baggage.

"Messalina told me you like a good whipping before you're fucked," he said, taking off his belt. "So stand up straight and spread those long legs of yours. Good. Now put your hands on your head."

He was worse for wear, but still in control of his faculties. He knew what he was doing when he wrenched off her loincloth and whistled the belt across her bottom. Africanus, mouthing silent and deadly threats against Messalina, gritted her teeth.

"I'll belt you 'til you start coming," he told her, winging the leather under her legs. "Then when your cunt's dripping, I'll give it to you."

"Thanks, bastard," she muttered, unable to do anything but endure another fierce stroke landing on her breasts.

He was powerfully built with muscles honed from much military training. But he wasn't the only man desirous of dipping his hardened cock inside the sweet pot of the black woman. The guards piqued at being obliged to stand duty, whilst everyone else was drinking and fucking themselves into oblivion, watched from the shadows, licking their lips and just itching to have at least one small slice of the cake. For a moment or two, they exchanged glances and reached an unspoken agreement.

"Wait until the bitch starts panting for it and then move."

"He's so drunk, he won't even know what hit him," the other returned, picking up a discarded peg mallet.

The third hurried off into the darkness to where the boat lay moored at the water's edge and deftly freed the mooring rope.

"A few more lashes under your legs and you'll be begging for it," the man belting her announced, quite oblivious of the guards creeping closer.

Africanus clenched her fingers against the pain throbbing through her sex. With her legs wide open, he couldn't fail to land the belt inside her labia, and once or twice even caught her clit. Her breath started to come in short, staccato pants, and then a groan escaped her lips. The belt left her sex and landed on her bottom, six strokes quickly followed, bouncing from her buttocks and jerking her body forward. He gathered the belt in his hand and winged it under her breasts and that was the last thing he could remember doing that night.

Something dull and heavy cracked over the back of his skull and he fell to earth.

"Come with us," the first guard rasped, grabbing her hand.

Africanus' heart leaped. They must be emissaries of Queen Hatentita, sent to rescue her before the impending slaughter. Eagerly she trailed behind running from the camp to the water's edge. Without thinking, she stepped into the

173

boat. Strong eager arms rowed her into the centre of the lake.

"When is it going to happen?" she asked eagerly. "You see I've got a young slave who..Aaagh!"

A pair of hands grabbed her from behind and threw her over one of the seats.

"It's going to happen now," she heard a voice inform, and another pair of unseen hands grabbed her ankles and spread them wide.

She fell forward, temporarily winded as her stomach thumped over the front seat. Then someone sat astride her back and pinned her arms to the gunwales.

"What the fuck is going on?" she muttered, struggling against yet another pair of hands mauling her tits.

"You're about to be fucked. That's what's going on," a voice chuckled.

"Open your mouth," a harsh whisper ordered.

"I'm Africanus, the governor's favourite concubine and when he gets to hear of this you'll all be...Mmmghhl!"

The throbbing cock rammed between her teeth silenced her.

"Now suck on that, you mouthy cow," the owner told her, shoving his balls against her chin.

There was nothing much else she could do with another throbbing length driving hard inside her cunt. A pair of strong hands gripped her hips and slammed her back and forth, riding her over the seat, whilst the man seated on her back reached under and started groping her breasts.

"Get a feel of these," he muttered. "I've never felt such a pair. Talk about udders."

His fingers painfully pinched her nipples, squeezing until her eyes watered.

The man at her front had taken the tip of his plum to her lips. Contentedly, he let it linger on her tongue, savouring her hot blasting breath. It didn't help with the weight bearing down on her back and she fought for air as he

174

leaned right over squashing her breasts in his palms. At her rear she could feel the cock cork screwing inside her vagina, angling hard into its sides and then coming right to her labia before slamming hard into her womb. Her body bucked over the seat and someone laughed. Then the flat of a hand smacked into her rump.

"C'mon, giddy up," a voice guffawed, and the man on her back bounced up and down as if on a horse.

"I've never had such sport," a voice declared, and her breasts were squeezed so hard her heart almost stopped.

She knew she wasn't in any real danger, but the cocks pumping her sex and mouth were real enough.

And they were hard, made harder by the remembrance of everything their owners had glimpsed going on inside that tent and of which they were denied.

Well, any red blooded male has to get his jollies somewhere and the black woman was providing them right this minute.

Spread eagled over the boat there was little she could do but endure her punishment. But the man at her mouth came a lot quicker than she imagined and accompanied by a fearful, foul-mouthed oath, gushed his spunk into her throat. She coughed and choked, then the man on her back slapped her hard between the shoulder blades and she swallowed the lot.

"Please, a drink." she begged.

The man at her front leaned over the boat scooping up a handful of water and held it to her lips.

"There, there," he consoled, as if comforting a small child.

Then the man on her back dismounted and went to her front, grabbing her ears and holding up her head. He was in her mouth quicker than she could blink.

"Now suck on that, you dirty cow," he said, pulling her head and jerking his loins.

He was bigger than the last.

And longer.

So long, it went right to the back of her throat.

"If you spew your guts, I'll make you lick it up," he threatened.

He might've been joking, but at that moment, Africanus was not in a position to argue either way. His cock was in so far his coarse pubic hair grazed against her face. She closed her eyes and sucked hard, wiggling her tongue inside her mouth, desperately trying to make him come. Now the man at her rump had withdrawn his cock and was playing it up and down her arse crease. She jolted and uttered a grunt when his forefinger went inside her bottom. He wormed it into the knuckle and stroked her anal walls. Then that peculiar tingling in her skin, which had started when Dorla had oiled her, returned with a vengeance. Every pore of her skin was alive. It was as if thousands of ants were crawling and biting everywhere at once. It didn't take much imagination to realize the stupid girl had oiled her with an aphrodisiac, designed to make her hot and horny when at last Cellenius decided to have her, but now it was happening right when she was being fucked by three of his guards in a boat on a lake and there wasn't a thing she could do to stop it.

"How would you like me to piss all down your back and over your bald head?" the man who had spunked in her mouth challenged.

"Yes, please," she returned, wiping the imbecilic grin from his face.

Her sex tingled so much she couldn't stop wriggling her bottom, and the man wiping his cock through her arse crease stopped abruptly.

"This cow's desperate for it!" he said on a note of amazement.

"Work it up her fat arse, that'll cool her," one of his companions advised.

Africanus, her hands now freed from the gunwales,

176

reached clumsily behind and placed her fingertips in her arse crease, opening it invitingly.

It seemed there was nothing she wasn't prepared to do.

She grunted when his cock rammed into her anus, splitting her cheeks and slamming in with all the finesse of a rutting camel.

"Piss on her, if that's what the filthy whore wants," the man who had taken his cock from her mouth snarled.

The boat rocked and threatened to capsize when he stood up and aimed his cock over her back. A fast stream of hot urine splashed all over her back and head. She uttered a moan at the curious sensation of warm urine jetting into her tingling skin and reached for the man at her front, grabbing his weapon and thrusting it back into her willing jaws.

But the three men were not so amused. They were used to taking whores and tarts whenever they felt like it, and the more they struggled the greater the thrill. But this one had no scruples about doing anything, and that seriously robbed them of their pleasure, not to mention their masculinity.

One of the three slipped off his belt and coiled it around his fist. The one at her front wisely withdrew his cock and stuffed her mouth with a ball of tarred rope. It wouldn't do having the governor's favourite concubine bawling and screaming in the dead of night. None of the occupants of the boat saw or heard a horse reining in about a hundred yards from the lake. A passenger clinging onto the rider dismounted, glanced at the boat, shrugged and then legged fast into one of the tents.

"Give it to her over her back," the man riding Africanus' arse said.

He lashed between her shoulder blades, then over the base of her spine. Two more lashes cracked around her ribs.

"She felt that all right. Her arse has tightened a treat," he announced, feeling her anal walls contract from the shock.

The tingling had not abated, but the pain was there, beginning to blaze into her skin.

Careful not to inadvertently strike his companion, the man with the belt began lashing her buttocks, keeping more to the sides than over the crown. Under the moonlight, they saw her cheeks quivering from the blow, flexing away from the singeing leather, then hollowing at the sides and going soft again. The man at her front reached under and jiggled her tits on his palms, chuckled and slapped them, making them swing back and forth.

And for the first time since being penetrated, she sobbed.

The belt continued to lash over her bottom, coming in fast short strokes, turning her skin blacker and leaving its dull but unmistakable marks. He lashed the sides of her thighs, wrapping the belt all the way around her leg, then working on the backs of her knees. Now the pain was greater than the tingling and sinking in fast. Struggling against the pain, she reached for the tarred rope and dragged it from her mouth.

"Stop beating me," she pleaded. "If you want to fuck me just go on and do it."

That was what they wanted to hear, but pretended not to.

"What is it you want, you rotten whore?" a voice rasped.

"Just fuck me and let me go," she wailed, sobbing.

The belt smacked hard into the centre of her back and her neck cricked. He just managed to wing the leather under her chest and whip into her nipples. The man at her rear was still pumping her bottom, but much harder, giving her all she could take.

"We'll let you go after you've sucked both of us at once," he promised. "So open your mouth. After all it's big enough."

She dropped her lower jaw and reached for the first cock, guiding it into her mouth and holding the length against her left cheek. The guard gripped his shaft and, angling his hips against his companion, slipped the plum between her stretching lips. He gave a gentle shove making her chest heave as she slowly took in his length. She hesitated, angling her neck to let them slip into her throat, and then using her hands to press their balls together, she started working her lips, sucking and pursing them over the hot throbbing meat. Her cheeks bulged and stretched at taking in so much cock at once, but she just managed to keep the plums from choking her. Her head moved slowly, riding the shafts and letting her hot tongue lick over the purple heads. She heard them groan and suddenly felt a jet of spunk squirting up her bottom. The man at her rear uttered a satisfied moan and slapped her arse.

"The whore gives a good ride, I'll give her that," he complimented.

His companions made no reply. They knelt with their eyes closed, feeling the delightful sensation of her hot mouth bringing them off. They came one after the other, the first squirting into the depths of her throat, the other filling her mouth. They withdrew letting the final drops splash over her shaven skull and face.

The boat rocked as the men settled at the oars, rowing noiselessly back to the bank. Africanus sat up and rubbed her bruised bottom. One of the men thoughtfully filled his cupped hands with water and washed the lingering spunk from her teeth.

"Are you really the governor's favourite concubine?" he asked, giving a sly glance at his companions.

"I am," she hissed, spitting over the gunwale.

They said nothing, but her tone had a ring of truth about it. They knew the governor's preference for black women and plied the oars faster.

The boat nudged into the bank and they scrambled out leaving Africanus alone and naked at the water's edge as they bolted far into the night.

"The governor's waiting for you," a voice purred and she almost wetted herself.

"Tamara! Where did you spring from?" she asked, shivering.

"Never mind that. If I were you, I'd clean up and get your arse into that tent before he has you flogged."

She rushed to the water's edge and quickly bathed her limbs. The party was still going on and it seemed no one had missed her, which was hardly surprising. Slaves and concubines were holding out bowls whilst their highborn mistresses drunkenly lurched towards them throwing up the contents of their stomachs. The orchestra was playing but driving up such a discordant racket that no one paid them any heed. Those still able to stand or hold anything resembling a coherent conversation urinated against the tent walls or into any convenient bowl. Many were copulating with anyone within reach, or performing outrageous acts of depravity. One of the contortionists amused onlookers by firing pomegranates from her vagina only to be caught in mid air by her companion using her open mouth. One of the jugglers, not to be upstaged fired darts from her sex and into the buttocks of a young naked concubine suitably bound hand and foot. Every time one of the darts shot into her bare rump, she let out a deafening howl that had the onlookers splitting their sides. Upturned furniture lay in heaps and many of the bottles and jugs lay smashed and scattered about the floor. A drunk lurched towards her, slipped in a pool of stale vomit and knocked himself unconscious on a table. Dorla was emitting high-pitched giggles as the man between her legs vainly tried to penetrate her.

This was the time to run. No one was in a fit state to stop either Africanus or Dorla from legging across the desert. She thought she could find her way to the Nile and possible steal a boat. It was also possible to loot the jewelry hanging from the necks of the drunken female guests. There was probably enough there to buy her way back to Rome. She went over to where Dorla was lying and kicked the man off her.

180

"We're getting out of here now," she said, grabbing the girl's arm and hauling her to her feet.

"You're going nowhere except into the governor's tent," Messalina said. "And this pig turd can get out of my sight."

Africanus wondered whether to floor the bitch there and then. A swift left hook would do the trick. But just as she bunched her fist a hand lighted on her shoulder.

"Do as the lady says, unless you want to be strung up by those plaits."

He stood six feet four inches and was as wide as a barn door. His cock was massively erect and nodded invitingly at Messalina whom he was obviously trying to impress.

She grinned smugly. "Deliver her safely and I'm yours for as long as your strength lasts," she offered.

"Come along," he said, dragging Africanus by her side locks.

They went swiftly from the scene of debauchery and into the orderly calm of the governor's tent. He was seated on a rug with one of the concubines kneeling beside him: naked except for her smile, she held a plate of fruit and wine.

"The black woman," the guard announced, releasing Africanus' hair.

"Ah, yes," he said softly, his tone betraying no evidence of liquor. "Please come in and make yourself at home. Mela, offer my favourite concubine a drink, if she wishes."

Africanus seated herself beside him and accepted a glass of wine. She plucked a grape from the plate and bit on it.

The serving girl discreetly retired to a cushion and sat cross-legged, placing her hands in her lap, a perfect picture of obedience and humility. Yet Africanus instinctively knew something was wrong. Whatever it was she couldn't quite fathom but it hovered all around her like a storm cloud. She glanced uneasily at the serving girl who smiled obsequiously in return and both hated each other on sight.

"You have a reputation," Cellenius began, staring her straight in the face. "It seems you have fucked your way

181

through half the harem when you were supposed to keep yourself chaste. Isn't that right Mela?"

"It is master," she grovelled.

"You see, even a slave girl agrees with me."

She would have stood chest deep in shit if he had ordered it.

"That's not true," Africanus protested. "If I've been fucked, it's because I was forced to."

"By whom?" he asked, showing sudden interest.

"By Messalina for a start off," she rasped back.

"Are you accusing the principle concubine of forcing you into having sex against your will? Because if you are that is treason. I am the only one who makes such accusations against her."

She knew now that he was determined to turn her into a criminal no matter what she offered in defence.

And treason was rewarded with heinous punishments too horrible to contemplate.

"Mela, I am not at all impressed with this liar," he said dangerously. "What do you think is a suitable punishment?"

"Not flogging," she answered. "She's far too used to that, and her arse could withstand any amount of whipping."

"Shall I have her put to death?"

The question so effortlessly delivered made Africanus' blood freeze. She instantly recognized the terrible cat and mouse game they were playing with her life.

"Death is too final," the grovelling little bitch answered. "If so much cock is to her liking, why not mate her with one of the stallions?" She may not have meant it, but the idea was enough to have Africanus' bowels churning. She thought for a moment and then her face lit up. "Why not stage a combat; after all it is now common knowledge that she's good at brawling."

"Who would you suggest?" he said, warming to the idea.

"What about her little friend? The one with rings through her tits."

"Fetch her!" he rasped, and Mela was gone like a shot.

"This is unfair, your Excellency," Africanus said tearfully. "I've only done what was ordered and..."

"You are a liar!" he barked. "I know you have slept with half the harem, and even offered your services to one of the guards not two hours ago."

Now she understood, and just had to admire Messalina's craft, suggesting she should fuck the guards for her own pleasure and then artfully betraying her.

Mela came back dragging Dorla behind her. The girl had rapidly sobered and stood petrified before her master.

"Call the blacksmith and have rings fitted to the black slave's tits," he said. "Then chain and arm them. They can fight to the death and the victor will be crucified."

Even the unspeakable Mela baulked at that. "Yes, master," she said, and again rushed from the tent.

The blacksmith came in carrying two enormous bronze rings, chains and his tools.

"See that the rings are well secured," Cellenius said, summoning a guard. "Bring shields and swords," he ordered.

And he settled on his couch while the blacksmith took a long sharp awl from his bag.

"Lift your tits," he snorted, angry at being summoned when at last he had managed to coerce one of the young concubines into his lair.

She cupped both breasts in her hands and raised them. Mela watched intrigued as he pinched the black woman's left nipple and pulled it from her breast. Without any emotion, he shoved the sharp end of the awl straight through the base of the teat and twirled it in his grubby fingers.

"You, girl," he barked at Dorla. "Pass me that ring."

She lifted one of the rings from his bag and held it in her trembling hand. She had still not really understood the implications of what Cellenius had commanded. It seemed beyond comprehension that Africanus would seriously kill her in combat.

The blacksmith took the ring and gave it a meaty shove, passing the open end clean through the hole, and then clasped it into place. He pinched the right teat and repeated the exercise, ignoring the wincing pain distorting the black woman's face. Quickly, he snatched up a length of chain and slipped it through the ring. A hasp clicked quietly through the links and he let the chain fall. He hoped that the concubine had not decided to run off and seek more cock elsewhere. Silently he cursed for not having chained her ankles to the forge before wasting his time on this useless exercise. He chained the other ring and told Dorla to come closer. He took both lengths of chain and hasped them through Dorla's breast rings. On his way out of the tent, he passed a guard coming in carrying shield and swords. He paid him little heed and rushed back to the forge. The concubine was still there, naked and about half his size. He need not have worried. The idea of being ravaged by this huge bearded savage was one that had her sex dripping.

The guard bowed to his master and neatly handed Africanus her sword. Now that she was armed, the sword blade gleaming sharply in the lamplight, Dorla instantly wetted with fright. It was true then, they were going to fight to the death.

"I won't do it," Africanus said contemptuously, throwing the sword to the ground. "This is no contest. It's just cold blooded murder. You know she hasn't got a chance, so why not just crucify me if that's what you want. And fuck Messalina. She's a lying shit."

Stunned silence.

No one knowing what to do next.

"Well, well," Cellenius rasped. "If nothing else you have spirit. So I'll give you both a sporting chance. Guard unhasp the slave."

The guard fumbled with the hasps and freed Dorla's breast rings. Cellenius cast his eyes to the roof of the tent. The wooden pole running across the canvas seemed stout enough for what he had in mind.

Both women were ordered to stand either side of the pole whilst Mela willing fetched a couple of chairs. Wordlessly the slaves mounted them and stood facing each other. The guard threw the loose ends of Africanus' chains over the pole and re-fitted them to Dorla's rings.

"Now reach up and grab that pole," Cellenius told them.

They obeyed, lifting their arms and grabbing the shaft.

"Hang on tight," Africanus said, knowing what was coming.

The chairs were wrenched from their feet leaving them hanging by their arms. The chains draped loosely over the pole but still firmly in place at the rings.

"Eventually one of you will tire," Cellenius said calmly. "And you know the result."

Mela, not quite understanding the purpose of the exercise, looked blankly at the slaves. Then her face lighted up as it suddenly hit her. When the first to drop hit the ground the chain would suddenly go taut, her weight would haul the other to the pole and she would hang in mid air suspended by her breasts. It might not be fatal but the pain would be unbearable, the rings tearing at the nipples threatening to rip them from the breasts. How long would Cellenius leave her hanging? That was anyone's guess.

And he went back to the main tent looking for a whore, leaving the guard and Mela ensuring that neither of the slaves would attempt to free the chains and vanish into the night.

"Our concubine has done well," Queen Hatentita remarked. "She has exceeded all my expectations, giving us the exact time and location of Cellenius' camp."

She was in her chamber at the Temple of Anubis, dressed only in a white linen robe and bereft of her wig. The information that Africanus imparted had allowed her army to set off at night, and within two days, they would be encamped just over the horizon, unseen by any of the camp's occupants. They would rest until nightfall and then begin the first stage of the assault.

"And what of our other assistant?" she inquired, pacing the floor. "Has she made her preparations?"

Nefru watched her long legs striding up and down the chamber, their shimmering beauty silhouetted through her transparent robe, slit to the hip, and revealing only glimpses of the warm flesh beneath. Her breasts were covered but he could see their unrestrained weight bouncing as she walked, the gorgeous nipples now stiff in anticipation. The magnificent profile of her head caught in the sun's rays and he wondered if she truly was the incarnation of the glorious queen now long dead. For a few seconds he contemplated her beauty. She would look good in anything, even an old sack. There really were women like that. But only a few.

"She has contacted us at the rendezvous, your imperial majesty. Everything is ready. At nightfall she will set one of the tents ablaze and the flames will lead us directly into the camp."

A deep inhalation filled her lungs and she clapped her hands in exultation. Nefru watched her heaving chest, the nipples poking at the thin material and had to turn discreetly away. No red blooded male could possibly avoid an erection throbbing in his breeches confronted with that.

"I am she on whom the sun never sets," Hatentita spoke, raising her arms. "Daughter of Amen-Ra, King of all the Gods. I shall ascend the throne of Egypt and take up the mantle of she who is gone. By divine right I shall become a Goddess and shall be known as Haten, Goddess of Light, Strength and Wisdom."

"Yes, your majesty," he said, overawed at the sheer power of her delivery.

She turned, the exited flush on her face subsiding into the pale translucence of her flawless skin. Her blazing eyes returned to their smouldering gaze, her lips softened and he marvelled at the transformation.

"The black woman will be rewarded," she said flatly. "As well as our other agent. Both have done well. And you too shall be rewarded, Nefru. After I have been crowned you may name your price and it shall be met."

He already knew what that price was, but kept silent. Given the gravity of her speech, asking to get between her thighs didn't seem appropriate. But he did wonder whom she might take as a consort, or would she take no one at all, but summon whoever took her fancy and just have him between her legs, pumping her belly just for the love of it?

One never knew with Hatentita.

"I want the governor taken alive," she said suddenly, her face clouding. "He shall be fed to the crocodiles. I think it would be quite amusing, watching him crunched between their jaws. Don't you think?"

"Yes, your majesty," he said, watching her nipples going erect again at the thought of the Roman governor being eaten alive.

She turned and walked slowly to the window, her buttocks tightly closed, squeezing at the cleft, but always round and firm. Her back was as straight as an arrow, the shoulders narrow and compact. She bent over to pick up a wine goblet and his throat went dry. The robe, pulling taut, sucked into her bottom cleft, and he would have given anything to tear it from her and throw her naked on her back. She made a half turn, still bending over and her breasts swung free, wobbling beneath the robe. The hardened nipples pointing to the floor only served to increase the desire throbbing at his groin. It would be taking one hell of a chance, going over and making a play for her voluptuous body. She might be right up for it, but then again, she might have him executed.

Again, one never knew.

She came upright and arched her fine brows.

"Have a slave girl whipped as a sacrifice to the Gods. Her screams will arouse them from their slumbers and bring us fortune."

"Your majesty," he bowed, and rushed off to the slave quarters.

He selected a slave girl, well proportioned but slender, not above eighteen summers, and had her brought to Hatentita's chamber. Incense was lighted in the bowls and a priestess summoned to chant the devotions. The girl was ordered to prostrate herself over a table, lying across the top, her pert bottom resting on the edge. It was Nefru who was given the honour of flogging her.

He chose a three-tailed whip with long tails and laid it gently over her back whilst the priestess summoned the Gods. The girl clearly terrified trembled over the tabletop, her breasts squashing against the marble, legs widely spread, and her sex lips visible and quivering. Nefru made up his mind that after she had been flogged he would summon the Gods after his own fashion. It was not impossible that her ecstatic moans might arouse them further.

The priestess completed her devotions and Nefru raised the whip. It went sailing over the girl's twitching buttocks, and then lashed between her open legs, going right into her slit. If the Gods did not hear her howling, they never would. He lashed over her back beginning at her rump and labouring his way to her shoulders, leaving not an inch untouched. Hatentita folded her arms under her breasts and watched the proceedings censoriously. This was to be no light flogging. The greater her agony, the more likely the Gods would respond. Nefru returned to the girl's bottom and thighs, winging in the whip at full strength. It hit her skin with a loud snap and dug deeply into her flesh, leaving long scarlet welts. But she held on, not flinching, just screaming and writhing from the agony blazing her welted skin.

"Have her turned over and flog her front," Hatentita ordered, when Nefru finished beating the slave's bottom and thighs.

Groaning from the pain, she sat up and then rolled over onto her back wincing as her welted spine and buttocks touched the cold marble.

"Arch your back, girl," Hatentita said, coming closer. "Thrust out your bosom."

She groaned and raised her slim back into an arch, digging in her heels and shoulders for support. Nefru sent the whip over her front with slow measured strokes, designed to cause the maximum hurt. He began with the tops of her thighs and worked the whip over her pubic mound and belly, lashing across the navel and up her ribs. Her mouth opened but uttered no sound. Her numbed body was beyond pain. Even the tails slicing into her nipples brought only a subdued whimper.

"Not good enough," Hatentita said flatly. "She must do better than that. Drop your breeches and ride her."

Nefru could hardly believe his luck. What had started as no more than manly desire was now going to happen and on her majesty's command.

He wrestled his breeches to his ankles and cast them aside. In no time, he was between the girl's whipped thighs and penetrating her with savage pelvic thrusts. Beneath him she humped and bucked, bouncing her whipped bottom on and off the table top, already she was starting to come. Deep throaty moans escaped her lips as she rushed headlong into an orgasm.

Hatentita sipped from her glass, her eyes furtively riveted on Nefru's powerful buttocks. She knew the effect she had on him when she bent over to pick up that glass and had given the girl to him as a present. She also had thoughts of her own watching his thrusting pelvis, his powerful torso rocking on his arms as he rode her hard. She also watched the curious changes of expression on the slave's face, her squinting eyes opening and goggling at the ceiling, mouth open gasping for air as her climax erupted. Her slender legs went around his back hugging him tight as she jerked and wriggled from his deep penetrations. She uttered a deafening howl, then a long low groan, and laid still, her eyes slowly rolling in her head.

"I think the Gods have heard us," Hatentita smiled artfully.

"The Gods have answered," the priestess dutifully echoed, shaking her rattle.

Nefru gave a final thrust of his loins and for a moment cupped the girl's face in his hands. Then he dismounted and put on his breeches, his royal duty done.

"Have the slave taken to the baths and washed," Hatentita said, wrinkling her nose at the earthy smell drifting from her sex. "She is now favoured and will join my retinue."

"Your majesty," Nefru acknowledged.

He noticed that between her legs a damp patch, which hadn't been there before, now stained the linen. He guessed correctly that watching the girl being whipped and then fucked had brought on her own orgasm. Dimly, he became aware that was why she frequently had her slaves whipped and was not above delivering the punishment herself.

"That woman needs my cock," he thought, turning away and helping the girl to her feet.

Idly he wondered if she would actually have it up her bum. But he dismissed that as irreverent. After all, once she ascended the throne she would become a Goddess and having it up her bum would not be in keeping with such an elevation.

He left her alone and escorted the hobbling girl to the bath house.

Hatentita quickly cast of her robe and dived for her cosmetics. She painted her face and selected an enormous wig. A robe of deep orange colour shielded her body from prying masculine eyes. Soon it would be nightfall and she would head for the guards' quarters. In the fading light no one would recognize her in that get up. She thought she could have at least half a dozen men thumping at her cunt before dawn. And she made her way silently across the courtyard, joining the other prostitutes hired to pleasure the guards. She kept a small bottle of goose grease under her robe. Having it up her bum was a thrill in itself providing her lover's cock was well greased.

"What's your name, girl?" a guard asked, fetching over a goblet of rancid wine.

"Atata," she whispered, sliding her arm around his waist.

His hand dropped onto her thigh. "You willing to take me and my mate? Two silver pieces if you'll have it at both ends."

She giggled like an adolescent girl at her first date. "Are you suggesting you want to put your thing up my bum while your mate fucks my mouth?"

He nodded. "That's what I'm suggesting."

And she took the two men upstairs.

The habits of a lifetime are a long time in dying.

CHAPTER NINE

"One of you is going to drop eventually," Mela taunted. "My guess is it'll be the little one. Her arms are already tiring. I just can't wait to see her hit the dirt and pull the teats off the black one."

She was like someone who takes great delight in teasing a chained dog, safe for as long as it remained tethered, but would never have the courage if it were free.

"Supposing I give her a little encouragement. What do you think?" She grinned stupidly at the guard who merely shrugged. He couldn't care either way whose tits were ripped off. "Maybe I should give her a caning. What do you say?"

Again, the guard merely shrugged. He ran his eyes over the chained women, feasting his eyes on their hanging bodies and just had to admire the long and shapely legs of the black one. Nevertheless, the little one had her charms, a pretty pert arse and well shaped tits. He wouldn't mind having either of them.

Mela searched the tent and found a long cane that had recently been used by Messalina on a girl slave who had committed no crime but was nevertheless beaten just for the pleasure of it.

"What about beating the little one's bottom, or shall I beat the soles of her feet. What do you think?"

The guard sighed impatiently. He couldn't put his thoughts into words, but had already taken a dislike to the insolent bitch taunting her captives.

"Do you as you please," he said absently, making it clear he wanted no part of her silly game.

Mela reddened, piqued at his lack of interest, and marched behind Dorla swishing the cane with exaggerated gusto. Africanus saw her wince and whispered, "Just hang on Dorla whilst I think of a way out of this."

But at that moment, she couldn't think of anything.

Mela tickled the soles of Dorla's feet, running the tip of the cane up and down the soles, and then tickling her toes. She wriggled and tittered, more from fright than the infuriating tingling going through her feet. Mela guffawed and lightly ran the cane up and down the backs of Dorla's legs. The girl's body twitched and shivered and her tormentor laughed so much tears came into her eyes. She prodded her victim's bottom, driving the cane into her anus and corkscrewing it around and around.

"I haven't laughed so much for a long time," she announced, poking the cane under Dorla's breasts, and then digging it into her nipples.

She left off for a moment or two and poured herself a goblet of wine, which she offered to Africanus.

"No?" Mela said, well aware the helpless woman could do nothing but cling to the pole. "Another time then," she said sarcastically, and drank half the wine in a single gulp.

She put down the goblet and without warning whistled the cane under Dorla's bare feet. It landed with a dull smack and her legs shot out sideways.

"I'll drop you, you little bitch," Mela hissed. "Now let go of that pole, or I'll whip you senseless."

No more taunting now, but real threats hissing from her teeth. She struck again, this time under Dorla's toes and the girl's whole body swung outwards to the accompanying high-pitched laughter of her tormentor.

The guard regarded her suspiciously. There was something about that laugh that wasn't quite right. And he definitely felt sympathy for the girl she was beating. In his own peculiar way, he was developing quite a liking for her. And she was pretty in a girlish sort of way. He was powerless to put a stop to her sufferings but he could suggest an alternative.

"If you're going to beat her hit her arse," he said, hoping she could take a caning more readily on the fat of her bottom.

"As you say," Mela said, happier now that she had aroused his interest. "Twenty strokes," she exclaimed, swishing the cane over her head.

"For the God's sake, hang on," Africanus whispered, gritting her teeth to stop herself from calling Mela everything she could think of.

The cane whistled into Dorla's bare bottom, at dead centre, lashing across both buttocks and instantly leaving a livid welt.

"Nice?" Mela asked, waiting a few seconds before delivering the next lash.

It came whistling under the girl's buttocks and hard enough to make them lift.

"What about another one in your arse crease?" she laughed.

She stood a little to the right and brought the cane down vertically, slicing it deep into the crease. The next blows landed in rapid succession on each buttock, smacking into the sides and crown. She stood back watching the welts forming on the surface, pale pink to start with, then turning a deeper scarlet.

"Thighs next," she announced. "At the crease to start with, then all the way down to your knees."

She may have been an amateur when it came to caning, but her taunts were doing as much damage. Dorla choked back a tear and clenched her tiny fists.

"I can't take much more," she sobbed at Africanus. "The pain is killing me."

"Please, my love, just hang on," Africanus said, bringing her arms closer together.

If she could just find the strength to hang with one arm, her free hand might be able to unlock the hasp. It was only held in place with a pin. She glanced over her shoulder at the guard looking angrily at Mela. The slave girl was sobbing and he didn't like it. He visibly muttered as the cane lashed into the crease between buttock and thigh, then again near the top and again at mid thigh. She fulfilled her promise and went all the way down the backs of her slim legs, not stopping until she struck the backs of her knees.

Then it happened; the one thing Africanus most feared.

"Hang on for fuck's sake," she screeched, seeing one of Dorla's fists slip from the pole.

The girl swayed like a drunken puppet, her body at an angle as her remaining arm took her full weight. Her free hand thrashed the air and she just managed to regain her hold, but it had been close. If she had lost her grip her body would have crashed to the floor and the chain ripped the teats from Africanus' breasts.

Mela, sensing victory, abandoned her cane and made for one of the flaming lamps. She picked up a sword and held the tip over the flame.

"I'm going to brand your arse," she grated, turning the blade.

"You'll do no such thing."

She abruptly turned and met the blazing eyes of the guard. One glance told her he meant it and she was certainly no match for his towering height, let alone his bulk.

"Beat the black one, if you must," he grunted.

Mela made a mental note to have him severely punished, and went back to her cane.

"I'll whip you until you drop," she whispered savagely, and whistled the cane into Africanus' bare rump.

Her pace slowed and she caned with an almost mechanical precision, striking across the buttocks with hard unrelenting strokes. Now that she had Mela's attention, Africanus couldn't possibly release the hasp without her noticing. Her bare bottom, hot and throbbing took at least twenty lashes before her tormentor showed signs of tiring. But still Africanus clung to the pole, and that infuriated Mela. It didn't assuage her anger when she saw the guard grinning at her.

Then her face suddenly brightened. She ceased caning the black woman's bottom and looked up to where her fists gripped the pole. If there was a weak spot that had to be it. She fetched a stool and reached up, flicking the tip of the cane over Africanus' knuckles. She struck with short, sharp strokes, rapping the cane over the backs of Africanus' hands, lashing into her fingers and wrists. It took one final savage lash and the black woman crashed to the ground. The chains on her breast rings shot over the pole like a rope through a pulley. Before Dorla could even realize what was happening the rings suddenly tore at her nipples, lifting her upwards, thumping her breasts into the pole. A deafening scream echoed around the tent and she frantically grabbed the pole trying to support her weight. But her arms were already exhausted and fell lifeless at her sides, the chains now rigid strained at the rings and she hung suspended by her breasts.

The guard moved faster than Mela could ever imagine. He was behind Dorla with his strong hands on her pert buttocks, lifting her as high as he could. Her belly drew level with the pole and the chains suddenly relieved of their burden went slack. In the confusion, Africanus fumbled with the hasps, withdrawing the pins and tossing the chains harmlessly to the floor. The guard lowered Dorla to the ground and with his bare hands, stretched open her breasts rings and slipped them from her teats.

"You'll all be punished for this," Mela sneered, backing away as Africanus rose to full height.

"I don't think so," he rasped, cradling Dorla in his arms.

Mela made rapidly for the entrance and didn't see the fist winging into the side of her head. She spun full circle and fell flat on her face, unconscious.

"By all the Gods, what do we do now?" Dorla stuttered, looking at Mela's crumpled body.

"You should've left that bitch to me," the guard muttered, slipping Dorla from his arms.

But it was too late for recriminations. When she came to, Mela was sure to report everything that had taken place and would probably greatly exaggerate her own injuries.

"I'll get rid of her," the guard said, mindful that if she did report them all three would be crucified.

"Take her into the desert and dump her," Africanus advised, rubbing her swollen knuckles.

"That would be a waste. I intend to take her to Thebes and sell her. I think she'll fetch at least ten silver pieces. And," he said sternly, "the little one's coming with me."

"You're not selling her," Africanus retorted.

"Who said anything about selling her? I meant as my wife."

Africanus thought fast. Getting Dorla well out of the way would save her a lot of trouble. "Head for the river," she said softly. "Whatever you do, don't head east into the desert. Move fast and don't look back."

He regarded her suspiciously. She obviously knew something he didn't and wondered what it was.

"Go, and may the all the Gods protect you," she whispered, and went immediately to Dorla fondly embracing and kissing her.

"I want to stay with you," the girl sobbed.

"You're better off with a man between your legs. Let him ride you as much as he wants. There's no substitute for a real cock inside your cunt."

Dorla choked back a tear, and helped the guard to carry the unconscious Mela to the horse lines. Africanus watched as they threw her over the saddle and galloped off into the night.

Too tired to do anything but wander to the concubines' tent, she found a vacant mat and curled up in a ball, resting her head one arm, and slipping the hand of the other between her legs, softly stroking her sex lips. Almost immediately, her juice started to flow. She put three fingers into her sex and started stroking. She touched her clit and her heart jumped. A cold thrill fluttered in her stomach. Her fingers moved faster. She had no need of anyone now. She came with a soft moan and kept her hand between her legs as she always did. There was nothing on her mind. She fell into a deep contented slumber.

Africanus knelt in the governor's tent, her shackled wrists resting on her thighs, ankles manacled to a long length of chain secured to an anvil. Cellenius was seated in his chair eyeing her malevolently. Around her neck, the blacksmith had fitted a broad iron collar with long spikes protruding from the perimeter. The side locks had been cut from her scalp and her head shaved. Dimly she recalled Ustane gently awaking her with the sole of her foot pressing into bottom.

"Govnor wants you," she had said seriously. "You've dropped yourself right in it this time. The shit's deep."

There was no disputing that when the blacksmith was summoned to shackle her wrists and ankles, and a concubine to shave her head. Ustane stood behind her wielding an ivory handled riding crop as Africanus kept her head bowed in submission.

"Well?" Cellenius grunted his eyes bleary and head throbbing from a torrid night with one of the drunken concubines. He had come into his tent at dawn expecting to find one of the women lying on the floor and the other hanging by her breasts, but instead discovered the tent empty and only Africanus had been found quietly snoring on her mat.

Africanus lifted her eyes. "It was the guard, he struck a bargain with Mela that if she let Dorla go with him he would take her along with them and set her free," she lied.

He had to think about that. "So why didn't you raise the alarm instead of going to your tent?"

Before she could speak Ustane intervened, "It's true master. One of the guards saw all three of 'em coming out of the tent."

"So why didn't he report it?"

"S'pose he thought they was just goin' off fuckin'" she delivered nonchalantly.

Africanus lowered her eyes wondering why Ustane had so valiantly aided her.

"That may be true, but that still doesn't excuse you for not reporting their disappearance," he said to the black woman. "I have a strong suspicion you were involved in this caper. And because of that, you will be punished. After you have taken your punishment you will be reduced to nothing more than a beast of burden. I'll have you hitched to a cart and you can spend the rest of your miserable existence pulling it." He laughed aloud. "And you will be fitted with blinkers and a bit through your teeth. The driver will have my permission to horse whip you as much as he likes. You may be thankful that

I don't have the blacksmith nail horseshoes to the soles of your feet."

He emptied his goblet and sent a long jet of wine hissing onto the top of her head and into her eyes.

"And you," he said to Ustane, "Will see that she carries that anvil the whole length of the camp whilst you flog her bare arse. Then take her to the baggage train and have her put in the shafts."

And he got up and left.

"Phew, that was close," Ustane breathed. "I thought you were done for. Now get up and do what he says."

Africanus struggled to her feet, lifting the anvil and holding it over her belly.

"I'll have to flog your arse all the way round the camp," Ustane said apologetically.

That was mild compared to what might have happened, and she walked slowly to the camp perimeter, struggling under the anvil's weight. Ustane followed behind lashing into her buttocks, herding her forward as if she were an animal. The crop stung left and right and it behooved Ustane to ensure the black woman was well whipped. If the governor had the slightest hint she was being gentle she would doubtless suffer the same fate.

Sweat streamed from Africanus' face and breasts as she trudged past Tamara piling up jars of oil and brushwood outside the tent where all the rugs and clothes were stored. She gave them a sidelong glance and returned to her task. The guards stood in line bawling suggestive obscenities as the black woman's legs bowed from the weight. Ustane lashed into her bottom, gripping the handle tightly and swinging her arm. Africanus' back cricked from the fiery pain going through her bottom. Her nipples had gone erect and one of the men rushed over and pinched each one in turn. Another ran to her side and patted her bald head. It was bad enough being flogged let alone having to suffer further humiliation. Ustane said nothing, allowing the men their sport and whipped the crop into Africanus' flanks. She made it to where the previous night's debauchery had taken place and dropped to her knees.

"Can't go on," she gasped, dropping the anvil.

"Get up!" Ustane ordered, making sure that anyone within sight would see she was doing as she had been ordered.

Africanus took a deep breath and lifted the anvil at chest height. The sun blazing on the broad expanse of iron had heated the metal to burning point and she sucked her breath as it pressed hard against her breasts, squashing them over the rim. She supported her weight on one leg and then, as she came upright, quickly brought up the other. Now on her feet, she dragged her sweat soaked body towards the lake where a dozen concubines wrapped in their fishnets were preparing to board the boat. Cellenius sat in the prow with Calla seated beside him, naked except for a short skirt wrapped under her enormous belly. Seeing Africanus driven along by Ustane's whip, she burst into hysterical laughter. Her massive breasts wobbled and shook and Cellenius couldn't resist burying his head between them and rolling the globes against the sides of his head.

"Move!" Ustane shrieked for the governor's benefit, and she whipped the crop hard over Africanus' rump.

The boat drifted into the centre of the lake and Ustane paused to admire the perfect symmetry of the rowers, swinging their oars with grace and precision. As on the Nile, their breasts and backs strained into the nets emphasizing the contours of their lithe bodies and sweating thighs. Even from where she was standing, she could see their pointed nipples poking provocatively through the mesh. The boat swung astern and she struck the black woman a final stroke as she completed her pain-racking journey. Her knees buckled and hit the sand with a resounding crunch. The anvil fell onto its side dragging her after it, and she knelt in a heap, reeking of sweat.

As instructed, the blacksmith came from his forge and removed the manacles and chains. He unfastened the spiked collar and effortlessly returned the anvil to its proper place.

"I'm supposed to put you in the cart shafts," Ustane said, helping Africanus to her feet.

"I'm not pulling a cart," she retorted, and cast her eyes to the horizon.

As yet, there were no signs of Queen Hatentita's army and she began to wonder if it even existed and had been no more than a product of her wild and demented imagination. Then she remembered Ustane's promise of supplying her with the drug. Already an escape plan was forming in her mind and the drug would be its lynch pin.

"I always bring it with me," Ustane said. "Comes in useful when I have to fuck some of these animals."

Africanus cursed herself for not going with Dorla and the guard. Mela would have fetched a good price in the fleshpots of Thebes, but the promise of Hatentita's gold and her own greed had held her back.

"Fetch me that drug," she said ominously, and walked boldly to her tent.

On the horizon, she caught sight of a dust cloud. It was far away and she dismissed it as nothing more than a passing sand storm. Tamara ceased her labours and looked at the dust cloud, smiled a knowing smile and went on with her work, stacking up more jars and humming to herself.

Ustane went to her tent and, rummaging in her belongings, took out a small earthenware bottle. She made her way through the camp to where Africanus was resting and made up her mind that by nightfall, one way or another the black woman was going into those shafts.

Cellenius reclined on a cushion groping Calla's monumental breasts. She made a good fuck and he had felt comfortable riding her wobbling belly. Her enormous thighs were warm and soft wrapped around his back. He made up his mind to have her as his favoured concubine, and tore away her skirt.

Women always looked so much better naked.

CHAPTER TEN

"So why did you help me?" Africanus asked when Ustane brought her the bottle. "You knew I was lying."

"You're a good fighter. I knew if he thought you were really involved he'd have you crucified. The fat bastard."

"I was involved," Africanus said softly, and she told her what really happened, and reminded her that Lady Octavia had given her to the gladiatrix as a companion, "A slave to a slave," she laughed bitterly.

"That was in the govnor's palace," Ustane grunted. "And I don't think she really meant me to be your slave. But that doesn't stop us fucking. Or me hitching you to that cart."

"Just try it," Africanus warned dangerously.

"I'm only obeyin' orders," she said.

Africanus regarded her for a few moments. There was one thing she wanted to know. "Supposing you were trained to fight in the arena, had taken the loyal oath, and then matched against your best friend and ordered to fight to the death, would you do it?"

"If I 'ad taken the oath, yes," she said. "I would 'ave no choice."

"When we were brawling in front of that painted bitch, you gave the salute. We're you just trying to be clever, or what, because no one belittles the gladiatrix."

"I've seen it done in the arena. My former master said I was the best fuck he'd ever 'ad and let me watch the games once. No one got killed, though."

"It doesn't happen that often. We cost too much to train for a start. Only sword fodder actually dies, and there's no kudos in that; slaughtering unarmed slaves."

"Have you ever fought with a lion?"

"Not yet, but I suppose it will happen one day."

Ustane's eyes narrowed. "If you really were a real gladiatrix, how come you're a slave now?"

"It's a long story," Africanus said ruefully, thinking that

if things had worked out differently she might be the one of the best gladiatrices in Rome. And rich.

"I want to hear all about you. We have time. That fat bastard is too busy with those women on that lake, and he's probably forgotten anyway."

"I need a drink first," Africanus said.

Ustane went off and fetched a jar of wine. In an hour, it would be dark and the governor would probably host another wild night of drinking and fucking. Already the musicians, concubines, acrobats and dancers were painting their faces and oiling their bodies.

"So let's hear it," she said, shoving the jar into Africanus' belly. She also brought some bread and fruit and waited patiently until the gladiatrix had taken her fill.

She laid herself full length on the mat and put her arms behind her head, looking magnificent with her long shimmering legs, full breasts and shapely hips. Ustane sat beside her cross-legged and taking the jar that Africanus offered.

"Are you sitting comfortably?" the black woman joked. "Then I'll begin."

"I was a slave working in a grinding house…" She told her story from start to finish, giving most of the essential details, her training and combat in the arena, the shipwreck and her adventures in Britannia, and finished close to the present day, but carefully avoided any mention of her encounter with Hatentita. "And now you know," she said.

She raised the jar to her lips, quenched her thirst from so much talking, belched and tossed the jar across the tent.

Ustane sat stunned at everything she had heard. How could she even think of putting so great a woman in a cart like a beast?

Overawed at the sight of Africanus and the greatness that lay within her, she leaned over and kissed her full on the lips, pushing her tongue into her throat and not stopping until their lips were sore.

"I might've guessed," Messalina said wryly, coming into the tent. "You can't get enough of it, can you? Even mating with this worn out whore."

Ustane would have floored her but Africanus grabbed her arm. She had already narrowly missed being crucified; knocking out the chief concubine would make it a certainty.

"The governor is giving some of his slaves to the guards in return for their loyalty," Messalina announced, casting her eyes around the tent. "So this place will do as well as any. Oil your cunts' and get ready for a long hard ride," she laughed, and went off in search for the two roughest and brutal men she could find.

Ustane and Africanus glanced at each other, and with that remarkable understanding that only happens between women, reached for the earthenware bottle. Quickly they applied the drug to their nipples and breasts, thumbing the teats to make them erect and going all around the pimpled areolas. They took generous amounts and smoothed their fingertips over their sex lips, just touching the clits and coating the labia. Then they parted and laid themselves on their mats, knees bent and open, displaying their charms; waiting in silence.

They came in, eyes immediately going between the parted thighs and liked what they saw.

They were tall, passably handsome, unshaven and already erect.

Their torsos were well-honed and muscular, a few battle scars marking their chests.

"I'll take the black one," the first remarked, throwing off his tunic.

"Good enough," the other replied, unbuckling his sword, moving towards Ustane.

The man kneeling between Africanus' thighs did not mount her at once but straddled her belly, seating his weight over her sex mound, feeling its tender pulp brushing softly against his buttocks. His hand went out and grabbed her left breast, squeezing it with a gentleness that surprised her. His fingers and thumbs rolled the nipples until they throbbed. He watched the changing expressions on her face, her lips parting and inhaling a sudden gasp, her eyes glazing as he pinched her nipples hard enough to make her jolt. His cock reared up fully erect and nodding a slow beat in time with his heart. Without being told, her hand closed around the shaft and began a slow up and down movement, not squeezing, but with a touch so light, he almost believed he was inside her and it was the soft petals of her sex embracing his length. Her fingers fluttered over the silky plum and she felt a quickening in the throbbing veins. He was long and hot, the girth wide enough to fill her sex, and hoped he wouldn't suck her nipples so soon.

He had no intention of sucking her breasts, but instead cupped the globes and lifted them from her chest. He squeezed harder until she squinted with pain, then he let them fall back into place. With both hands, he slapped her breasts simultaneously; hitting the sides and watching them wobble and jiggle. He pressed them tightly together and smiled broadly at the lengthening cleft between them. Then he struck harder, slapping underneath the nipples, bringing both hands down hard at the place where each globe swelled from her chest. His thumbs pressed over the nipples and forced them flat into the ballooning flesh. Her hand was still on his cock but squeezing harder from the pain searing through her nipples. He let them spring up again and pinched the teats until she sucked her breath.

"I want to see you suck your own tits," he said, pushing up her breasts

Panic seized her. That was the last thing she expected. The drug would render her unconscious in seconds and only the Gods knew what he would do then.

"I'd rather suck you," she smiled broadly.

Her mouth opened and he quickly shuffled over her belly ramming his cock deep into her mouth. Inwardly, as he almost choked her, she breathed a sigh of relief.

205

"Now suck," he said, his tone growing more severe.

He kept his cock deep in her throat and felt only her tongue licking around the shaft. Her hand groped clumsily at the root of his cock and cupped his balls, gently manipulating them in her palm. Inside her mouth she let his plum rest on her tongue and licked slowly and carefully into the groove. All the tension in his massive frame seemed to evaporate and, emitting a purring groan, he cupped her face holding her head rigid. He rode gently back and forth, letting his cock glide in and out of her mouth while her lips pursed and sucked from plum to root. It was a rare woman who could take the whole of his length into her throat, and he laughed at the sheer ecstasy of it all.

Ustane was not being treated with such finesse. Her man went instantly into her sex, ramming home with all the strength he could muster.

"Have that, you dirty bitch," he rasped, slamming between her thighs.

"Jupiter!" she gulped, as he slipped his arms under her legs, lifting them high over her head.

She bent double and couldn't remember being so deeply penetrated. He was one of those men who firmly believed that the more women were punished during sex; the more they loved it, and reached under her bottom and pinched her buttocks. She yelped and he started slapping her thighs, stretching as far as he could reach and then winging in with full strength. The shock was enough to make her whole body jolt and through tear-filled eyes she saw his lips curling into a snarl.

"Now let me feel you work your hips," he commanded, in no mood for argument.

She began a slow rolling of her pelvis, performing magnificent gyrations, making them twist and roll, forcing her pubic mount harder into his balls. He responded with a savage thrust of his loins and her head bucked backwards, tongue drooping from her mouth. She was breathing hard through dilated nostrils and he laughed at that, watching mucus blasting from her nose.

"When I've fucked you, I'm going to whip your bare arse all the way to the sea," he promised, and slammed so hard her neck almost snapped.

But no mention or any indication of putting his mouth where she really wanted it.

The man stuffing Africanus' mouth had withdrawn his cock and was playing the plum around her nipples and rubbing it through her breast cleft. His hand went between her legs and crushed her sex mound. Her eyes winced and he slapped her flank.

"Over on your belly," he grated, rolling her onto her stomach. His hand slapped her bottom. "Now up on all fours."

She was up on her knees and hands, opening her thighs and bracing herself. Taken from behind penetration would be much deeper. "Open your mouth, and keep it open," he rasped, shuffling behind her.

With incredible precision, he sent his belt flying around her head and landed it between her teeth.

"Bite on that," he ordered, pulling it tight and buckling it over the back of her head. He looked at his comrade bearing down on Ustane, almost crushing her under his great weight. "Look at my fine mare, isn't she a beauty?"

His comrade laughed when he saw him tugging on the belt and slapping her flanks.

"You're just built for riding," he continued. "I only wish I had a pair of spurs to dig into your ribs."

Africanus' lips stretched half way around her face and her neck was already feeling the strain. He guided his rampant cock into her sex and penetrated her to the hilt.

"Aaaroogh," she blurted, unable to utter as much as a single syllable.

The noises she made when he tugged her head had tears running down his face. Africanus' eyes were also watering but not from merriment. The belt was creasing her face until the pain was unbearable. He gave the side of her buttocks a hefty slap and juddered his pelvis against her bottom. The cheeks were round and soft and felt warm against his skin. He rode her with gusto, rocking on his knees and all the while tugging at her head and slapping her thighs and flanks.

"I'm going to suck your hot cunt after I've finished with you," he announced, driving his cock in as deep as possible.

"I wish you'd suck it now," Africanus thought, her mouth sore and dry.

He paused and looked down watching his shaft gliding out of her sex and went wide eyed at her lips enveloping the slowly emerging length. He came right out of her and joyfully teased her labia, playing the purple glans around her sex pouch, and tickling her clit. Her back shuddered and he caught a muffled groan at the back of her throat. He was not in a hurry to penetrate her sex; her splendid arse looked much more inviting. He tickled her clit until he heard her gasping through the belt. Not being free to give vent to the sexual frustration racking her belly, she jerked her hips and buttocks, desperately trying to reach her climax. To increase her sufferings, he reached under her body and softly manipulated her breasts, not squeezing until it hurt, but just lightly teasing the nipples with the barest touch of his fingers. She sobbed and shook her head, emitting more warbled grunts.

"Release the poor bitch," his comrade sympathized.

Ustane, with her knees banging against her ears, could just glimpse Africanus sobbing and snorting, so close to her orgasm but still unable to come. She saw him reach forward and slacken the belt, saw it drop from her mouth and heard the sighing gasp of relief. But if Africanus thought his cock was going to plunge back into her sex she had another think coming.

"Oh, by the Gods, no!" she grunted, and braced herself for what was soon to follow.

His hands were on her arse cheeks, forcing them open as he mounted her rump, positioning the plum right at the centre of her bottom hole. He gave a gentle shove, only penetrating her a fraction and, when he felt her anal muscles relax, rammed against her bottom. She gulped and choked, feeling his entire length slamming into her.

"It hurts," she protested. "It's too long!"

She ought to have known by now that complimenting a man on his great length or sexual prowess only drives him on to further exertions. He snatched up the belt and lashed between her shoulder blades, then again on her flanks.

"Now wriggle your arse," he told her, belting her ribs.

How could she do that with a cock of that length grinding inside her? She squeezed her anal walls and shook her bottom from side to side. She rotated her hips and let them rise and fall in time with his thrusting. She did everything possible to make him come and then suck her sex, but he was not in a hurry. It was not often he got to ride one of the concubines.

Ustane's lover had graciously retreated from her chest and was kneeling between her thighs with his cock still fully immersed in her sex. One of her legs idly draped across the mat; the other was dead straight and pointing to the roof. His arms were around the thigh and gripping it fast. His free hand rested firmly on her belly whilst he pumped his loins. Thankful that he was no longer attempting to snap her spine, she smiled lovingly up at his torso and whispered softly, "come on…come on…come in me."

Usually it worked, the softly spoken words encouraging her lover to shoot his load, but he seemed deaf to her whisperings and just went on pumping, occasionally groping her pert breasts and tweaking her nipples. As with her suffering companion, she began to wonder whether if either of them would ever get round to sucking their nipples or sex'.

Both men came almost simultaneously, the man at Ustane's belly, quaking his loins and uttering a loud snort, the other riding Africanus' bottom with long, purposeful thrusts, flooding her bum tunnel with more spunk than she ever dreamt possible. They withdrew and congratulated each other on their efforts, made for the wine jar and finding it empty let loose a barrage of curses. After all fucking is thirsty work if you've got any imagination.

The man who had been fucking Africanus stumbled into the night in search of wine and her face fell, but not for long. His companion, seeing the vacant black woman's sex, was there at once, diving between her legs, and licking all around her nipples. She lovingly stroked the back of his shaggy head and angled it into her throbbing teats. He sucked each one into his mouth and bit hard. She held her breath not daring to scream despite the excruciating pain. Instead, she gave release to a long throaty groan and bent her back, thrusting her whole breast into his face. He sucked until her nipples ached, then rolled over and fell into a grunting sleep.

"It worked!" Africanus exclaimed.

"Of course it fucking worked," Ustane retorted, then sat up as his comrade came lurching into the tent, wine bottle swinging in his hand.

"Look at that," he remarked disgustedly. "One fuck and he's finished. So now that leaves just the three of us."

Africanus, astute as ever, dragged him to the floor and straddled his middle, aiming his cock straight into her dripping sex.

"Have the pair of us," she offered, bouncing her hips. "One at each end. Fuck me and suck my friend."

What man in his right mind would argue with that?

Ustane was just as quickly there, swinging a leg over his head and settling her bottom on his face. His tongue went into her sex, sucking on the clit and lapping his tongue all around her pouting lips. Her juice tasted of the usual feminine musky odour but flavoured with a slight taste of almonds. But constant grinding between her thighs and the diluting effect of her sex juice had weakened the drug. He buried his face deeper into her lips and contentedly swallowed the rich, creamy rivulet streaming from her cunt. Africanus sensed that something was wrong and signaled to Ustane to get off him. Her breasts had not been sucked and the drug would still be on her nipples.

She lifted her bottom and, in one dexterous movement, swung her body in a semi circle, dropping her breasts over his face and pushing her nipples into his mouth. Africanus rode hard, bouncing and wriggling her bottom, writhing like a demented eel. Ustane uttered genuine cries of ecstasy while he sucked hard on her teats, biting and nibbling until she cried in pain. Then he pushed her away and concentrated again on the black woman whose gleaming body he found irresistible. He reached up and cupped her breasts, swung their weight from side to side and rolling them under his palms.

Africanus lifted her body and popped his cock from her sex. Before he could utter a word, she was on his face, grinding her sex against his mouth. The black woman's smell was a lot more powerful than Ustane's, a rich earthy aroma and that strange essence of almond was there, but more ardent, especially on the inner petals of her sex. His tongue licked her vaginal walls and there the essence was even stronger. He swallowed the juice pouring into his mouth and bit on her clit. Africanus uttered a silent oath and leaned forward resting her hands on his thighs. Her hips rocked faster and then, as she reached her climax he suddenly ceased his sucking and biting.

"Fuck, I was so close," she swore, lifting her bottom.

"The bastard's asleep!" Ustane cried joyfully.

Africanus plunged her fingers into her sex and jerked her wrist so fast it ached. She came with a shriek and rolled onto her back panting like a racehorse.

"Now what?" Ustane asked, when her breathing abated.

"We get the hell out of here, that's what," Africanus replied, scrambling to her feet.

"Yeah, sure. Stark naked and not as much one bronze coin between us, and nowhere to run. Fucking great idea."

"This is the only chance we're going to get, you stupid fucking cow. It's now or…"

She stopped and looked at the ruddy brightness suddenly illuminating their faces.

"Shit," Ustane uttered. "The fucking rug tent's on fire."

They rushed out and saw flames leaping to the sky. Sparks were flying in great clouds and another tent was already ablaze. Africanus squinted her eyes at the raging conflagration. She was sure she saw the figure of Tamara strongly silhouetted against the fire and hurrying quickly away into the darkness. One of the oil jars stacked against the tent exploded and shards of pottery shot through the air. A river of burning oil poured into one of the concubines' tents' and naked, screaming girls came bolting into the night air.

The ground beneath them suddenly trembled and in the distance hoof beats of horses galloped towards the fire.

"By all that is sacred," Africanus breathed.

And she grabbed Ustane's hand and dragged her to the safest place she could think of.

"Don't argue, just get in and start rowing," Africanus shrieked, clambering into the boat.

Taking the oars, they slowly rowed the boat away from the bank and towards the centre of the lake, not looking back until they were well clear of the blazing encampment. The fire had spread rapidly from one tent to the next and many were already reduced to ashes. Frightened horses reared and shrieked, men and women were running in all directions screaming and swearing, all sense of discipline abandoned.

"How the hell did that happen?" Ustane wondered, gazing mesmerized into the inferno.

Another jar of oil exploded with such force, the two women could feel the heat on their faces. Some of the more astute concubines had rushed for the lake and were swimming towards the boat. Africanus shielded her eyes and saw Cellenius and Messalina making for the horse lines. They might have saved themselves the trouble for by now Queen Hatentita's cavalry were already there, dismounting and unsheathing their swords.

"That fire was started on purpose," Ustane fathomed, watching more horsemen thundering around the camp perimeter.

With consummate skill, they leaned over and scooped up the nearest concubine, throwing her over the front of the saddle and taking her to where all the rest were already gathered. Dimly, Africanus saw the women being chained and fettered. Most of the guards had tactfully surrendered and were being herded away as prisoners of war. The great slaughter that Africanus had anticipated had not taken place after all. But then again where was the sense in carrying out mindless butchery when the camp occupants could be taken as slaves and sold.

"What do we do now?" Ustane asked, leaning on her oar.

Africanus watched as one by one the remaining tents caught fire. "Nothing," she said quietly.

CHAPTER ELEVEN

Dawn saw nothing left of the camp, just smouldering wreckage and the concubines seated sobbing on the ground. All were naked and chained, but yet unmolested.

Africanus and Ustane rowed to the shore and picked their way through the charred remnants, heading to where the concubines were fettered. It seemed the logical thing to do. Cellenius and Messalina were shackled together and seated in the very cart into whose shafts he had ordered the black woman, and she smiled at the irony.

"You!" exclaimed the captain of horse, marching up to Africanus. "Tell me your name, girl."

She told him and to her utter amazement, he bowed and offered his cloak, draping it around her shoulders. "I am to take you to the Red Sphinx. Is this your slave?"

"She is my friend," she informed, avoiding the astonished look on Ustane's face.

He escorted both women to a troop of awaiting cavalry and they trotted into the desert mounted behind the riders, heading into the rising sun.

The reached the Nile and followed it for several miles, only stopping to eat a morsel of food and ease their aching limbs.

At a ruined temple, they headed west and into the desert proper, nothing to be seen except endless sand dunes and the occasional skeletal remains of perished beasts. Strangely, the cavalrymen ignored the two near naked women, not even going anywhere close to them, except to offer food and drink. They rode on through the monotonous landscape, and descended into a deep depression at the bottom of which rearing up from the earth stood a gigantic sphinx of red sandstone. From a distance, it looked like a crouching lion but with a woman's head, her featureless eyes gazing enigmatically into the infinity of the desert. Africanus cast her eyes upwards and shuddered. The face was the living embodiment of Hatentita. The horsemen helped the women to dismount and ushered them to a doorway between the lion's paws.

"Her imperial majesty awaits you," the captain said, and the two women walked tentatively over the threshold.

"Phew!" breathed Ustane, staring in wonder at the gigantic statues lining the hallway.

They were all the various deities worshiped long ago; many of human form with animal heads, some of women wearing crowns, others were animals still inhabiting the borders of the Nile. The women walked on unguided, their footsteps echoing along the chamber. At the end they passed through a low door and found themselves in a great hall, the walls freshly painted with colourful murals and thousands of hieroglyphs, meaningless to the women. The sandstone floor was liberally covered with animal skins and rugs, expensive and elaborately carved furniture stood in abundance, and there at the centre of it all sat Hatentita, resplendent in her transparent robe and enormous wig. She looked every inch a queen, bedecked in jewels and ornaments. In the lamplight, Africanus saw concubines of various ages and races, some fanning the queen with ostrich feathers, others merely languishing on the rugs, some busy with bottles and goblets; all completely naked apart from their customary wigs and ornamented belts.

"Yes, come," the queen beckoned.

The two women approached her throne and dropped to their knees, heads bowed.

"This is my other agent," the queen introduced, as Tamara came out of the shadows, dressed in a fine transparent robe of white linen, her feline contours standing out in stark relief. "She is the one who started the fire which guided my army to the camp, and as you can see has been suitably rewarded, as you soon shall be. The governor and his mistress will be arriving shortly and you shall witness their demise."

Her lips distorted into a horrible triumphant grin as she motioned Tamara to her side.

"Take the black woman and her slave to the baths and see that they are well prepared, then bring them to my chambers."

Tamara bowed so low her head bumped her knees. "Your majesty," she whispered, and taking Africanus by the hand led her and Ustane to the bathing chamber.

"Just what the fuck is going on?" Ustane asked, following Tamara along a passage and down a steep flight of steps.

"That was Queen Hatentita," Africanus replied, and motioned her to keep silent.

They went into a subterranean chamber illuminated by shafts of light descending from overhead. Africanus quickly recognized that the red sphinx and its attendant corridors and chambers were a secret bolthole to which the queen retreated in times of trouble. Now Cellenius had been captured she wondered what her next move would be. However, that was none of her business. She just wanted to grab the gold and run. The sooner she was back in Rome the better.

"I suppose you had quite a shock, meeting me here," Tamara purred, placing the sole of her foot into the small of Ustane's back and plunging her into the bath.

"You're a traitor," Ustane uttered, spitting out a mouthful of water.

"So I might be, but then, so is your friend, she's as guilty as I am, but then again, I should say it was worth it with all these delicious little concubines at my disposal. Whipping their little bums is going to be great fun, wouldn't you say? The queen has already given me one of them as a pet."

Her foot went flying into Africanus bottom and she fell headlong into the bath.

A couple of nubile concubines duly arrived to wash and perfume the women and Tamara retreated to her own quarters laughing like a demented hyena.

"What did she mean; you are as guilty as she is?" Ustane asked, flicking water from her eyes.

Africanus filled her in on all the bits she had left out, her first encounter with Hatentita in the brothel, their escape and the strange interlude at the temple of Anubis, and her subsequent entry into the governor's harem.

"Well, I suppose I would've done much the same had I been in your position," Ustane agreed. "So what happens now?"

"I'll wait until I get my reward, then I'm out. You with me?"

"Better with the bitch I know than the one I don't," she said dully, and flicked water into Africanus face.

The black woman retaliated with a playful slap across Ustane's breast. She came swiftly back with a hard slap on the black woman's bald head and followed with a ribald joke. Africanus pushed her under the water and they broke into a fight, slapping and punching, grabbing each other's breasts and nipples, letting all the tension, and fears evaporate whilst the concubines watched on in dumbfounded amazement.

Overhead the sun shone directly down the shafts and it was towards midday when they had been finally washed, perfumed and dressed, looking and feeling better now that they were no longer naked and looked like real women again.

Hatentita's chambers comprised a suit of rooms brightly lit with dozens of lamps and candles. Murals adorned every wall and the furniture was magnificent. She had changed into a bright orange coloured robe, her left breast and right arm bare in ancient Egyptian fashion. She was wearing a different wig with golden pendants weighting the braids. Only the Gods knew what all this must have cost.

"I said I would reward you and so I shall," Hatentita said, motioning the women to her side. "You may choose any of the concubines as your slaves, and I have already made a suite of rooms available with their own private baths. You may eat and drink as much as you please. Soon, I shall travel to Luxor and attend my coronation. I hope you will be happy here, and I offer my heartfelt thanks in return for the services you have rendered and welcome you as my guests. The slave will show you both to your rooms."

Africanus, too stunned to speak dumbly followed the slave to her rooms along with Ustane muttering savage obscenities.

"That woman is fucking crazy," Ustane swore, flopping onto a bed. "If she thinks the Romans are just going to sit back and watch Egypt slip from their grasp, she's got another think coming. A soon as they find what happened in that camp, they'll have a whole legion marching up the Nile. Killing Cellenius isn't going to change a thing."

She bit on a grape and spat the pip over her shoulder.

"We'll have to make our own way then," Africanus whispered, suddenly struck by the horrible reality of Ustane's words.

"That might be difficult," Ustane muttered. "Because we're not her guests. We're her prisoners."

Africanus had to think about that. Ustane was pretty astute when it came to these things, recognizing any given situation and quickly analyzing it.

"But there must be more than one way out of here," she mused. "It's just a matter of finding it."

"Yeah, providing we can pass the guards. You can bet your tits this creepy hole is crawling with them."

"There is a way out," a tiny voice whispered, and both women turned their heads so fast they span.

The slave who had showed them to their rooms stood timidly in the shadows, not daring to venture into the lamplight.

"Come out, whoever you are!" Ustane bawled, leaping off the bed and instinctively grabbing a heavy candlestick.

She took a couple of steps forward and stood trembling before the women towering over her. She was no more than four and a half feet in height, a tiny waist and slim legs but blessed with an enormous bosom that seemed ridiculously out of proportion with the rest of her diminutive frame.

Ustane burst into laughter and dropped the candlestick.

"Her tits are bigger than her head," she chortled. "Did you ever see anyone like this in your life?"

"Come over and sit on the bed," Africanus consoled, putting her arm around her. "No need to be frightened. Now tell us the way out of here."

Her voice was soft but quietly menacing. The girl, embarrassed at the size of her breasts, covered them with her arms. Her eyes were abnormally large and lustrous but strangely beautiful beneath her plucked brows.

"The only way is through the labyrinth," she whispered. "But no one knows the way through the passages."

"Fucking great!" Ustane blurted, snatching up a wine jug. She took a hefty pull and belched. "Big help she is. Tells us how to get out of here, but doesn't know the way."

Nevertheless, it was a start.

"So where is the entrance?" Africanus asked softly, hoping she would at least know that.

She had to think for a moment, and it didn't help the poor girl's state of nerves when Ustane disgustedly pronounced her as thick as shit.

"Give her a chance," Africanus chided, and took her frightened arms from her chest. "You've got splendid tits," she admired, putting the girl more at ease. "I wonder how the God's blessed you with such a magnificent pair. You're making us jealous."

That compliment at least brought a flicker of a smile to the girl's voluptuous lips. "The entrance is in the punishment chamber," she remembered. "Behind the great wheel."

"What the fuck is that?" Ustane asked, shoving the wine jar into Africanus' breasts.

"It's where the queen's slaves are punished," the girl said tearfully. "My twin sister is due for a flogging as soon as the chief concubine is free from her duties."

"You mean there's another one exactly like you?" Ustane laughed.

"No prizes for guessing who the chief concubine might be," Africanus said without laughing.

"Take us to the punishment room," Ustane said harshly. "And we'll have a look at this great wheel."

That made immediate sense, and the young slave girl padded softly across the floor followed by the two women.

Unsurprisingly the punishment room was deep underground and the great wheel its main instrument for punishing the slaves. At first glance, it looked nothing more sinister than a huge cartwheel with a massive hub and wooden spokes projecting outwards to the rim. Closer inspection revealed spikes and iron shackles that could be moved into varying positions depending on the slave's height or length of limbs. At the side of it, massive chains and weights hung from pulleys hooked into the ceiling. The whole ghastly apparatus had Africanus shivering, but Ustane merely shrugged. Around the walls chains hung in profusion and a variety of whips, rods and canes lay openly displayed on a table. A stone statue of the wolf-god Upuat stood ominously in the shadows, his massive phallus rearing up from its belly. There was need to guess what that was used for. In one corner of the chamber, a bowl of milk rested incongruously on a plinth, its use baffling the onlookers.

To their chagrin, Tamara arrived much earlier than they had anticipated and girl visibly trembled at her approach and hid herself behind the taller body of Africanus. She came noiselessly into the chamber leading a girl slave by a golden chain. Behind them came the girl's twin and at first glance it was impossible to tell them apart. Ustane was about to make another of her dirty remarks but thought better of it. The naked twin looked terrified, her wide eyes goggling at the wheel.

"What brings you here?" Tamara purred, running her eyes over the unexpected intruders.

No one answered. Their eyes were riveted on the slave Tamara had now loosed from the chain. She was on all fours and crawling towards the bowl and, to both women's

220

utter astonishment, began lapping at the milk. Tamara crouched and fondly patted her head.

"This is my kitten," she beamed lovingly. "Hasn't she got such a beautiful body?"

That couldn't be denied. The slave was slim and lithe, her breasts small and pert, a stark contrast to the twin sister whose enormous breasts heaved from her slim shoulders.

"Her majesty has ordered our presence to witness the punishment," Africanus lied without as much as a flicker of her eyes.

Ustane nodded in agreement and moved towards the edge of the wheel and saw behind the axle a small doorway leading into a darkened passage, and wondered whether this means of escape was such a good idea after all.

"As her majesty commands," Tamara acknowledged, and slipped her robe from her shoulders, revealing only a short pleated skirt that barely covered her bottom.

She pointed to the wheel and without a murmur, the girl stepped up and swung her legs over the hub, sitting astride it as she reached up to the spokes, spreading her arms wide. Tamara speedily manacled them and then went to her ankles, taking hold of each one and stretching them over the spokes. These were quickly fastened into place and the girl's body now formed an X shape, her legs and arms stretched as wide as possible. Her bottom rested on the hub, the cheeks parting from the narrow crease flexed with fright. Her narrow back seemed to ripple all down the spine because she knew exactly what would soon follow.

"You have been disobedient and rude to your mistress," Tamara proclaimed joyfully, selecting a whip from the table. "You are to receive seventy lashes anywhere I please. So I think we'll start with your bum. A good place to begin, wouldn't you say?"

Her twin sister hiding behind the tall black woman was already sobbing at the fate of her sister, but Africanus could do nothing to console her.

There was nothing anyone could do except watch and wait until the punishment was complete.

"Kitten!" Tamara rasped. "Set the wheel in motion."

The girl slave left the bowl and slunk obediently to the wheel, reached for a lever and pulled it downwards. Overhead the pulleys clanked into life, creaking in their stays as the chains slowly passed through their rims. The onlookers gazed at the weights rising and falling in opposite directions and then at the great wheel grinding on its axle.

"By all the Gods," Ustane uttered, for once in her life lost for words as the wheel began to turn.

What evil genius had invented that contraption was anybody's guess, but the effect on the manacled girl was galvanic. Her body turned full circle before Tamara even lifted her whip, the limbs straining at the shackles, her head going upside down, and blood rushing to her face as she gulped for air. Her enormous breasts, carried by their own weight pressed over her shoulders, and then as she became horizontal ballooned from her ribs, only to assume their natural position as she came upright again.

"Unbelievable," Africanus whispered, and shielded the girl at her side, sparing her the terrible sight of the whip now lashing into her twin's naked buttocks.

"She's too thin," Ustane mumbled. "Her arse will never take seventy strokes."

Tamara started by teasing the girl, just flicking the whiptails over her bottom as the wheel began its circle. Now the onlookers realized the awful intelligence that had created it for as the girl's body slowly turned the whip couldn't fail to strike every inch of her flesh. Now it fell faster and harder, lashing across the centre of her buttocks and, as her body became horizontal, lashing into the sides of her thighs and hips. She went right upside down and the tails struck into her open legs, her sex splitting open from the force of the blow. The wheel cranked its deadly course and again she became horizontal and this time the whip lashed the other side of her back and shoulders. How many had she taken so far? It seemed like fifty she was sobbing and gasping so much, but Africanus counted only a mere handful, no more than ten at the most.

"Stop the wheel!" Tamara shrieked when the girl was upright again.

She crept softly behind her and patted her welted cheeks, smoothing her paws in circles and running them down the length of her thighs. Africanus knew well what was going through her devious mind, and it was only a matter of time before she had her brought to her chambers and fucked. The kitten shot her mistress a sly glance, her cat like eyes glinting from the pleasure of watching the girl's humiliation.

"She's got big tits," she purred, trying to imitate her mistress' throaty tones. "When we've finished can I suck the milk from them?"

"Of course, my precious, you can do whatever you like, after I've finished with her. You can even sit on them and bounce your beautiful little bum on those big soft cushions."

"I'd rather sharpen my claws on her back," the kitten hissed, and crooked her fingers baring her nails.

Ustane saw that they had been carefully filed into deadly points and made a mental note that when they decided to make a bolt into the labyrinth and might have to despatch Tamara into the bargain, the kitten would be the first she would knock unconscious. Caught unawares those claws could do a lot of damage.

The wheel was set in motion and Tamara aimed the whip into the arse crease, lashing deep into the cleft. The bottom cheeks suddenly rippled and quivered, each cheek shaking so fast the skin seemed alive. She struck at the tops of the thighs, aiming under the cheeks and then at the backs of her knees. The girl's slim legs went rigid and Africanus could see the muscles tensing. The thighs went hard at the sides, the calves bulged and seen like that with all her muscles flexing, she had to admit that despite being thin, her limbs were very shapely. Her pert buttocks were now squeezing tight into the cleft as the wheel brought her upside down.

"Kitten, as you are now under my charge, you must learn your craft. Let me see you whip that miserable wretch's cunt."

She sprang forward and took the proffered whip, lashing it through the air, delighting in her sudden newfound power.

Her arm swung wide lashing between the girl's legs. Her howls filled the chamber with such a heart-rending pitch that even Tamara winced.

It was too much for her twin sister who came suddenly from the black woman's side, her enormous breasts shaking and wobbling as she marched straight up to the kitten, snatching the whip from her hand.

"She's had enough," she shrieked, and swung her tiny fist into the kittens jaw.

Tamara was there at once, felling her with a sharp slap into the side of her breast. She hit the ground and lay winded on her back.

"Now your wish has come true," Tamara said to the stunned kitten. "Fetch those irons."

The kitten, nursing her bruised face, speedily brought over two pairs of shackles. It only took a few moments to slip them around the felled girl's wrists and ankles.

"You can bite on her tits," Tamara offered, kicking the girl in the ribs.

The kitten sat on the girl's thighs and lowered her head uttering a throaty purr. Her mouth opened and snarled and Africanus wondered if she had gone into a demented dream. The kitten's eyeteeth had been sharpened into gleaming points. Ustane watched in horror as the fangs sank deep into the girl's breast, puncturing the areola and crushing the nipple between the grinding teeth. Her face distorted into a mask of searing pain, the eyes bulging from their sockets and her mouth wide open snatching for air. The kitten shook her head as if playing with a captured mouse, then pursed her lips sucking on the throbbing bud. She sucked until the teat went hard then lapped her tongue all around the pimples.

"She's coming along well, don't you think?" Tamara beamed, looking at the girl's writhing hips.

The two women made no reply, just stood and watched in stricken silence as Tamara gathered the whip and sent it whistling at the sister on the wheel. It was revolving once more and the spread-eagled girl turned full circle bearing the lash on her buttocks, thighs and back. She was still conscious, but only just, her breathing coming in slow measured gasps. Tamara ceased her whipping and looked at the twin sister the kitten was still biting and sucking, and then back again at the twin on the wheel, a sinister smile creeping across her face.

She unfastened the manacles and the whipped girl collapsed backwards. Only a timely leap from Africanus prevented her skull from cracking on the floor. She held her in her arms as the kitten unshackled her sister and stood back admiring the deeply indented teeth marks surrounding the dark areolas.

"Lay one over the other," Tamara commanded. "And let's see how well they fuck."

"If they don't fuck hard enough, I'll whip them," the kitten quickly offered.

To demonstrate her sincerity she lashed the already whipped sister forcing her body harder onto the one beneath. Their breasts squashed and ballooned against one another, the nipples pressing into the breast flesh. Although they were belly to belly, sex to sex, neither moved, but lay rigid determined not to perform the outrageous act that Tamara and her horrible protégé were so eager to witness.

"They are disobedient," Tamara rasped, blasting impatient air through her nostrils. "And disobedience must not go unpunished. We'll put them both on the wheel; the head of one can go between the legs of the other, one facing outwards and the other against the spokes. You," she addressed Ustane, "can help my kitten shackle them."

"I'd rather you and the kitten sucked my tits," she returned, to Africanus' amazement.

"She has a good pair, mistress," the kitten acknowledged.

Ustane quickly bared her breasts, full, ripe and mature, the nipples erect and almost begging for a pair of eager lips to suck them.

"On the condition you fuck both of these miserable wretches afterwards," Tamara said.

"Done!" Ustane laughed, and turned her back while she fumbled with her robe, reaching under the pleats and then slowly throwing it over her head. Her arms tangled in the pleats and for several seconds she wrestled with the folds and finally threw them off. She stood stark naked, cupping her breasts and offering her nipples, flicking her thumbs over the teats and lapping her tongue around her lips.

Tamara and her kitten bent their heads and sucked on each breast so hard their cheeks fanned in and out. They reached under Ustane's legs and rubbed her sex mound until the lips were wet. Africanus, disgusted at how Ustane could so easily offer herself to these monsters, turned away, but as quickly turned back. Both Tamara and the kitten slumped to the floor in a heap.

"Told you I always kept the drug handy," Ustane laughed, and they went to the twins, unfastening the shackles and lifting them upright.

"We have about an hour before the drug wears off," she said. "May the gods help us through the labyrinth."

"You'll need light," one of the twins advised, lifting an oil lamp from its holder.

The other three women quickly took up more lamps and they all processed through the arch, Ustane leading the way, the twins following and Africanus protecting the rear.

The narrow corridor seemed to go and on, the lamps

throwing eerie shadows and catching carved reliefs of long extinct deities and rulers. Nobody spoke and only shuffling feet broke the silence. After what seemed an age the tunnel suddenly divided into three separate branches, each vanishing into darkness.

"Now which way, for fuck's sake?" Ustane swore.

None of them had any idea.

"I want to go back," the whipped twin snivelled.

Ustane looked her straight in the eyes, her face angry.

"We're coming with you," her sister said, quickly diffusing the situation.

"I think we should try each one in turn," Africanus suggested. "If we reach a dead end, we come back and try the next."

"What if they just go round in circles," the twin said.

"Supposing the oil runs out," her sister rejoined.

A hard slap on their faces silenced them.

"One more peep out of either of you and the rats'll be having a feast," Ustane sputtered.

And they all set off along the middle tunnel. At intervals, more tunnels branched left and right, some with steps ascending and descending, others leading into the blackness. One of the lamps sputtered and went out. They trudged on through the gloom in a frightened oppressive silence.

"Let's face it, we're lost," Africanus said, verbally expressing everyone else's thoughts.

They turned a corner and one of the twins shrieked. In an alcove, a statue of Thoth peered at them with his gimlet eyes.

"I'd like to piss all over that," Ustane snorted, and then her lamp guttered and failed.

"Any more of those go out and we're well and truly fucked," Africanus said, turning a corner and coming face to face with a blank wall.

They turned and retraced their steps, going down a tunnel

they had not tried. The twins still naked started shivering, their nipples erect from an icy blast of air coming from a slit in the wall. It took a couple of moments to recognize the significance of that.

"It's coming from outside!" Ustane declared, holding her hand over the slit.

They walked on considerably cheered. At a junction of the tunnels another statue reared up, this time of Bast, the cat headed god in human form and one of the twins promptly pissed all over the tunnel floor, which made Ustane break into frightened laughter. Africanus lifted her robe and turning her back on the statue, bent over and fired a stream of urine all over its middle. It was what they all so badly needed, something as silly as that to allay their fears. One of the twins farted and Ustane laughed so much her laughter echoed along the tunnel gradually fading into its infinity. Then, as the laughter died, they heard the sound of footsteps, seemingly neither near nor far, but definitely somewhere ahead. The footsteps died away and all four women gazed at each other. One of the twins opened her mouth about to cry for help but Africanus clamped her hand over her lips. It was wise not to reveal themselves until they were sure as to whom the footfall belonged. At least they were no longer alone.

Cheered, they walked along the tunnel and ahead caught the distinct sound of voices.

Ustane put her finger to her lips and they continued like thieves, tiptoeing and not speaking.

Ahead a dim light cast by a lamp led them to a chamber, empty except for a pile of discarded sacks. Ustane and Africanus looked at each other and shook their heads. None of this made sense, but they knew that they were getting closer to the outside world.

Going in single file, the twins hugging their breasts against the cold draught now wafting through the tunnel, they came across a spectacle that had them all riveted in shock.

"Where in the name of the Gods did all this come from?" Ustane blurted.

They all stood gazing in amazement at a great pile of treasure; funereal masks of pure gold, caskets of precious stones, golden crowns, a cabinet inlaid with lapis lazuli filled to brim with golden and silver ornaments, and what looked like a coffin filled with ornate jewelry and silken robes.

"I would say all this has been looted," Africanus guessed.

She looked at Ustane who nodded, they grabbed handfuls of rubies, and sapphires, thrusting them into their robes, lifted a heavy sack full of necklaces and pendants and threw it over Ustane's shoulder.

Voices, louder this time and fast approaching came along the tunnel. The distinct shape of Marius Aquinus came into view leading a troop of slaves carrying more sacks. They emptied the booty in a pile and left as quickly as they came with the women trailing in the shadows. The brightness had them shielding their eyes. Sunrays poured into the entrance and Africanus grabbed Ustane, kissing her full on the lips. The twins hugged each other and burst into tears.

"We've done it," Ustane breathed.

And they walked gratefully into the sunshine.

A valley opened up before them and they followed its course, the twins nakedness now partially covered with segments of sacking ripped from the pile, enough to cover their buttocks but leaving their breasts bare.

Like fugitives, they went through the valley bottom and in the distance saw a shimmering band of water.

"The Nile!" Africanus cried. "We're free!"

Her words might have come true if it were not for Marius Aquinus and a band of tomb robbers mounted on horseback and coming straight for them.

"Oh shit," Ustane swore and dropped her sack. "Now we are well and truly fucked."

CHAPTER TWELVE

"Where the hell did you spring from?" Marius Aquinus asked, staring in disbelief at the black gladiatrix.

It seemed she had a habit of mysteriously appearing from nowhere, first in Akara's brothel, then at the banquet, and now here just as he was looting another ancient tomb.

In this line of work, witnesses were something he could well avoid.

She related the story of the encampment, its destruction and her fleeing into the desert without mentioning anything at all about her involvement with Queen Hatentita or the labyrinth.

He regarded her speculatively and knew she was lying, but had a quick and intelligent mind, well, for a woman, anyway. She had already stumbled upon the loot, and might, if she were desperate enough ask for money in return for her silence. He had abandoned all plans of getting her back to Rome, or staging combats in Egypt, it wasn't worth the candle now that he could raid the tombs without involving any of the dignitaries. There was another factor he had to consider, she wasn't alone and the dark one had already helped herself to his booty.

"I could take you down river as far as Thebes," he suggested. "After that you are free to go wherever you like. I'll not betray you. After all you have suffered you deserve your freedom."

Knowing the devious minds of Romans, it was an offer she did not want to accept but was not in a position to refuse. The women climbed behind the robbers and they galloped to the river where a number of boats docked at the quay. She guessed rightly that he was looting all the tombs he could find and used the labyrinth as a holding store until it could be shifted, probably to Alexandria and thence to Rome.

"I don't like the look of that bastard for a start," Ustane remarked, as they boarded the nearest boat.

"We'll jump off at Thebes," Africanus said. "And make our own way to Rome."

"What about this pair?" she asked, indicating the twins.

"They can either make their own way or come with us as our slaves."

The women went below deck and into a cabin, which Marius Aquinus had generously offered. Loaves of bread and bottles of wine were in abundance, and they all fell on them, tearing at the loaves and quenching their parched throats. The boat rocked gently and through a small opening Africanus could see the craft was heading into midstream.

"Where do we piss?" one of the twins asked, squeezing her stomach.

Good question. There were no pots or buckets for that usage, so the obvious place was on deck, probably meaning that she would have to put her bare bum over the gunwale and empty her bladder into the river.

"They've locked the door," she wailed, clutching her stomach.

It was a couple of seconds before the implication of that sunk in.

"Oh, fuck," Ustane swore.

"I ought to have known," Africanus, sighed, banging her fist on her forehead.

Then the cabin went into a spin. The walls grew to twice their size, and then went very small. Ustane crashed into her and fell headlong onto a pile of cushions. Both twins staggered about like drunks and fell together in a tangle of bouncing breasts and buttocks.

"Bas..tar..d," was the last word Africanus uttered before the sleeping draught did its work.

The crew gave the women a few minutes and when they heard them contentedly snoring, entered the cabin and shackled their wrists and ankles. Collars slipped softly around their necks and their chains fastened to the cabin walls. While they slumbered, the boatmen quietly groped inside Africanus' robe and helped themselves to the looted jewels.

"When they're awake, we'll fuck them one by one," he said, squeezing the sleeping black woman's breast.

If he thought he was going to have the black woman, he had another think coming.

"These other three pieces of worthless horseflesh you can use as you please," Marius Aquinus offered, as the women slowly stirred into life. "But the black one stays in here with me. You know my instructions."

The boatmen unfettered Ustane and the twins, only releasing their ankles and the hasps at the cabin walls, ushering them on deck and throwing them bottom up over the gunwales. Marius Aquinus waited until the heaving and swearing began before he eased Africanus on her back.

Knowing why he was there, she opened her long silky legs, offering no resistance as he penetrated her. Nothing comes free and her fare would be paid in kind if not in coin. Her calves went over his back and locked at the heels.

"You can fuck me all the way to Thebes," she laughed, playfully slapping his ribs.

"Of course," he said, unconvincingly. "All the way to Thebes."

He propped his weight on his elbows and rode her steadily, ramming his full length inside her and nibbling her nipples, not showing much enthusiasm or imagination. He seemed distracted and she didn't even reach her climax before he erupted in her. Nor did he show any inclination to have her bottom or mouth, but merely ordered her on deck to take the air.

Shrugging, she came into the daylight and saw Ustane and the twins chained together at the wrists, on their knees and sucking any of the crew who took their fancy. The collars were still around their necks and linked from one girl to the next.

"You might've at least unchained them," Africanus tutted,

smiling at the amusing sight of all three vainly trying to stroke each cock.

"They're fine as they are," he grated. "Bo'sun, carry out my orders."

Faster than she could blink, the boatmen whipped their cocks from the girl's mouths and jumped on her, forcing her to her knees and shackling her wrists. The chain hanging from Ustane's collar was quickly fitted to her own, and all four women dragged to the gunwale.

"You treacherous bastard!" Africanus shrieked, watching a slave boat hoving into view.

"I have a choice," Marius Aquinus told her. "Either slit your throats, or sell you as slaves. I thought you might prefer the latter."

The slave dealer came aboard the boat and quickly inspected the slaves. Reeking of sweat and grime, he opened their mouths checking the quality of their teeth, squeezed their breasts, and poked their thighs and bottoms.

"Name your price," he said gruffly, expecting a long argumentative bartering session.

"You can take them gratis," Marius Aquinus said to the amazed dealer.

The black woman alone was worth two thousand sestertius, and the twins would probably fetch five thousand. The dark one was he was not so sure about, he had already marked her as a troublemaker.

"What's the catch?" he asked warily.

"No catch. Sell them to whom you like, preferably as sword bait, just as long as they're well out of Egypt."

"That's a bargain," he grunted, herding the women over the gunwale.

"I need female slaves as sword fodder." he lectured, standing the women in a line. "Men pay handsomely to see big breasted, pert bottomed women naked in the arena, and you are just what I'm looking for," he continued, slapping Ustane's buttocks. "Some are fed to the beasts, others pitched against gladiators. Either way you are all dead meat." He turned his eyes away from the paralyzed women and smirked at the crew, and then back again just in time to see the twins urinating all over the deck. "However, while you are still alive it would be a pity to waste your charms idling in the hold. The crew can make use of you until we dock."

The women were unchained and led away to various parts of the boat. Even before they were on their backs the crew had discarded their loincloths and stood naked and erect. The first mate steered Africanus to the prow, seating her at the tiller, stretching her arms along its length and binding them fast. He seized her legs and lifted them high in the air, bent them over her shoulders and lashed her ankles along side her wrists. Her sex was open and defenceless against his massive erection aiming into her quivering labia.

She stared blankly over his shoulder at the fading landscape; the twinkling lamps lighted in the village hovels, the lowing of oxen returning from the fields and the exited chatter of women slaves pleasuring their masters. Her snorting lover settled between her thighs and grinned horribly, rubbing week-old stubble against her face and clumsily groping her breasts. Ustane lashed upright against the mast, her legs spread wide, took one man after another, gritting her teeth and swearing audibly. The twins bent over a pile of caskets and bared their buttocks, their huge breasts bouncing and swaying from their chests as they were rapidly penetrated.

It was dawn before the crew slaked their lust and the women, naked and exhausted returned to the fetid hold. They sat back to back, chained at their neck collars and wrists.

"Are we really going into the arena as sword fodder?" Ustane asked, unusually subdued.

"That's where we're headed," she confirmed, shifting her aching bottom over the floor.

The hold hatch slid open and a shadowy figure came furtively over the boards. Even in the semi darkness, she could feel the heat arising from his throbbing cock.

"Open your mouth," he rasped, forcing the silky plum between her lips.

She sucked on the shaft, swallowing it right to the back of her throat, wondering how many more men would have her before she met her end in the arena as nothing more glorious than naked killing meat.

"I'm not being sword fodder just to give everybody else a laugh," Ustane said bitterly, when at last the women were alone.

"You might have to fight," Africanus warned. "Not that you'll have much of a chance against a fully armed gladiator."

"What if we told the Romans where the Red Sphinx is," one of the twins suggested. "They might let us go if we did."

Africanus stared at her for a few moments. She banged on the door of the hold until her fist numbed. Sometimes information was worth more than life and could fetch a high price. After her escape from the labyrinth, she bore no allegiance to Queen Hatentita.

"You'll tell me everything you know," the slave dealer said, eyeing her intriguingly.

If she was telling the truth, selling her as dead meat would be a waste and he already knew the Roman sixth legion was preparing to move up river to avenge the sacking of the governor's palace.

"I'll only tell the general of the legion," she said firmly. "He'll pay you anyway."

He thought fast. It was possible he could strike a deal and be well rewarded and might even get to keep her.

"Keep this tart under close guard until we dock," he ordered the mate. "And see she is never left alone."

The mate, following instructions, escorted her to the

forward rope locker and tied her hands behind her back. He sat her against the wall and spoon fed her soup and porridge until the boat thumped into the wharf at Alexandria.

"So where is this Red Sphinx?" General Petronius asked.

It was part of the bargain that the twins and Ustane should accompany the gladiatrix to the Roman encampment. After all, they knew as much as she did and could corroborate her story.

He showed her maps and she pointed out the location of the sphinx, as well as the entrance to the labyrinth. He seemed satisfied. Tactfully she omitted the destruction at the oasis and her dealings with the queen. Treachery was not something the Romans' forgave easily. Crucifixion was not a very pleasant way to quit the earth.

He paid the slave dealer and ordered the four women released.

The twins were immediately offered positions as contract whores in one of the most lucrative brothels in Alexandria, and accepted faster than the procuress could wink.

"You said you were a gladiatrix," the general said, motioning her to a seat.

"We both are," Africanus lied, remembering how Ustane had saved her in Cellenius' tent.

"I happen to know of a former gladiatrix in Rome who, I'm sure would welcome you both into her ludus."

Africanus' heart leaped.

"Fortuna!" she blurted.

"That's the one," he acknowledged. "Tall woman with freckles on her bum as I remember. Do you wish to join her? I can arrange it. You and your friend. My price is that we spend a few hours together before I head up river and deal with this Queen."

"Your wish is our pleasure," Ustane willingly broke in.

"No, only you," he said to Africanus. "Taking you both on would leave me too exhausted. And I have another hard ride tomorrow," he laughed, dismissing Ustane and closing the door.

She stood naked before him, arms by her sides, neither welcoming nor resisting, just offering her body for whatever purpose he chose.

"You can do anything you want with me," she said softly. "I am at your disposal, my lord."

He threw off his toga and paced slowly towards her. At once, an unspoken sexuality filled the room.

They embraced as if they had known each other for a long time. His strong hands pressed her buttocks, forcing her against his torso. Her arms were around his body feeling the strength in his arms and back. His erection stood hard and proud embedding into the soft mound of her belly. Her magnificent breasts squashed into his chest and he slapped her buttocks hard.

Without uttering a word they fell to the floor, rolling over and over, limbs locked tight. She caught her breath and held it as his rampant cock glided easily into her soaking sex. Her long legs opened wide and went over his back, ankles crossed and hugging his buttocks.

"I'm going to ride you until sunrise," he whispered, and she thrilled to his coarse stubble grazing her face.

He rubbed it against her breasts and nipples, moving his head like a bear scratching on a tree trunk.

"Ooh," she softly muttered, feeling the length of his cock rubbing into her bud.

"Good?" he asked, biting her nipples.

"Very good," she purred, and bucked her hips.

They made love for hours on end, unhurried, just riding each other, sometimes she sat astride him, at others she was on all fours with her bottom slamming against his middle, he stood her against the wall and fucked until she cried from so many orgasms. Finally, he sucked her sex lips and almost drove her hysterical with longing.

Trumpets sounding the call to arms separated them at

last and wordlessly he buckled on his armour.

"If you're short of money," he spoke, swinging a red cloak around his breastplate. "I know of a ship heading to Rome. You and your friend will be well paid for your services. You will have your own cabins and can choose your lovers from amongst the crew. A woman like you could ask and get at least ten gold pieces per man. Up to you."

It was an offer she couldn't refuse and slipped on the robe he gave her.

He was gone, mounting his horse and heading up the banks of the Nile.

She watched him leading the legion into the rising sun and linked arms with Ustane, walking happily towards the docks.

General Petronius stole a lingering glance at the two women, wondering who in hell was Fortuna and omitted to mention the ship was a man 'o war heading directly into battle with the mad queen's warships.

The crew had a right to a last free fuck before the ship was set ablaze, and he spurred his horse south, wondering if the mad queen would make a good lover.

END

Africanus is a beautiful North African girl enslaved by Rome from an early age and then given a chance to train at a 'ludus' for a career as a gladiatrix. Her owner's business affairs depend on her success in the arena but immediately she becomes the centre of a web of deceit.

The treacherous slave girl Nydia spies on her. The lady Octavia, wife of her owner is having a torrid affair with the games sponsor and the creditors are closing in on the ludus.

Filled with all the decadence, sex and danger of life in ancient Rome, the first instalment of Africanus' adventures is a headily erotic read in the best traditions of Silver Moon books.

Africanus, the beautiful black slavegirl has escaped the brutality of the arenas in Imperial Rome but her ship is wrecked far to the north and she finds herself a prisoner of the Celts.

The warriors lose no time in taking full advantage of such an unexpected piece of good fortune and for Africanus it seems as though her fate is sealed.

However, worse awaits her as she finds herself swept up in savage rituals from which she barely escapes with her life. To make matters even worse she earns the enmity of the Celts' High Priestess herself.

From the brothels of the legions' garrison towns and their arenas, to the sinister standing stones in the forests, Ritual of Pain features an intensely erotic array of beautiful slavegirls, and dominant masters and mistresses who are all intent on possessing Africanus' body.

There are over 100 stunningly erotic novels of domination and submission in the Silver Moon catalogue. You can see the full range, including Club and Illustrated editions by writing to:

Silver Moon Reader Services
Shadowline Publishing Ltd,
No 2 Granary House
Ropery Road,
Gainsborough,
Lincs. DN21 2NS

You will receive a copy of the latest issue of the Readers' Club magazine, with articles, features, reviews, adverts and news plus a full list of our publications and an order form.